FALL FROM GRACE

Also by Leye Adenle

Bobby Fatokun
Cell One

The Amaka Thrillers
Easy Motion Tourist
When Trouble Sleeps
Unfinished Business

Standalone Novels
The Beautiful Side of the Moon

LEYE ADENLE

FALL FROM GRACE

SIMON &
SCHUSTER

London · New York · Amsterdam/Antwerp · Sydney/Melbourne · Toronto · New Delhi

First published in Great Britain by Simon & Schuster UK Ltd, 2026

1 3 5 7 9 10 8 6 4 2

Simon & Schuster UK Ltd, 7th Floor
199 Bishopsgate, London EC2M 3TY

Simon & Schuster Australia, Sydney
Simon & Schuster India, New Delhi

www.simonandschuster.co.uk
www.simonandschuster.com.au
www.simonandschuster.co.in

The authorised representative in the EEA is Simon & Schuster Netherlands BV, Herculesplein 96, 3584 AA Utrecht, Netherlands. info@simonandschuster.nl

A CIP catalogue record for this book
is available from the British Library

Paperback ISBN: 978-1-3985-5050-6
eBook ISBN: 978-1-3985-5051-3
Audio ISBN: 978-1-3985-5052-0

Typeset in the UK by M Rules
Printed and Bound in the UK using 100% Renewable Electricity
at CPI Group (UK) Ltd

FSC www.fsc.org
MIX
Paper | Supporting responsible forestry
FSC® C013604

For Mum

Trigger warning

Reader discretion is advised: this book contains references to suicide, rape, and mental illness.

If you or someone you know needs support, the following organisations offer help and assistance

Samaritans (UK): https://www.samaritans.org

Rape Crisis (UK): https://rapecrisis.org.uk

NHS Mental Health Services (UK): https://www.nhs.uk/mental-health/

1

Francis Mouland was at his office in Clarence House at nine a.m. after swimming fifty laps in the pool at Buckingham Palace. At seventy-two, he was only two years younger than his boss, the King of England. Francis liked to think of his job as a reward for losing an eye in service to his country. Other people had lost life and limb in battles and wars; Francis had lost his eye when he was a spy in MI6.

He quite preferred his new life hobnobbing with the rich and powerful, but every now and then he would give in to sweet reminiscing about the past, the familiarity of fear, the excitement of pursuing a recruit, and the joy of hunting down an enemy's spy.

He settled behind his ornate desk and promptly went about dealing with the letters that had arrived for his attention. Five envelopes later, he placed an invitation for the King to attend the Loughborough Junction Christmas Gala on a pile of similar invitations he would later respond to in writing. He suspected that the people who made such requests only did so in the hope of receiving a letter from the King, or at least something on paper bearing the insignia of the throne. Responding to the ones that merited a reply was a tedious task often delegated to other staff, but thankfully, AI had made researching something to say about their town, their festival, or their tragedy a lot easier than when he'd first got the job. Once in a while, a truly significant letter turned up, and he had real work to do. Those tended to be addressed directly to him and sent via registered delivery, as was the next envelope in the pile. So it was with muted zeal that he picked it up, inserted the sharp tip of his envelope opener into the tiny space above the adhesive on the edge, and cut the envelope open in a clean slice.

He extracted the letter and saw that it had been written in the same hand as the address on the envelope.

He sat back to read.

To His Majesty, the King of England, c/o Francis Mouland

Your Majesty,

Dear Sir,

I am a pastor and a partner of the law firm whose letterhead appears above.

A young woman of Caribbean descent in my congregation recently approached me, seeking counsel and representation on a matter that might be of interest to you. Specifically, she made wild claims and allegations regarding a prominent member of the British Establishment. Her claims are of a sexual nature, and due to the alleged date of the encounters, amount to statutory rape.

At first, I was inclined to dismiss her as a mere

fantasist, but upon scrutiny of her so-called evidence, I felt the need to take her more seriously. It is my opinion that, were her claims and evidence to be made public, the truth would be irrelevant in the court of public opinion.

As your loyal subject, I feel duty-bound to bring this issue to your attention. I intend to maintain the lady as a client for the sole purpose of preventing her from going public with the accusation she shared with me.

I wish to stress that I do not seek, nor would I accept, anything in return for this information. This is neither a scam nor an extortion attempt, both of which could see me struck off by the Solicitors Disciplinary Tribunal. I implore you to consider the greatly compromised position I have placed myself in by revealing confidential client information to you. I would not have done so if I were not convinced beyond all doubt that not to do so would be to put major institutions of the state at risk.

I await your advice and instructions.

Your loyal subject,

Pastor, Dr Dolapo Daniel, D'Don

Francis read the letter again. He picked up the envelope and scrutinised it as if searching for clues as to the sender's motivation. He read the letter one more time, then placed it on his desk, clasped his hands behind his head, reclined his chair, and stared at the ceiling.

*

The law chambers of Osinuga & Associates occupied the first and second floors of a Victorian terrace on Camberwell Road, above an estate agency on the ground floor and a hairdressing salon in the basement. Francis paid his taxi fare and pressed the bell to announce his arrival for his appointment. He took in the busy road while he waited to be buzzed in.

A soft click sounded. He pushed the door and stepped into a narrow hallway that smelled of fresh paint. A steep staircase rose ahead of him. Halfway up, he heard footsteps approaching from above.

Pastor Dolapo Daniel D'Don was shorter and slimmer than he appeared in the photographs that Francis had found on Google. He was clearly a gym-goer. Dressed in a fitted black suit and a white shirt, the uniform of his trade, the lawyer–pastor did, however, have a pair of white trainers on his feet, a plethora of bracelets on both wrists, and a sizeable diamond-encrusted crucifix hanging from a gold chain around his neck. His eyes were wide behind the lenses of his rimless glasses as he welcomed Francis with an effusive smile and pulled him into a non-consensual embrace.

Francis spoke as soon as they had settled down at the lawyer's desk. 'Mr Daniel, before we begin, I have to let you know that I am here purely of my own accord. I am not here on behalf of anyone else.'

'Please, call me D'Don,' the pastor said. The smile on his face had not waned or wavered.

He'd better not expect a reciprocal gesture, Francis thought. The informality felt premature, but then again, this was a man obviously used to steamrolling his way through life.

'All right, D'Don. I need you to confirm that you understand that I am not representing anyone.'

'Ah, my friend, I understand,' the pastor said, rubbing his palms together so that his bracelets rattled. 'Let's just say that this meeting never happened.'

'That is not what I said. But let's get on with it. It is only fair to also let you know that I have not done anything with respect to your letter. Frankly, I don't know what to do with it. Should I send it to the police? They might be interested in talking to you. Or do I send it to be filed away with the millions of other hoaxes we receive each day? One thing intrigues me, though. Why did you send it to me?'

'Well, Francis. May I call you Francis? You are His Majesty's secretary. I know there's a title for it, but in the end, you are like his PA.'

'PA?'

'Personal assistant. It was my hope that you would read the letter before it reached His Majesty, and I hoped you would know how to deal with such a delicate matter without involving innocent people who don't need to be bothered with this mess. Ah. I see that you are laughing at me.' D'Don chuckled.

Francis composed himself. 'I apologise, Mr Don. And thank you. I think I have what I came for.'

He stood to leave.

'There is a video I think you might want to watch,' D'Don said.

The pastor waited for Francis to sit back down, then

he picked up a Nokia phone that had been charging on the table. He freed it from its cable, typed in the code to unlock it, and played a video clip on it, turning the screen towards Francis.

When the clip had ended, Francis sat back and regarded the pastor with new eyes. He watched as D'Don slipped the phone into his pocket.

'She was on holiday with her relatives in the Caribbean,' he said. 'He was staying on a private island nearby. At the time, she didn't know who he was. An older woman took her and two other girls to him. She was just a child. Just a little child. As were the other girls. When she returned to England, she kept the entire thing to herself. She tried to pretend it never happened. She felt ashamed of her own abuse. Years later, while in therapy, the suppressed memories from that period of her life began to return. She realised she had been groomed, drugged, and trafficked. She remembered filming the man she was made to sleep with, but she had lost the phone long ago. Still, the next time she went back home, she searched through her things at her grandmother's place. Miraculously, she found the phone and finally recognised who had taken advantage of her all those years ago.'

Francis sat perfectly still as he listened to the pastor.

'My client brought the phone to me herself,' D'Don continued. 'She is in an office upstairs.'

Francis gripped his armrests and pushed himself to his feet.

'Calm down,' D'Don said. 'And please, sit down. I know you do not want to meet her. I asked her to bring the phone. Usually, she keeps it in a safe deposit box – I made her promise that to me.'

He opened a folder on his desk, spun it around with his fingers, and pushed it towards Francis.

'I made her sign that undertaking.'

Francis looked down at the document in front of him.

'I agreed to represent her on three conditions,' the pastor said. 'One, she had to account for every copy she had made of the video; and two, she had to give me the full details of everyone she had either talked to about it or shown it to. She promised me that it had not occurred to her to make any copies, and she was too afraid to talk to anybody, which is why she came to me. The third condition was that I would have sole custody of the phone, to keep it safe and to ensure that she would not be tempted to show anyone or make any copies. She refused to give it up. Instead, she suggested that I change the PIN so that only I could unlock it, while she would continue to hold on to it. Very clever. She's a very intelligent woman. You'll agree with me when you meet her. She could even be prime minister one day. Anyway, I had no choice but to accept.'

Francis looked up from the document and stared at the pastor.

D'Don continued, 'A clause in the contract states how much she would owe me in compensation if any copies of the video suddenly turn up. You can see the amount there. Currently, she is awaiting God's instructions through me; that is also in the document she signed. It states that she cannot reveal, or cause to be revealed, the existence of the video or any parts of it unless by direct instruction from me, her spiritual father. She will not do anything unless I tell her to.

'I did all of this to make sure that the video would never come out, by the grace of God.'

For days after his meeting with the pastor, Francis endured questions about his health, concerns over his weight loss, and more attention than he needed as he planned, plotted, and reflected, trying to decide what to do.

He did not sleep, and he did not eat. All he did all day long was think, think, think: What would someone else do in his place? Could he trust the pastor? What if it all got out of hand? And amid all the thinking, something more alarming was already in sharp focus: it all felt too familiar, and he knew exactly why. It felt as if an agent of a foreign country had just tried to recruit him. And the more he thought about everything – what to do, who to trust, who to use – the more he kept circling back to his old friend, John Quarrel, who was still a spy catcher at MI6.

Francis had first encountered the prominent ridge of John's aquiline nose at six a.m. on Magdalen Bridge in Oxford, during May Morning, some fifty years before. He had been searching the crowd of students for Stephanie Engle, the German blonde. He spotted her just as the bells of the Magdalen College tower began to toll and the choir to sing. She was staring at a tall guy with an eagle-like nose raised to the air, mouthing the Latin hymn. Francis would later learn that John had once been one of the choristers at the top of the tower.

Years later, they met at the Foreign Service in Beirut.

Francis always wondered if John had also been recruited back in Oxford. In the evenings, they would sit outside the shops on Hamra Street, catching up on gossip over thick coffee and practising their Arabic with Lebanese men sipping tea and smoking traditional narghile pipes. On one such evening, John had asked when they could talk. Francis still remembered how John had interrupted him mid-sentence to say it. He remembered waiting for John to say more. Later in the evening, in John's flat, they'd talked over a bottle of sherry that Francis had brought with him. John's eyes had gleamed in the dim lamplight.

'I've found myself in a bit of a pickle,' he said, 'and I need you to unpickle me. As a courtesy, however, you need to know that once I tell you what it is, you're going to be in a pickle, too. And it's a rather tricky one. The way I see it, you'll either have to report me up the chain of command or get your hands soiled saving me. Take a moment. Think it through. And no, I can't tell you what it's about until you've decided you're going to help.'

A lot had happened since then. They'd both ascended the rungs of the espionage ladder like circus monkeys let loose, and eventually, inevitably, both their names were being mentioned for the same job. They'd met for coffee to chat about the rumours and how great it would be if either of them got the posting, and as John was speaking, Francis had asked if they could talk. Later that evening, in the flat that Francis shared with his girlfriend, Siobhan, he'd poured two glasses of sherry and asked John to step aside so he could get the job.

*

John was sitting on a bench in St James's Park and tossing grain at the birds when Francis arrived. They had not seen each other in thirty years. Francis sat, and they shook hands and asked after one another's families, covertly assessing how much older the other looked. When all that was done, Francis said, 'I hear you now use external contractors to train agents.'

'Can you believe it?' John replied. 'It's disgraceful. Utterly disgraceful. Good on you for getting out when you did. It's all going to shit now. Tory cuts and leftist apologists in the House of Lords.'

'I would like to come back as a contractor,' Francis said.

'You? Why?'

As John left the park that day, Francis sat back on the bench and took a moment to enjoy the first piece of his plan falling into place. He watched the birds scrambling for John's seeds, and a smile crept onto his face. He was going to enjoy this.

2

Kenny's breath came in short, sharp gasps that fuelled the apprehension filling his chest. The blindfold he was wearing pressed his eyes into their sockets. The calluses of the hand gripping his bicep made him itch.

The door closed behind them, shutting out the sounds of Woolworth Road at ten p.m. on an autumn night. The smell from the fishmonger next door lingered. He heard his own breathing in the tiny space and shifted on his feet, the soles of his trainers sticking to the dirty carpet. He pictured the door in front of him. Anytime now, it would open. He waited and listened, his heart pounding, the knots tightening in his stomach, and his knees threatening to give. The man holding him remained silent. What were they waiting for? Was this a test? What would happen next? Had he been rejected? What had he done wrong?

'I will walk you through the floor today,' the man said. 'Count your steps and memorise everything.'

He moved forwards, pulling Kenny with him. The sound of the door opening. A cool breeze. Air conditioning. The smell of rubber. They stepped through.

Grunting. Everywhere. Grunts of effort and words forced out between them: 'Jesus, help me.' Grunt. 'Jesus, grant me strength.' Grunt. 'Jesus.' Grunt. Over and over. Different voices. All male. 'Jesus', 'Jesus'. And the clank of heavy metal. The slap of feet on treadmills. The squeak of pulleys bearing heavy weights. Grunt. 'Jesus, give me power.'

The man spoke into Kenny's ear. 'I will take off the blindfold now.'

Not seeing what awaited him had been terrifying. But now Kenny considered not opening his eyes. He wouldn't have seen anything. He could say he wasn't ready after all. Maybe the man would let him go. He thought of everything he would lose.

The blindfold came off. He opened his eyes. Darkness. No light. Nothing. Just darkness. Darkness and grunts and pleas to Jesus.

'I will guide you to a treadmill,' the man said. 'We'll start with a warm-up. There are six in a row on your left. Four metres left and two metres forward. Don't stick your hand out. Just let me lead you. Now turn. Stop. Step forward. Slowly.'

Kenny took a short step forward. His arms began to stretch forward. He returned them to his sides and took the next step in faith. His foot hit something solid and he froze.

'You are behind a free one now,' the man said. There was panting and pounding on both sides. 'I will let go of you, and you will get onto it.'

Kenny searched for the handrails and gripped them.

He raised his leg high and stepped onto the rubber. The next time he heard the man's voice, it was in front of him. 'Give me your hand,' the man said, snapping his fingers. Kenny stretched out his hand. The man took it and placed it further along the rail. Kenny gripped hard. The man lifted his hand again, moved it forward a few inches, and brought it down once more. Kenny felt a smooth protrusion beneath his finger. 'This controls the speed,' the man said. 'Forwards to increase and backwards to decrease. Start slowly and be mindful of your steps. Most people fall the first time.'

Kenny pushed the lever forward once. Nothing happened. He waited. Maybe he hadn't pushed hard enough. Then the rubber track beneath him began to carry him backwards. He panicked, stepping forward too quickly and losing his balance. His belly hit the central console. He recovered and, holding on to the rails, adjusted himself to the speed. A slow walk. As he brought his breath under control, he searched for the lever and pressed it twice. He began to go faster. Metal weight plates crashed behind him. He turned his face into the darkness and the 'Save me, Jesus' that followed the commotion. The treadmill punished him. He lost his balance again; his arms flailed, his legs splayed, then his face hit the moving belt, and the machine spat him out onto the rubber-covered gym floor behind. Bundled and bruised, the darkness like a heavy blanket over him, Kenny lay still and listened to the machines whirling, the feet pounding, the metal clanking. The grunts, prayers to Jesus, and, close by, someone whimpering in the dark.

3

One year later: Bobby

I've just bought the best property in Malibu. It's right on the Pacific. The waves crash against the eighteen-foot concrete caissons that support it above its own private strip of beach. The glass walls and wraparound terraces provide unobstructed views of the ocean. It's an engineering marvel. Everyone talked about it when it was constructed. The house was a star. She even went viral.

It was advertised for thirty-four million. I offered twenty. They accepted.

I would have paid thirty-four.

The guys were over from Lagos. We were on the terrace, under the stars, standing on chairs from the dining table, and peeing over the glass balcony into the Pacific because, why not? We were young, Black, and rich. The world belonged to us.

My phone rang. It was the doorbell app; our food delivery had arrived. I opened the app and saw Mike Tyson's face peering into the camera. Mike Tyson. I didn't even know he was our neighbour.

I passed the phone around, then we all went to let Iron Mike in. I opened the door, and I saw the disappointment in his face.

'You guys,' he said. 'You buy a house like this, get all this security, then a superstar shows up on your doorstep and you let him in. You defeat all your own security yourself. And I'm not alone. My gang is with me. Oh, did you think they were my entourage? This is a robbery, motherfucker!' And he pulled out a .45 Magnum.

I awoke with a start. The landline in the living room was still ringing. I stayed on my back and stared up into the darkness, my head throbbing. For some reason, for the past couple of weeks I'd been waking up with a headache. But it wasn't morning yet. I couldn't have been in bed more than a couple of hours.

I reached for my phone, yanked it away from its charging cable, and squinted at the glow of the screen. It was just past midnight, and I had seven missed calls from a withheld number. The landline stopped ringing. Who still calls a landline, anyway? I'd even taken the number off my website.

Sitting up, I reached for my dream journal on the bedside table. I had to write it all down before I began to forget. It had started as a dream. And then, like every dream I'd had for months now, it had taken a sudden twist and turned into a nightmare. Tyson. Fucking Tyson. Really, who wouldn't open the door if Mike Tyson showed up on their doorstep?

The landline started ringing again. I knew I'd lose it if it was a marketer. A wrong number would be okay, but if it was someone asking if I wanted to make a claim for an accident I wasn't in, I would go crazy.

I had to squat and reach behind the TV stand to fetch the handset. I really never used it. It stopped ringing, and I held it in my hand, hoping it wouldn't start again. By now I was curious who it was and why they had called so late.

I was thirsty, so I went into the kitchen to get a glass of water, the phone still in my hand while I thought about the dream. Tyson. Fucking Tyson. Now, what could that mean? The whole dream. A mansion on the shore in Malibu was well beyond my dreams' usual reach. A house like that represented the kind of capitalist overconsumption that I found wasteful and lewd. How many rooms does one person need?

The mansion in the dream probably had several bedrooms. Say, six. Single and childless, sometimes my two-bedroom flat felt too big, especially when the cleaner wasn't due and I needed to tidy and dust. How many rooms could a person possibly sleep in? Did the super-rich who lived alone in gigantic mansions go to bed in all the different rooms on rotation? I bet there were homeless people in Malibu, too. What a vulgar, in-the-face-of-your-poverty thing to do – to buy a house so big with so many empty rooms that you could barely ever use them all. I didn't even own a car. How wasteful is it to carry an entire living room with you wherever you go – burning the immense energy that it takes to move tonnes of metal around – just for you? For God's sake, take a train!

With my head tilted up as I quenched my sleep-thirst with tepid tap water, the handset that I'd forgotten I was still holding in my other hand began to ring again.

'Hello, who is this?' I said, and I heard the annoyance in my own voice.

'Mr Fatokun?'

'Yes?'

'Sorry to wake you. It's Roger Bainbridge. From the Met. You coached me last year.'

I was instantly fully awake. I noticed the sudden tightness in my chest and the quickening of my heartbeat. I knew exactly what my face would be doing if I were to look into a mirror: my lips would have tightened, my nostrils would have flared, and my gaze would be steady and alert. I took a deep breath and exhaled slowly. What is this? I asked myself, attempting to label the emotion. It wasn't anger; it wasn't loathing. It was something else, and I couldn't quite place it. I needed to name the emotion and bring it under my control. I'd long since stopped educating people who casually declared, 'I'm triggered.' But right then, I found myself experiencing all the symptoms of a trauma reaction simply by hearing this man's voice and name. I was indeed triggered.

He was a former client. I meet people like him in my line of work.

My coaching practice is unique in that over ninety per cent of my work comes from one source: the Metropolitan Police. I am an external contractor there, and with that comes a very specific clientele: police officers who get themselves into trouble. Typically, these individuals are first-time offenders, and their transgressions, although unsavoury, usually remain on the edge of criminality, not severe enough to warrant immediate dismissal. However, this is not the case with the man on the phone.

My mentor, Sir John, had told me that a day like this would come. He'd warned me to be prepared for it. I wasn't. Sir John Farquharson was the only Sir I knew in person. I always referred to him as 'Sir John', which he'd initially objected to but had eventually become our thing. It was he who had got me the gig with the Met, and it was to him I turned on the occasions that I needed advice on dealing with the force. We'd first met years before, when I was pursuing my postgraduate degree in coaching, following a master's in IT and a stint in Lagos with the Nigerian police force. He was one of the many postgraduate lecturers and his thing was NLP, neuro-linguistic programming. His module was halfway through the course, so we all repeated our introductions, starting with him. He'd been a soldier, a policeman, an artistic chef – something he promised to explain but never did – and now a coach. He had travelled around the world and had come to consider some of the places he'd lived in to be as much his home as the UK. Syria, Argentina, France, Nigeria. He'd met and married his wife, Ngozi, in Nigeria, and she was the reason he now lived between London and Lagos – she refused to move to the UK.

When it was my turn to introduce myself, I felt emboldened by his personal revelations. So, for the first time, I revealed to the class that I was 'Bobby Fatokun, recovering IT project manager, coach-in-training, and former

Nigerian police officer.' The connection was immediate. We spoke through the lunch break. He invited me to dinner at his house, and we exchanged numbers. I met his Ngozi and they both met my then Yemi, and after the course he referred my first paying client to me, one of many he would subsequently send my way. He was the one who'd initially secured the Met gig, but due to the high demand for his services, he was already seeing three to four clients a day. It just wasn't sustainable for one person. All that focused attention, all those hours spent sitting and listening to each client work through their problems, all that involuntary internalisation of their issues, all that empathy, and all the notes to write afterwards were simply too much for one coach to handle.

Over a bottle of Pinotage at the IoD – the Institute of Directors at 116 Pall Mall, and his favourite place to meet – he told me about the fascinating work he did with police officers. How it was so rewarding both professionally and financially; how he had to turn some officers away because he just couldn't fit them in. He finished by asking me if I'd like to take some of his clients off him. Of course, he had to introduce me to the Met, and I had to go through some security vetting, but he knew I'd be okay. 'Some security vetting' turned out to be six months of filling out forms, taking calls to answer single questions, filling out more forms, providing yet more information about things on which I'd already provided all the information I had, and interviews with an array of people in my life, but in the end, it was well worth it. The work was as rewarding as Sir John had claimed: both professionally and financially.

When the Met sent Roger Bainbridge to me, he had, until recently, been working undercover at a church, and had been accused of the sort of crime that attracted immediate censure even before the facts of the matter were known. My job was not to know the facts; my job was to make him aware of the errors in judgement that had resulted in his out-of-character behaviour. It had to be out of character, or else he wouldn't have been given a second chance through me – the last obstacle in his journey towards redemption. Despite him having a spotless record and no prior accusations, I instinctively sensed that this wasn't his first offence. Had he been a private client, I would have turned him down, but to have him sent to me by his superiors indicated that they, who did have all the facts, had judged him innocent of the crime.

I had hoped never to hear from him again.

My mind tends to erase the existence of people I'm not in constant contact with. It's a curse. But in Roger's case, I had looked forward to forgetting him after our last session together. He must have found the landline number on my business card.

I drew in a deep breath, held it, then let it out slowly. The hum of the refrigerator filled the silence. I grounded myself in the room: the sink, the hob, the extractor above it, the stacked oven, the microwave.

'Hello? Mr Fatokun? Are you there?'

'Yes, Roger. Is everything okay?'

I was aware that I sounded unwelcoming. I didn't care. What did he want? I took another deep breath.

'We need to talk,' he said.

No, we didn't. It was the last thing I wanted. And besides, I am paid to listen. He wasn't paying me, and I didn't want his money anyway.

'Is the Met paying?' I asked, sounding like a snobby shopkeeper who tells you the price of a suit they've determined you can't afford when all you've asked for is to see it in your size.

'No,' he said, impervious to my condescension. 'I would like to keep this between us.'

I knew that I hadn't given this man any reason to think he was welcome to contact me after the Met had forced me to sit alone with him for ninety minutes twice a month for six months. I hadn't asked him for feedback, I hadn't asked for any referrals, and I sure hadn't invited him to call me if he ever needed the services of a coach again. Our last session had ended with a very brief, perfunctory handshake, and I remembered washing my hands after he'd left, looking at myself in the mirror, and realising what he must have seen. It was the exact face I'd be looking at now if I were staring into that very same mirror over the basin in my guest bathroom.

'Sure.' I said it coldly. 'You can book a session through my website.'

Hopefully, he would get off the phone, and I could ignore his calendar request.

'That's not it. I just have to see you. It's really important.'

'I can't see a former client unless I know what it's about,' I said. I actually frequently meet with former clients, even if it's just in response to a simple text message asking to meet for coffee. I live by my hourly rate; every call and request to talk could result in more coaching. At my hourly rate, a terrible coffee in a train station café is always well worth it, but not with this one. Not with the man on the line.

'Sure,' I said. 'Call me in the morning.'

He didn't have my mobile number and I would mute the landline. I had no desire at all to hear from him again, to see him again, or, worst of all, to spend hours alone with him in my coaching room. No way.

'Wait. I'm really sorry I woke you up. I promise I didn't know how late it was. But there's something I have to talk to you about, and it can't wait.'

'Sure. Call in the morning.'

'You don't understand. This is really urgent.'

'It can't wait till morning?'

I was tempted to ask what it was about. But only fleetingly. I wasn't going to encourage him. I wasn't going to see him. Then a thought occurred to me. What if he told people at the Met that I didn't want to see him? I could lose my contract with them. I was sure he had as little reason to like me as I had to tolerate him, but he could really hurt me if he wanted to, and he had nothing to lose. He could find me on an online list of coaches and leave a terrible review.

'Okay, I'm listening.' I sighed. I felt like a fraud.

'Not on the phone,' he said. 'I'll be on the concourse at Marylebone Station at twenty past ten.'

I bit my lip and cursed silently as he hung up.

4

'Hi. I'm Bobby Fatokun. I have bad dreams, and I'm a person living with paranoia.'

My exaggerated smile looked stupid in the mirror. I looked as if I were happy to have a mental illness. Do people actually introduce themselves like that at AA meetings, or is it just a Hollywood thing? I shook my head and opened the medicine cabinet to find the packet of Panadol, then gathered up the mental health pamphlets next to the sink. I'd filled out a lengthy form on a website just to request them. I dropped them in the bin on my way out.

As I stepped back into my bedroom, I remembered Roger's call, and a shadow fell upon my morning. I set my phone's alarm for six a.m. on weekdays and it felt as if it had started beeping just as I'd finally managed to go back to sleep after talking to him. He just wouldn't get off the phone. In the clarity of the morning, I remembered stupidly agreeing to meet him and I hissed at my own foolishness. My shoulders immediately tensed up. Then, just as swiftly, I reminded myself not to tell myself off; the body listens, Bobby.

I managed fifteen minutes on the treadmill machine in my bedroom before I ran out of willpower. My lungs were still bursting when I got into the shower at seven. By seven thirty, I was dressed and at my desk in my consultation room, the double room right off the entrance hall. The guest bathroom is adjacent, so clients don't need to wander into my home.

I started by checking my appointments on my laptop. The first one was a chemistry meeting at nine. That was why I'd woken up energised, before the memory of Roger had doused me. A chemistry meeting is the initial sit-down with a potential client. It's like a 'go-see', as a male model I know once put it. It's short, it's informal, and it's a chance for the coach and the potential client to check each other out – to answer the question, 'Do I want to spend ninety minutes with this person twice a month for six months?' I especially enjoy attending chemistry meetings because I rarely get to do them. Most of my clients are police officers sent to me by their superiors, so they don't exactly have the option of saying, 'No, I'd like someone else, thank you.' So I always relish the chance to conduct one – to meet someone who hasn't been accused of something, who isn't motivated to lie to me to save their job, who is paying out of their own pocket, and who is thus more likely to take full advantage of the sessions rather than be preoccupied with saying what they think I want to hear.

The nine a.m. was with Maria, a schoolteacher who'd found me through the register. Roger was after that. Ten twenty a.m. on the concourse at Marylebone Station. I contemplated calling him to cancel, but that could potentially give him a legitimate reason to leave a negative review. God, I disliked that man.

I'd worked with him about a year ago, so he would be thirty-one now. I wondered if he still had the crew cut, which I'd thought was careless for an undercover officer. He'd been a member of a Major Investigations Team, posing as head of security at a church when a member accused him of rape. That was all I knew. He'd denied doing it, claiming the victim had made it all up. 'Alleged victim', I suppose I should say. There wasn't enough evidence, so he was never charged nor was his identity revealed to his accuser, but he was taken off the case and sent to me.

He wouldn't be the first cop to get in touch after our sessions together had ended. Once they've experienced the deep thinking that happens in the coaching room, some return as private clients. Mostly they want help with their career at the Met: how to get promoted, whether or not to apply for that programme or that training, etc. Some are working on difficult cases and find themselves stuck.

Whatever they're dealing with, trying to change, or trying to achieve, they all come to me knowing that whatever is said in the coaching room remains in the coaching room. They also return to me because they know I'm a policeman as well. Or I was. A former officer of the Nigerian police force. I know the job. I know the life. I will forever be part of the universal law enforcement family. They are talking to a fellow detective when we discuss their cases.

Sometimes I already know about an investigation from

the news. Occasionally, my involvement extends beyond merely assisting a client. If the case is solved, they might even invite me out for a drink with the investigative team. I remember the first time it became clear to me that an officer I'd coached before was asking me to help with their current case. I didn't know what to do. What would the coaching look like? What exactly did they expect? Was it even legal? I called Sir John, and we met at the IoD. After explaining my dilemma, he asked me, 'So, how much are you charging them?' That was all the go-ahead I needed. I emailed my standard contract to the officer that evening, and a week later, I was listening to the intricacies of an ongoing people-smuggling investigation.

It was my first glimpse into the inner workings of a major Met case, and I was surprised to discover that, in many ways, it was similar to what I'd experienced with the Nigerian police – training and equipment aside. After collecting and analysing all possible evidence, questioning all witnesses, and following all leads, the investigator often relies on their gut instinct to make a breakthrough. My client's gut feeling told them something was wrong with a confession obtained early on, but they didn't know what. In the end, they were proven right. The confession had almost succeeded in prematurely halting the investigation. But because my client learnt to trust their intuition, they kept digging and uncovered an international criminal network many times larger than the solitary driver attempting to cross into the Port of Dover with fourteen desperate migrants huddled together in the back of their truck.

The officer thanked me for helping them solve the case,

but all I'd done was listen and ask questions. I'd thoroughly enjoyed working on it with them; it had felt like discovering a new joy in life. A new hobby. A new interest. It had made me feel like a detective again, and that's why I didn't mind that I'd slashed my hourly rate and even gone pro bono for the last few sessions. With what they earned, I knew they couldn't have afforded to pay my full rate.

That said, if it turned out that Roger wanted more coaching after all, I would charge him the full price. I had only agreed to meet him out of misguided fear of a negative review, and I would rather not spend hours alone in a room with him again. Of all the officers I'd worked with at the Met, he was the only one who had managed to make me feel uncomfortable. I decided to review the coaching notes I'd taken during our previous engagement, hunching over my laptop to read them. They covered the initial triad meeting with him and his first-line supervisor–manager, each of the ninety-minute sessions we'd had over the six-month period, and my reflective notes at the end of the programme.

It was a lot of reading. I'd forgotten just how much. The encrypted document showed sixty-seven pages – more than I'd ever typed for any client. As I read, each session came back to life. I recalled the non-verbal clues I'd spotted but hadn't been able to decipher. His side-glances mid-sentence. His confusing body language and random hand gestures that had made me think he could be trying to tell me something in code. In the end, I'd concluded that it was just manipulation. He was trying to misdirect me. To distract me so I couldn't read him.

His Met record, which I'd been shown with his permission, had portrayed a policeman through and through. He'd known from nursery that wearing the uniform was what he wanted to do. He was good at the job too, steadily earning promotions and distinctions along the way. Everything had been rosy for him until that one incident.

I decided to read the rest of the notes while making my way to him after my nine o'clock appointment. I scrolled to the end and found the entry I was looking for: 'Ithdi'.

A coach's notes are for the coach alone and are strictly confidential, but a court order can compel you to hand them over to the authorities. For this reason, I've developed a crude code that allows me to record my thoughts, concerns, or opinions without ever risking having them disclosed. I form a short sentence, and I write down the initial letters of each word. Sometimes I forget what the letters resolve into, but in Roger's case, I remembered all too well.

'Ithdi'. I think he did it.

5

Francis stared into the mirror on the inside of his locker door, watching a worker pull used towels from a bin and stuff them into a canvas bag before leaving through a side door. He didn't recognise the worker – a Black, middle-aged, slightly potbellied man. Recently, Francis had become suspicious of people he did not recognise and anybody he spotted lurking behind him. He knew he was being overly cautious, but he still let the old, familiar hypervigilance back into his daily life, and with it, certain memories from his past that he would rather forget.

John could have simply texted 'Done' to his most recent request. 'Done', 'OK', 'Cool', or even a thumbs-up emoji – that was all he had to do. But instead, he had asked to meet.

Francis checked the time. He placed his watch next to his wallet and phone in the locker, then changed his mind and picked up the phone. There was still no new message from John. The knot in his belly tightened.

He placed the phone back down, then took off his glasses and looked at his own reflection. The wire-rimmed spectacles left a ridge that had become a permanent wrinkle, like the ones radiating up from between his eyes, where he held many difficult thoughts from five decades of service to his country. He thought he could see how the past few months had aged him. His cheeks were sunken. His skin was paler. Even the birthmark in the middle of his bald patch looked different. A port-wine stain that had slowly revealed itself with the gradual loss of his hair, it had once been the shape of a tiny island in the bareness of his scalp; it now looked like a city spreading out at its edges.

Glancing over his shoulder, Francis turned back to the locker and reached into his bag. He held up a green A4 plastic wallet and stared at it. He pressed down on the manila folder that was just visible inside before replacing the plastic wallet in the bag and zipping it up again. He used the mirror to check behind him one more time, then brought both hands to his right eye. With his right index finger, he pulled down his lower eyelid and let the prosthetic eye fall into his palm. One hollow socket and one droopy eye stared back at him. He put on his swimming goggles and shut the locker door.

The pool in Buckingham Palace was empty after the handful of early morning regulars had left for work in the government offices in and around Westminster. Francis used the rails to step backwards into the coldness of the water. He pushed himself to float on his back, letting the momentum carry him and his thoughts as he watched the ceiling above. If John shut him down now, months of preparation would come to naught, and what had started with a letter from the Nigerian pastor could yet result in the scandal he had hoped to prevent.

He turned in the water and began the first of his fifty laps.

6

'Do you know why you work out in the dark?' D'Don asked.

Kenny thought of the first day he'd been taken to the blacked-out gym. The sound of equipment in use and the grunts all around him. All male, he had assumed – he hadn't been able to see anyone – and all young, like him. Teenagers working out for Jesus. He remembered his fall from the treadmill. The momentary pause as everyone turned towards the commotion. The feeling of eyes peering down at him in the dark, unable to see him but sensing his embarrassment.

For months, he trained in the dark, aware of others lifting heavy weights around him, preparing their bodies for the service of Jesus, if they were chosen. In the gym, the routines became progressively easier, and the weights felt lighter, but only when he was alone at home in the flat that he shared with his mentor was he able to admire his progress.

His body had responded well to all the training and protein shakes. His muscles were big and defined; his belly was a hard surface with distinct packs – he liked to run his hands over them. In time, he began to look forward to the evening trips to the secret gym on Woolworth Road. His body began to yearn for the burn, even as his mind wondered exactly how his strength was going to serve Jesus, but that was not what kept him up at night. He had no idea if he would be chosen or how. And when he was eventually chosen, it wasn't in any way he could have expected, and he didn't stop losing sleep.

He had finally been called to the home of the general overseer and founding pastor of WAITRN Church of Christ. He was standing, chest out, before the great man of God himself. 'Imagine you're wearing a cape,' his mentor always said. He wanted D'Don to see how hard he'd been preparing his body. How he had built his muscles to serve in the army of Christ.

'We do not build our bodies for our own gratification or our minds for our own edification,' the pastor said. He stood from his chair, walked to the window, and gazed out at the fields of the Hertfordshire countryside. 'We prepare our bodies and minds for the service of the Lord. Do not be deceived; there is war out there, brother.'

Kenny had been momentarily distracted by the pictures of D'Don standing alongside famous people that lined the wall behind the desk. He'd recognised the Pope in one, the prime minister in another, and the Queen in the largest of the framed photographs. Now he followed the pastor's gaze, looking out at the empty green fields, the blue sky, and the trees far away.

'The war is now, and it is upon us,' D'Don said. 'We

are in the rapture now. W, A, I, T, R, N, and it is not as the blind imagined. No, brother. It is a war, and we must be prepared. Ephesians 6:11: "Put on the full armour of God so that you can take your stand against the Devil's schemes." The Devil is waging war out there, and we must be ready to fight alongside Jesus.'

He turned around. The sun behind him blurred the edges of the muscle-bound frame on display beneath his fitted black trousers and body-hugging black turtleneck. A three-inch-high, diamond-encrusted crucifix dangled from a thick gold chain glistening just beneath his toned pecs. His belt had a curved snake as its buckle. Kenny recognised it. Gucci.

'One of the Devil's tools is pride. That is why we work out in the dark – so that we do not admire our own bodies. So that we are not tempted by the beauty of our own bodies or the bodies of our comrades as we prepare, because that is not why we build our strength. We build our muscles in preparation for the work that Jesus has for us, and we must not forget it. That is why we do not admire ourselves in mirrors. That is why we do not use our strength to fight, or to impress girls or boys, or to gather praise from admirers. We do not do it for likes. We build our muscles because we are Jesus' army. Do you get it now?'

Kenny looked up at the pastor's face. Their eyes met. He swiftly turned his gaze to the ground. The man of God was beautiful in a way that could only be the work of the Holy Spirit. Kenny had felt the presence of the spirit the moment he stepped into the pastor's presence. He felt it in his chest. It made him breathe faster. It filled him with a deep sense of joy, as if he were deeply in love with life itself.

'Raise your head,' D'Don said. He waited until Kenny looked up. 'There are two types of people: those who look down and those who look down at the bowed head. Never look down. Never bow before any man but Jesus. He is your Lord. He is your God. You serve in His army and His army alone. He has chosen you. You are chosen. He is your commander and your general, and He bows to no one, and you, too – his soldier – shall neither bow to man nor to the powers and principalities that we fight at His command.'

Kenny tried but could not bear to look straight into the pastor's eyes. Instead, he stared past him at the field outside.

D'Don walked up and stood in front of him. They were only inches apart. Kenny could smell the older man's cologne. He could feel the power of the Holy Spirit radiating from him. They were so close; he couldn't avert his eyes. The pastor stood there, looking into his eyes. Kenny yearned to look away.

The moment was broken when D'Don's phone rang, and he pulled the phone out of his pocket. As he turned, Kenny peered at the screen in the pastor's hand: 'Francis 666.' The beast! His head reeled with fear and his eyes shot away again. He feared that the pastor would notice his heart racing. Why did D'Don have a person's name stored on his phone alongside the mark of the beast? He silently began reciting the Lord's prayer.

The pastor rejected the call, returned the phone to his pocket, and walked around to stand behind Kenny. His whisper close to Kenny's ear jolted the teenager.

'We are at war, brother, and it is time to prepare. Ecclesiastes 3:8: "There is a time to love and a time to hate, a time for war and a time for peace." The time for war has come upon us, and you have been chosen. Jeremiah 51:20: "You are my war club, my weapon for battle – with you I shatter nations, with you I destroy kingdoms." Brother, are you prepared to serve your Christ and Saviour?'

Kenny nodded.

D'Don walked around and stood in front of Kenny once more. A smile softened the pastor's face. When he spoke, his voice had softened too.

'That day in the church,' he said. 'The day you were chosen. How did it feel?'

Kenny never stopped thinking about that day. His greatest fear was being asked about it, and now, of all people, Pastor D'Don was asking him, and he didn't have an answer. He swallowed hard.

If he kept quiet, perhaps it would go away. It worked with his mum. Whenever he couldn't answer a question of hers without getting into trouble, he would go silent. She would keep asking, getting louder and closer, her posture becoming more and more threatening, till she was close enough, and then she would ask one more time, giving him one last chance before the slaps began to fly from both hands.

If he ran, she would stay where she stood, make him come back, and the process would start all over again until his silence broke the limit of her frustration, and then the slaps would continue from her rested hands till his ears burnt red and the ringing in his head drowned out her enquiring voice. It was best not to run. He learnt to wait it out until she sent him off to the room he shared with his half-brothers, where he would spend the rest of the day without another meal. He learnt to take a beating at the hands of his mother – before social workers finally moved him for a while. From her, he also learnt how to keep quiet.

But this wasn't his mother. Perhaps it was time to confess.

He remembered to stand straight. He pushed his chest out and tightened his core, but he felt weak inside.

'It's hard to describe, isn't it?' D'Don said, smiling in Kenny's face, his calm voice, powerful with the Holy Spirit, reaching into the teenager's racing heart. 'How can human words describe such a divine experience? We are simply not equipped with the required vocabulary. Your gift is the ability to see things that normal eyes cannot see. What you saw that day wasn't a one-off. It was a revelation. A sign of greater things to come. I assure you, it is not the last vision you will have. Indeed, one day you will learn to master your gift. One day. I guarantee it. Tell me, do you know why you were chosen?'

Kenny shook his head.

'Oh, but you do,' D'Don said. He continued walking until he was behind Kenny again. 'You know God's purpose for you, for the gift he has given you; you just don't know that you know, but soon you will know. Soon you will learn how to listen to him and hear him clearly with your heart, just as you hear me now. In the meantime, you will hear his voice through me. I will guide you till you know who you are – who you truly are – and what your strange and important purpose is.

'Ephesians 6:12: "For we do not fight against flesh and blood, but against principalities and against powers, and the rulers of the darkness of this age, against spiritual hosts of wickedness in the heavenly places." So, therefore, my brother, we may prepare our bodies for war, but our battles are spiritual and will appear strange to men. Tell me, if I ask you to do something strange, will you do it?'

Kenny felt the pastor's breath on his neck. He nodded. He would do anything for the anointed man of God. Anything but talk about the day he was chosen.

'And what if it was God asking? Would you do it?'

Kenny nodded.

'Do you know the story of Jonah?'

Kenny knew this. He nodded with certainty. The pastor stood behind him.

'Would you have waited to be thrown overboard, or would you have leapt into that whale's mouth?'

Kenny nodded.

'You know the story of Abraham and his son, Isaac?'

Kenny nodded.

'Would you have hesitated or immediately killed your own son as a sacrifice to God?'

Kenny nodded.

The pastor remained behind him. He could feel his breath on his neck.

'One day, God will ask you to do something strange. I assure you, it will sound strange to you, but remember this: His ways are as far from ours as the heavens are from earth. But fear not; I will guide you till you know His plan for you, so that when He asks you to do something that seems strange, you will do it without hesitation because you will know it is precisely His plan for you. Are you prepared to obey God's commandment regarding your purpose?'

Kenny nodded, his heart racing.

'Show me your body,' D'Don whispered into his ear. 'Show me how you have prepared for the battle. Show me how ready my soldier is.'

In the six months since he had been chosen, Kenny had been living with his mentor, tagging along on errands during the day and working out in the dark at night. When his mentor had said it was time to meet D'Don, he felt sick to the stomach. What if his secret was exposed? Surely, D'Don of all people would know that he had no gift at all, and all the hard work would have been for nothing. He would have to return home to his life as a poor Black kid being brought up by a single mother who had two other children by two other fathers, none of whom were known to any of the children. It had been her choice. He had once overheard her on the phone telling someone how she wanted another child, but the man she had in mind wanted to have a family, and she didn't have space in her life for a man's problems. The fear of being found out and sent back to his mother and his half-siblings had kept him awake on many nights. On one such night, it had occurred to him that if he worked really hard and built the strongest body for the service of the Lord, all would be well. He had convinced himself of this, and now, as if the Spirit itself had inspired him, the pastor wanted to see his body.

'Show me,' D'Don whispered. 'Let me see my soldier. Take off your clothes. Let me see how you have prepared to serve in the army of Christ.'

Kenny tensed his muscles under his clothing, trying to flex them into readiness for display. He squeezed his pecs and curled his fists to tighten his arms. He had built his body well. Everything depended on it.

7

I got to the Hansom fifteen minutes early for my nine o'clock. I always try to arrive ahead of a potential new client. I like to watch them as they arrive. To see them in their normal state before we meet.

My favourite spot was at the back, at a set of two chairs and a table just to the left of the bar. Someone was already there, but another spot nearby was empty, so I hurried over to it. With some luck, they'd be done in time for me to reclaim my usual place.

As always, just before sitting, I stopped to admire the centralised, free-standing, marble-and-brass bar and the golden glow of its illuminated bottles. I draped my jacket over one of the chairs and sat on the long sofa on the other side of the table so I'd have a good view of the entrance. Then, as I glanced around, I noticed the person who'd taken my table standing up and walking towards me. She smiled and held out her hand.

She was tall and slim, with silky black hair like a L'Oréal advertisement, a face like a model, and a fitted skirt suit that looked more like a city worker's uniform than a schoolteacher's work outfit. It was my client. She was early. And she'd sat in my spot.

I got up, and we shook hands. 'Victoria?' I asked, somewhat redundantly.

'Hello,' she said, rather enthusiastically, flashing the most perfect set of sparkling white teeth. Then she came in for what turned out to be a soft hug, followed by a two-cheek kiss, from which I got a heady dose of her sweet perfume. Something felt off. Her perfume smelled expensive, her hello sounded like we were friends, and her hug and kisses were overly familiar.

She placed her bag and jacket on the sofa. I removed my own jacket from the chair I'd saved for her, and she sat down.

'Did you have to travel far?' I asked. It was my standard opening question. I was still thinking of the unexpected kisses and the wide smile that I couldn't quite place. Was it politeness? Was it enthusiasm? What was it? There was something about that smile that was puzzling me, and that wasn't always a good thing.

'Nah,' she replied, the same smile leaving her gleaming white, perfect dentition on constant display. 'Not really.'

'Great,' I said.

A waiter had meandered over. I asked for water, and so did she. We made it through the customary chit-chat, then I asked the standard, 'Have you had any coaching before?'

'Nope,' she said. Her smile stretched to her eyes.

'What about therapy?' I asked.

'Nope.' Still smiling.

She hadn't had either, so she wouldn't know what to expect. My first task was to dispel the usual misconceptions.

'Do you have an idea what it would be like?' I asked.

'Which?' she replied. 'Coaching or therapy?' This time her smile widened, and I couldn't tell if she meant the question as a joke.

'Coaching,' I said.

She shook her head.

'That's fine. Would you like me to tell you?'

'Yes, please,' she said. She leant forward, planted her elbows on the table, and rested her head on the hill of her palms. Her smiling eyes stared into mine.

'It's going to be a lot of you talking and a lot of me listening,' I said. 'Sometimes people new to coaching assume it's a process in which the coach tells the client what to do, how to solve their problems, how to fix their lives, that sort of thing. That's not how it works. I am not an expert on your life or your situation. That's your job. I will ask you a lot of questions, and I will give you time to think about them. We might do some activities or some exercises that involve movement, and I might give you some homework to do if you want it, but ultimately, you are going to do all the work yourself. I'm just going to be there, helping you think deeply and thoroughly until you arrive at your own solutions and answers, because you are the only expert on your own life and situation. What are your thoughts about that?'

I ended with an open question and got ready to hold the silence while she considered it. To experience a little of what our time together in the coaching room would feel like.

'I'm fine with it,' she said, without skipping a beat. Her smile had not wavered.

I had expected her to reflect a little before responding. Then it hit me. I'd nearly missed it as I focused on her smile. And she was still smiling. She had maintained the same smile throughout our conversation. I surreptitiously checked her eyes. Were her pupils dilated, or was I just imagining it? I would have to turn her down as a client if she showed attraction to me. The same would apply if I found myself drawn to her. Was I? It didn't matter now. What I had realised was that I had mistakenly called her Victoria – my ex's name – and she hadn't corrected me. It had felt strange that a schoolteacher had agreed to meet at nine a.m. on a weekday and had turned up dressed like a banker, wearing expensive perfume, and carrying a Prada handbag. In my gut, I began to get the distinct and familiar feeling that something was wrong. And in coaching, you don't just learn to trust your gut; you start to rely on it.

'What do you want from me?' I asked. It wasn't a question I'd ever asked a client. I watched her. I saw the slight twitch. It took her a second to recover, and then her eyes slid to the right. She was making something up. I didn't wait for the lie. 'Your name is not Maria, either.' The name she'd given me. It was a hunch. She hadn't corrected me when I'd called her Victoria because she had used a fake name to start with.

She looked deeply puzzled. Poor acting.

'And I know you're not a teacher,' I added.

My bullet-point delivery, like an aggressive barrister putting an accusation to a defendant, worked. The smile dissolved into a stern expression. I was disappointed. I'd hoped it was an innocent thing – that she'd wanted to use a fake name until she'd decided whether we could work together, at which point she would come clean and explain her need to be cautious. But the look on her face told a different story.

She spoke as if we were having a normal conversation. 'My name is Naomi Long-Fuller. You can google me. I'm an investigative journalist.'

I wasn't expecting that. What the hell did an investigative journalist want with me? Whatever it was, I'd bet it wasn't in my interest to stay to find out.

'I have one rule,' I said. 'No lies. I'm sorry, but we can't work together.'

I picked up my jacket and satchel bag and stood to leave, putting on an air of righteous indignation to mask my rising panic. She had lured me there for a reason. She had been waiting at my usual spot. I expected camera crews to close in on me at any moment.

Instead, she looked up into my eyes. 'You're the Bad Coach,' she said. 'You work with the Metropolitan Police. Your clients are police officers who've screwed up. Unconscious bias, racism, sexual harassment, excessive use of force – that sort of thing. That's why they call you the "Bad Coach". Because they send the bad eggs to you. Am I getting warmer?'

'What are you talking about?'

'Do you deny it?'

'I'm afraid you've got the wrong person,' I said. 'I just wish you'd been honest on the phone. We could have both saved each other the time.'

I stepped out from behind the table. As I made to move away, she grabbed my forearm to stop me and said, a little too loudly for comfort, 'I just want to know why the Metropolitan Police is so focused on reforming these bad characters. And why they're spending taxpayers' money hiring a convicted Nigerian police officer to do it.'

8

It was a grey autumn morning, besieged with clouds and the possibility of rain. From Buckingham Palace, Francis walked through Green Park, past chestnut, oak and plane trees that stood bare against the sullen sky. Fallen leaves, in shades of gold, amber and crimson, covered the ground, crunching beneath his feet. He continued past Lancaster House and towards his office at Clarence House, the cold air crystallising his breath all the way.

It had been years since he'd left the Circus and settled into his new role managing the royals. He had kept his past in the past – a wall between who he'd been and his new life meeting dignitaries from around the world, coaching presidents on royal protocol, responding to invitations from heads of state, and working on a memoir he would never be allowed to publish. It was his own personal brand of retirement, and he had grown into it, learning to enjoy his proximity to the heirs and heiresses, the tycoons and oligarchs, and even developing a taste for the occasional sip of champagne and canapés enjoyed on the sundeck of a tech billionaire's superyacht.

It was a wonderful life. And in the thirteen years he'd had the job, this beautiful life of his had only been interrupted twice: when Siobhan's Alzheimer's diagnosis had confirmed what they'd all feared, and when the pastor's letter had arrived on his desk. Now John could become another problem Francis had to deal with.

His phone vibrated in his trousers. He passed his duffel bag to his left hand, then grappled with his coat to fetch the phone, glancing ahead and around before looking at the screen. John had sent a message. Francis placed the duffel bag between his feet, and with fingers still wrinkled from his swim, he opened the text: 'Meet in ten.'

He checked the time on his watch. He could be there in ten minutes, give or take. John must have eyes on him. Francis looked around again. There were cameras anyone could see and more that only a few would spot, and then there were the walking cameras – wearable devices embedded in the clothing of agents deployed for specific targets. Why was John watching him?

Warily, he put on his gloves, then picked up his bag and turned around.

A year had passed since the letter first arrived on his desk, prompting him to seek out his old friend. He had read it so many times that he now knew every word by heart. At first, he would reread it line by line, scrutinising it for something he might have missed. Then, in time, as he made up his mind and began to put the pieces of his plan together, it became a ritual he performed to remind himself of what was at stake. Now, as he walked the ten-minute route to meet John, everything was at stake.

Francis walked through Marlborough Gate and swept his eye over St James's Park. The morning joggers were out. Most of them were government workers taking advantage of pathways that were relatively clear of tourists this early in the morning. He continued his solitary walk, registering every human that came into his field of vision.

John was alone on their bench, tossing cracked corn at a blackbird foraging in the grass. Francis sat and placed his bag between his feet once more. John threw another treat at the bird.

'It's quite chilly today,' he said without looking at Francis.

Both men had faces with set-in expressions: for Francis, a constant scowl of deep thought, and for John, a fixed squint of mistrust.

Francis tucked his hands into his jacket. He looked past the bird. A couple in tracksuits had stopped to take selfies. They pretended to sip from paper cups for the picture. A man in a dark suit was sitting with his briefcase on his lap, a copy of the *Financial Times* hiding his face. Francis watched the people jogging past. He would recognise anyone he saw coming around again.

'How is Marcus?' John asked, his eyes still on the blackbird, his speech as slow and deliberate as ever.

'Marcus?'

'Yes. How is he?'

Francis studied his old friend. He waited for John to fill the silence. Nothing. 'Why?' he asked.

'Why, what?' John replied.

'Why do you ask about my son?'

'Just asking.'

'He's well.'

'And the Mrs?'

'You know.'

'Yes. I'm so sorry. Give my love to Siobhan. And to Marcus, when you talk to him. He spends his time abroad these days, doesn't he?'

Francis watched John. Had he made a mistake reaching out to the spy catcher?

'I'm going to miss meeting you here,' John said, his gaze still fixed straight ahead.

'It's a no, then,' Francis said. He caught John's slight shrug. For a moment longer, he watched John watching the bird, then he looked over his shoulder at more agents pretending not to be agents. He had made a big mistake. 'What is this, John? A courtesy?'

'We're just talking.'

Francis looked behind them again. 'You've got what – seven, eight agents?'

John tossed another piece of corn at the bird. 'You know better than to look.'

'They're not for me,' Francis said in realisation. John would have noticed that he had assumed that they were.

John fetched more corn from his pocket. 'See that chap pretending to read his paper?'

Francis had already made the man with the *Financial Times*. He'd assumed he was one of the agents John had brought to their rendezvous.

'Anytime now, he's going to be done with the paper.' As John spoke, the man placed the paper down onto his briefcase, dusted crumbs off the front of his suit, then folded the paper in two.

'He's going to drop it into that bin, then he'll return to his desk at his job as a defence contractor in the service of His Majesty the King, and when he does, it will be without the tiny flash drive he had with him when he left work last night. Tiny thing. Almost as thin as paper. It would fit on the tip of your little finger.'

Francis watched the man stand up with his briefcase, walk to the bin, and drop the newspaper into it. The couple sipping coffee, a group of four joggers running by, and a park worker in overalls all ran to the man and seized him by his arms. Someone took his briefcase and walked away with it. More agents moved in from deeper in the park. They walked the man, his face a mix of shock and resignation, to a green van with the name and logo of a tree surgeon on its side. Two men in park uniforms were already at the bin, collecting the clear bag that lined it and replacing it with a new one.

'You know what's strange?' John said. 'Every time this happens, I feel bad for the poor sod. The thought of betraying his country would never have crossed his mind had he not met someone like you or me. Someone who had studied him for months, maybe years. Someone who had learnt his weaknesses and had neither the scruples nor the slightest hesitation about using them against him. And you know what else is strange? In the years I've been doing this, it has never been about the money. Not once. The money has always been a secondary motivation and not the primary driver. Wouldn't you agree?'

He turned to face Francis for the first time.

'I will miss meeting here. I assume you'll be moving up the road soon. I'm sure we'll work something out.'

'Why am I here, John?'

'It was your request, Francis. It gave me pause. A lot of people weren't happy when I brought you back. I told them that we were getting a different Francis, not the arsehole they all knew. I said it was something to keep your mind occupied while you looked after Siobhan. So imagine my surprise when I got your latest request. I stuck my neck out for you, Francis. I don't know what you're up to, but it seems you're back to your old ways. It doesn't matter anyway. They're not renewing your contract. It's over, and we're square.'

Francis sighed. 'I didn't want to have to do this,' he said.

He reached down into his bag and pulled out the green A4 plastic wallet. He removed the manila folder, opened it, withdrew the envelope inside, and handed it to John.

'What's this?'

'What I've been up to,' Francis said.

John stared at the envelope with scepticism, noting that it was addressed to Francis. He put on his glasses, removed the letter from its envelope, cast a glance at Francis, and then began to read.

9

Kenny pulled off his black hoodie and dropped it by his feet. He took off the black T-shirt beneath and held it tightly. He was aware of D'Don's presence behind him. The pastor's voice startled him: 'Everything.'

Slowly, uncertainly, Kenny unbuckled his belt, unbuttoned his black jeans, and waited. D'Don was silent. Kenny kicked his trainers off, then hesitantly pushed the trousers down and stepped out of them.

'Go on,' D'Don said.

It felt weird and wrong, but it was D'Don. He must have a reason. So Kenny pushed through his discomfort and pulled off his socks. Finally, he tugged his briefs down beneath his buttocks, moving his legs to ease them down his thighs rather than bending over. As he finished, he looked down at the discarded clothes at his feet. Since he had arrived at the mansion, he had not seen or heard anyone else. The building was so big it had to have twenty rooms or more, and maybe even a swimming pool. Why were they all alone in the big house? Why did Jesus need to see his naked body? Didn't Jesus know what he looked like?

'Pick up your clothes,' D'Don said.

Kenny considered the mechanisms of picking up his clothes. He repositioned himself – one step to the side so his back wasn't directly to the pastor. He kept his legs together, bent at the knees, and gathered the clothes to his chest before standing back up. He held the bundle over his groin.

'Give them to her.'

Her? Kenny hesitated before he looked. A girl was standing by the door that had been left open. She was wearing a pair of tight black jeans and a tight black turtleneck like the pastor, and she had a silver Gucci belt – the common one. She was about the same height as Kenny, but she looked older. Maybe twenty. She was also darker, and she was beautiful. Her face reminded him of an Afrobeats musician, but she couldn't be. He looked down when she smiled. Who was she? What was going on?

The young woman walked over and stood in front of him. When he finally looked up, she smiled and held her hands out for his clothes.

'You have become a new man today,' D'Don said. His voice was strong, as if he were speaking from the pulpit. 'Old things have passed away. Behold, all things have become new. You no longer need those clothes. That was the old you. Tashique will take them from you. She will clean you up and look after you. From now on, you will dress like a soldier of Christ. You are a warrior, and warriors dress in the garments of warriors. Give her the clothes.'

She was so close he could smell the sweetness of her

hair. It reminded him of his mother when she returned from the salon.

Tashique kept her eyes locked on to his as she reached for the bundle. She took his shoes, then, still looking into his eyes, she collected the rest of his stuff, held the bundle to her chest with one hand, and took his hand with the other.

'Come with me,' she said.

She tugged and he followed. D'Don walked behind them to the door, speaking in a rising voice that terrified Kenny and spread goosebumps along his exposed skin.

'You are now covered by grace. Anything you do is totally permitted. Soldiers do terrible things in war. They spill blood, they rape, they pilfer, they plunder. They destroy armies and nations, and yet, their victory is assured by the power of God who sends them. Second Corinthians 12:9: "But he said to me, 'My grace is sufficient for you, for my power is made perfect in weakness.'" He has chosen you. He sends you now with his power, and his grace is sufficient for you. Whatever you do is permitted. No matter how strange it first appears to you. One day you will know your purpose – the purpose for which you are called. From now on, you are covered by grace.'

10

The 'convicted Nigerian police officer' remark caught me off guard. Where did she get that from? Images from that time flashed through my mind, along with chilling thoughts of what could have been. My time in the Nigerian police force had turned out to be the second major traumatic event in my life. Remembering one always brought back memories of the other. I felt the tightening in my chest that I'd once mistaken for a heart attack and took a deep breath to counter my increased heart rate. If I spent too long in either of those pasts, I would soon start sweating, and dizziness would follow. Right there, in that beautiful space that I loved so much, I was experiencing multiple trauma responses from multiple traumas, but I couldn't let it show.

'Sit,' Naomi said.

I took care to hide my slow exhale as I maintained eye contact with her in silence, and she must have thought she had me. I took another stealthy deep breath, followed by a longer exhale while she watched, no doubt celebrating her victory. Oh, but she'd lost me at hello.

I had so many questions that I was tempted to sit and pretend to be checkmated so I could find out just how much she knew. But one thing I've learnt is that you cannot say something you'll later regret if you say nothing at all. I was already in a weak position. She knew about my practice, and she even knew my silly nickname, but all I knew about her was that she was a journalist. She'd got one thing wrong, though. I was accused of tampering with evidence. It was someone's word against mine. There was no evidence either way. I was never convicted. Which meant she was fishing. I wasn't going to bite.

I placed my satchel down on the chair and caught the smile returning to her face. It faded away when I picked up my jacket and began to put it on. She looked surprised. I buttoned it up, picked up my bag, and walked away.

I feared she would shout out her accusations as I left, so I increased my pace, but not so much that I'd draw attention. I'd not seen a camera crew. That was good. But they could be waiting out there with damning questions. What the hell was going on?

Outside was clear, as far as I could tell. Also, she hadn't followed me. I still needed to get far enough away from her to think. Of course, my practice would make a great story for anyone willing to bend the truth in favour of sensationalism. Something about rotten Met officers getting a second chance thanks to an unscrupulous Nigerian coach ready to give them a pass. No. They'd make it sound even dodgier than that. Nigerian coach sells waivers to corrupt officers.

But why hadn't she followed me?

It was a classic move: waylay a subject, tell them just enough to scare them, then see who they call or lead you to. I had to take precautions. It might yet turn out that I was overreacting, but I was trained to think of everything you might do to your adversary, then assume they'd do the same to you.

I'd planned to take the Metropolitan line to Baker Street, then walk to Marylebone for my ten twenty a.m. with Roger, but now I had to make a different plan. Then it hit me. Roger. Undercover cop, terrible misconduct, massive cover-up. Could he be the story? Did she know I was meeting him?

The more I thought about it, the more it made sense. Of course, I would never be able to admit that he was a client, never mind disclosing the nature of his misconduct, but if she already had an inside source who'd tipped her off, and I assumed she did, then nothing could stop her from naming me in the story she was working on.

She had accused me of being a convicted police officer. I could have corrected her on that point, but doing so would have amounted to admitting to something. I wasn't going to admit to anything when I wasn't sure what was going on. Invoking my Met nickname had made my practice sound shady, but while it wasn't openly broadcast, it wasn't exactly secret either. I was just one of thousands of private contractors working for them. And they had vetted me. I had been through every known vetting process, and because I was a former officer of a foreign country, I'd also been subjected to levels of investigation not in the public domain. The Met knew about my problem with the Nigerian police force. They knew the whole story.

It had all started when I was thirteen. One day, my father and his driver, Brother Biodun, did not return from the biscuit factory my family owned. There were no mobile phones or email messaging back then. By the time we realised they were missing, the factory had been shut for the day, and we couldn't confirm when they had left or with whom. My mother reported them missing at the police station, and then, with my father's younger sister, she visited every hospital and every mortuary in the area.

We received a phone call early the next morning, and then the terrible news was confirmed in the papers and, later in the day, on the news on NTA, the Nigerian Television Authority. I still remember the strangeness of watching the beautiful newsreader mention my father's name. He, along with fifty-three others, had been accused of plotting to overthrow the military government.

Nobody knew where they were being held. Even their lawyers had no access to them. Days became weeks, and weeks became months. Our home became overwhelmingly busy with worried relatives, neighbours and occasional journalists, but not one of my father's friends or business partners showed up – our house was being watched. Soldiers outside the gate searched cars as they came and as they left. Eventually, my mother started taking meals out to them, much to the chagrin of my father's sister, who had begun to come over after work to help with Mimi, my sister.

I'd been dreaming that the phone was ringing, and

somehow, I knew it was my father calling, and that I, specifically, had to take his call or else something really terrible would happen to him. But, with the phone ringing away in the living room, try as I might, I just couldn't move. I stayed glued to the bed, desperately fighting whatever was keeping me frozen, and with each unanswered ring, hope for my father's safety slipped away.

I was still focusing all my effort on willing my leg to move when I felt a hand shaking me. I woke, rescued from the grip of my sleep paralysis, and my mother was bent over me, her finger to her lips.

'Get dressed,' she whispered. 'Hurry.'

It was dark, but I could see wrapping cloth around her midriff. Mimi was tied to her back. And as she walked out of my room, my pupils adjusted, and I saw that she was dressed in a pair of jeans and a sweater and her running shoes. I knew that something was wrong. I knew I had to do as she said.

The rooms of the house were filled with staff and relatives. We didn't wake any of them. We didn't say goodbye.

We left through the kitchen. She placed the ladder the gardeners used against the fence in the backyard, then climbed and sat on top while I also climbed up. When I had reached the top, she pulled the ladder up and over the fence and descended into our neighbour's yard, which was patrolled by their Alsatian dogs. She waited for me with the dogs snarling and barking at her feet. I was so afraid. Mimi was crying, my legs were wobbling on the ladder, but my mother was looking only at me, holding the ladder steady and waiting. The look on her face that night is forever burnt into my brain. A steely determination beneath which I could see the extreme fear that was fuelling her unflinching resolve.

We climbed into the boot of Mr Okoro's yellow Mercedes 230. He drove us to a motor park, where we boarded a bus, the other passengers complaining about the smell of petrol on our bodies. My mother smuggled us to Benin that night, and all through the journey she had that same look – a look so powerful it was both reassuring and frightening. I just knew that she would kill anyone who tried to harm either me or Mimi that night. In the morning, in a motel in Cotonou, she washed our clothes, squeezed the water out of them with the only towel in the bathroom, and ironed them until they were dry. She counted the money she had on her, then took out the jewellery she'd stuffed into her bra and spread it all out on the mattress. She selected a thin gold chain that went back into her bra, then she told me to look after Mimi and not to open the door for anyone until she returned. It was the first time she'd ever put me in charge of my sister, and the only time she'd left Mimi alone since she'd been born three months earlier.

When my mother returned to fetch us, there was a taxi waiting outside. I still remember how Mimi hadn't made a sound while she was away. I'd sat on the bed and watched over my baby sister. She seemed so small. Her little eyes followed mine, as if somehow, she had become aware of the danger that we were in.

My mother eventually brought us to the UK, where I stayed for the rest of my childhood. Back home, and without any evidence, a court found my father and the fifty-three others accused alongside him guilty as charged. Treason. The men were mostly academics, along with a couple of journalists, a handful of high-ranking soldiers, and a number of wealthy businessmen like my father. Everybody knew there had been no failed coup or plot, but still the 'coup plotters' were executed – shot at dawn and the truth buried with them. The dictator had got rid of the soldiers he did not trust, and his civilian allies had got rid of their business rivals.

When I returned to Nigeria and joined the police force, I thought it would allow me to investigate those who had betrayed and framed my father. I was wrong.

11

John looked up from the letter and gazed into the distance. Francis watched him. He knew that the veteran spy catcher would take his time. If it were him, he would have been stunned into silence as well. He, too, would weigh and measure the brand-new information, ask hypothetical questions, and attempt to answer them. One question, more than any other, would be the most difficult to solve: What do I do with this?

'Fuck, Francis,' John said.

'I know,' Francis replied.

'Who is it?'

'Do you really want to know?'

'Fuck.'

John kept staring straight ahead. A mother pushing a stroller approached. John's stare sliced through her as she passed.

'When you asked if you could come back as a trainer, it wasn't for the money,' John said. 'You already had the letter.'

'Correct. I needed resources so I could have eyes on him and the girl while I figured it all out.'

'What were you planning to do?'

'I thought I could handle it on my own. I was wrong. I fucked up.'

John fell silent and continued to gaze into the distance. After a while: 'I take it the claim checks out.'

'Oh, it does,' Francis said. 'I researched the pastor after I got the letter. He appeared to be legit, so I went to see him. He showed me a video. Do you want to know what's on it?'

John met his eye and they stared at each other.

'All right, then,' Francis went on. 'In the video, the accused person uses his teeth to tear off one leg of the girl's black silk tights, then he uses his mouth on her. It's who she named. I checked, and it was easy to place both of them in the same place at the time she said it happened.'

'Oh, fuck. Who else knows about this?'

'Just you and me and the letter writer.'

'What does he want?'

'Access. When we met, he reminded me that he did not want any reward, as stated in his letter. I played along and asked him for a copy of the video so I could verify it. He claimed the video was never duplicated; the original file still sits on the girl's phone and it's kept in a safe deposit box somewhere. I haven't managed to find it yet.

'As for my request to have the video verified, he has been waiting for God to tell him whether he should hand it over to me. In the meantime, he's been asking for little favours – introductions, invitations, that sort of thing.'

'And have you given him anything?'

'I've thrown him a few scraps here and there. Introduced him to a lord here, a viscount there. I had him brought up to meet me in the Royal Box at Ascot. He loved that. He was there for all of five minutes, but it kept him happy for weeks. I steered a few clients his way – high-net-worth individuals I'd introduced him to at events. Conveyancing is his thing. That kept him busy and satisfied. Or so I'd hoped. I thought that was all he wanted.'

John turned fully towards Francis. 'Francis,' he said, 'I'm perplexed. What does he want access to? What's his end goal?'

'Well. He's got it into his head that the palace chooses the prime minister.'

John raised his eyebrows in disbelief. 'He wants to be PM?'

'No. He wants it for the woman. He essentially believes he can blackmail me into getting the palace to give her the nod.'

'Is that a joke?'

Francis sighed.

'You know, John,' he said. 'I would have put it above you to think that the idea of a Black female prime minister is a joke.'

'Fuck you,' John said, his firm face cracking into a chuckle.

They laughed together. For a brief moment, they were young men again, but a moment was all they spared.

Francis pushed his glasses up the bridge of his nose, wiping all emotion from his face. 'It's not as bizarre as it sounds,' he said. 'That's how it's done in his country, only the other way around. The president appoints the kings, so it's really up to him. This man doesn't just think that the palace can, if it wishes, choose the prime minister; he believes that's how every prime minister has been secretly chosen since the Glorious Revolution.'

'Is he crazy?'

'In a lot of ways, but on this, he is dead serious. He really believes that God speaks to him.'

'And he thinks that God ordained this lunacy?'

'I'm afraid so.'

'What if it's just what he wants you to believe?' John asked, sounding sceptical.

'The thought occurred to me. I did a background check on him. He's just a very delusional, possibly outright deranged, individual. You should hear the things he says in his church.'

'Church?'

'Yes. He's a pastor. He operates one of those American-style churches. He's a full-time pastor and a part-time lawyer with only one client – this woman. He's managed to brainwash her with some religious nonsense, and he even got her to sign a contract that basically gags her.'

'Why did he pick you?'

'I'm the King's PA,' Francis said, mimicking D'Don's accent.

'Do you think he knows who you really are?'

'If he did, he wouldn't have come to me. All he wanted was an old, loyal subject who would do anything to cover up a scandal this big.'

John fell silent again. 'You said you fucked up. How?'

'How much do you want to know?'

'We never had this conversation.'

Francis nodded.

'An opportunity came up,' he said. 'And thanks to you bringing me back in, I was able to have someone placed in his church. A copper. A couple of months after he started working there, my pastor friend called me, seeking my advice. He told me how a young man he had recently employed to head up security at the church had raped a girl. He said that her boyfriend had witnessed it. He said he was worried about what it might do to her mental health, considering the other alleged incident. He wanted to know if I thought it was a good idea to let her go to the police. I told him I trusted his judgement. She went to the police and gave a statement. I have a copy. She described in specific details how the lad used his teeth to tear off one leg of her black silk tights.'

'Same as in the video,' John said.

'Yup.'

'That was a message to you.'

'I'm afraid so. But he's only fishing. And there's no way the copper comes back to me. He doesn't know I exist – he thinks he was working on some money laundering thing.'

'Do you know how the pastor found out about him?'

'I'm not certain that he did,' Francis said, slowly shaking his head. 'But something spooked him – that's for sure.'

'Does your man know?'

'No. As far as he's aware, his cover was never blown. He thinks the girl set him up.'

'Explain.'

'He claims she was hitting on him, but he knows better than to have sex with a suspect while undercover.'

'Unless it's necessary and proportionate,' John said. 'What happened to him?'

'She withdrew her statement the same day she made it. There was no evidence, and she didn't mention a witness. Even though the case didn't go any further, the Met still had to do something, so they stuck him behind a desk and sent him to see a coach.'

'A coach? Like a therapist?'

'Similar but not the same. According to my understanding, a therapist has patients, and a coach has clients. A therapist fixes you, whereas a coach helps you fix yourself. I got that off the man's website.'

'Why did they send him to a coach?'

Francis shrugged. 'Something about working with women,' he said. 'He saw the man twice a month for six months, and then the matter was considered closed. I didn't bug their sessions. I didn't think it was important. Seeing the coach was just a formality. Procedure. I made sure he understood that. All he had to do was show up, talk about stuff, appear normal, and that was it.'

'But now you're thinking he might have said something?' John asked.

'There was nothing to tell. My only concern is the pastor. If he were to hear the voice of God telling his client to go public now, an attempted cover-up would make things much worse. There would be an investigation; he would mention me, he would mention the copper and everyone would know that you brought me back in after you were told not to.'

'Fuck you, Francis.' John held his face in his hands and hung his head. '*Fuck*. What were you thinking?'

'I thought I could handle the situation without anyone ever needing to know about it,' Francis said, his voice calm as he stared straight ahead.

'What are you going to do now?'

'I'm going to clean up the mess I made.'

'Fuck, Francis. Fuck.' John took a deep breath and exhaled slowly. 'Okay. Your request has been approved. You have your reclassification.'

He stood to leave.

'One more thing,' Francis said.

John tucked his hands into his pockets and stared down at him.

'I need a specialist,' Francis continued.

A moment passed, then John turned around and walked away.

Francis exhaled as if he'd been holding a deep breath. John had come through. Francis was no longer training spies; he was now running live agents. The letter was in his gloved hands. He carefully folded it up, put it back into its envelope, put the envelope back into the plastic wallet, and put the plastic wallet back into his bag.

John's fingerprints were all over the letter now.

12

Tashique led Kenny up the arched glass balustrade staircase to a wide landing on the first floor that was bathed in light from a large skylight above. Then, still holding his hand and leading the way, she took him through a doorway and into a hall with many more doors leading off it. At the end of the hall, she opened the last one and pulled him in with her.

It was a huge bedroom, larger than any bedroom he'd ever seen, except on TV. It was even bigger than his mother's front room, maybe even bigger than the front room and the kitchen of the council flat combined. A massive four-poster bed dominated the space, but it was a framed black-and-white picture of Tashique on the dressing table that drew his attention. She looked younger in it, and she was smiling, but not like when you smile for the camera; she looked genuinely happy, as if someone had taken the photo because she was happy. He wondered who.

She let go of him, and his hand snapped onto the other over his groin. She walked to the dresser and dropped his clothes on top of a pile of other clothes in a colourful woven basket.

'I'll wash them and take them to a charity shop,' she said, turning to him then taking him all in. 'First, we need to get you cleaned up, then I'll find you something to wear till you get new clothes.'

She walked up to him. 'Did he tell you everything?' she asked.

She was so beautiful.

'Well?' she said.

He had no idea what she meant.

'You know why you're here, correct?'

This he knew. It was because he was chosen. He nodded.

She smiled and pulled off her top. His eyes darted about, trying to look away, but they kept returning to her chest. What was she doing?

She dropped her top and continued to undress. He looked at her picture on the dressing table. What was happening?

'Can you do me a favour?' she asked.

He looked at her and nodded. He didn't dare move his eyes from hers.

'When he takes you shopping, can you get something for me too? A perfume.'

He nodded again.

'It's okay to use your voice, you know,' she said, smiling into his eyes. 'I bet you sound good, too.'

He looked to the ground. Adjusted his hands to conceal his condition.

'Look up, soldier.'

He looked up.

She took off her bra and tossed it towards the bed. He watched it fall short by a foot. His eyes darted to the door. His heart was beating fast again. The door was unlocked. The pastor could walk in at any time.

She kicked off her shoes, wiggled out of her trousers, and stood straight, staring at him. He looked at the floor. He looked back up. He turned his face towards her picture. He looked the other way.

She walked towards him, then raised her hand up to his chin and lifted his face towards her. 'We are covered by grace,' she said, taking his hand. 'Come with me.'

He walked behind her, her arm extending backwards as she led him to the bathroom. He glanced back at the closed door to the hallway. What if D'Don walked in? What if he saw them naked together? Why was she doing this? Could it be a test? Were they testing him? Satan tempted Adam with a woman. That had to be it. It was a test. Everything was a test. They were testing him to see if he was really born again. When the pastor made him take off his clothes, he was testing his obedience, and when Tashique took her clothes off, she was testing him to see if he could resist temptation. This was just a test. He relaxed. When D'Don sneaked in to catch him, he would have passed the test.

The shower was behind a floor-to-ceiling pane of glass beside a freestanding bathtub. Tashique let go of him to turn on the water and test the temperature. Kenny looked up and froze. Above him was the sky. In all his life, he had never imagined standing in a mansion, taking a shower, and looking out through a skylight.

She pulled him under the rush of warm water, reaching for a bottle of shower gel from the alcove and a loofah hanging from a suction hook. He averted his eyes as she turned to him.

'Look at me,' she said.

He looked up.

She stepped closer. His heart began to race again. He flinched as she placed the loofah on his chest. In gentle circular motions, she bathed him with a minty green soap that tingled his nostrils and peppered his eyes.

'Turn around,' she said. He turned. He longed for her touch. She drew a line down his spine with the loofah, from his neck to his tail bone. Beneath the rushing water, engulfed in minty steam, the loofah in her hand drawing circles on his back, his body began to betray him. He squeezed his eyes, trying to recite the Lord's prayer but never making it past 'Our Father'.

She placed her hand on his shoulder and spun him around.

She rinsed the loofah, soaped it up again, then held it out to him and said, 'Your turn.'

13

I got a black cab. As I stepped in, I scanned the front of the Renaissance Hotel to see who might possibly be following me. I'd already checked everywhere else from where I'd been standing with my back to the hotel. If I was being followed, I didn't want them to know that I knew.

I got off on Harewood Avenue. I'd been checking throughout the ride, and I was sure no car was following us, but I still wasn't taking chances. Chance is what gets you, and your adversary only needs one. I walked the rest of the distance in a meandering manner, crossing the road, stopping in front of a restaurant, and pretending to read the menu in the window while I looked behind me in its reflection. A man in a green cardigan, who had also previously been on the other side of the road, walked past. I looked again to be sure. Slender build, five-ten, mid-twenties, green cardigan, blue chinos, nubuck boots. Definitely the same guy. My skin tingled as oxygenated blood was redirected to essential organs. This was happening.

I had options. I could follow Green Cardigan to see

where he led me or I could shake him off, but most importantly, I had to keep moving. Just as I made up my mind, I caught my own reflection in the window and recognised the face staring back at me. The young detective tailing a ransom bearer who had arranged his own uncle's abduction. Only I wasn't in my twenties anymore, I wasn't in the heart of Mushin, and I'd not held a firearm or been shot at in decades. If indeed I was being followed, it wasn't a matter of life and death; it was just journalists looking for a story.

I knew exactly what Margaret, my supervisor coach, would say if I told her I'd had another episode. We'd done so much work together on it. It had been months since my former self had last jumped to the fore at the slightest whiff of something. The first time had been 'a pattern' I'd noticed in the sequence of delivery vans arriving at a shop on the other side of the road from a café I used a lot. I was in the queue at the post office, holding a box addressed to that same shop. Inside was a cheap table clock I'd bought from one of those spy gadget shops on the high street, the kind with a tiny camera hidden behind the numbers that could transmit to my phone. I'd only come to my senses when I found myself at the counter and the clerk asked what was inside. There was nothing I could say that wouldn't make me sound insane.

If I told Margaret that I'd had another paranoid episode, she'd ask if I still had the details of the therapist whom she'd suggested I speak to. I still had their card in my phone case wallet. I had no plans to call them.

Green Cardigan sidestepped a pram and kept on

walking, totally oblivious to the pair of eyes on him. I took a deep breath and let it go, before crossing the road and hurrying on to my appointment with Roger. I'd wasted time on a fantasy, and I was now running late.

A police van was parked close to the entrance to Marylebone Station as I arrived. More sirens were approaching, and officers appeared to be cordoning off the area. I instinctively searched the ground around them for blood. I feared there'd been another stabbing. It seemed to be happening fairly regularly – kids with knives stabbing other kids.

I searched for Roger in the crowd that had been evacuated from the station. I was already ten minutes late, but I couldn't see him. I checked for missed calls, then I remembered that he didn't have my mobile. I scanned the crowd. Had he left? Could he be watching me? Had his train been delayed due to whatever was going on? A suspicious package, no doubt. Maybe he hadn't even arrived.

I spotted a woman in a TfL vest on her phone. She was also watching from the crowd that had formed around me. I pushed my way over to her and made it obvious I meant to talk. When she lowered her phone, I asked, 'What's going on?'

'There's a casualty on the track,' she said, and returned to her call.

Of course, all trains to or from Marylebone would be delayed or suspended. I pictured Roger in a carriage stuck on the tracks, with precious little explanation coming from the driver. What if he hadn't planned to arrive by train? I'd assumed he had because he'd asked to meet on the concourse. Right now, he could be watching me. Or maybe he'd got cold feet. I had to talk to him. I had to know what the journalist had on him and what it had to do with me. Regrettably, I found his mobile number and I sent him a message: 'Call me. I need to ask you something. This is Bobby Fatokun.'

Now he had *my* mobile number.

There wasn't much point in hanging around. I searched the crowd for Roger one last time, and my eyes swept past Green Cardigan. I did a double take. It was him. He was looking straight at me. My skin tingled. A rogue thought flashed through my mind: I should have trusted my instincts. He kept staring. Throat dry, I looked behind me and caught the back of a camerawoman. A reporter was facing the camera and speaking into her microphone. I recognised her from a reality show. Other people had recognised her as well and were filming her and taking pictures. I checked on Green Cardigan again. He wasn't brazenly staring at me. He was gawping at the reality show star turned reporter.

I turned away and began walking, struggling to breathe against my racing heart.

14

Francis stayed behind and watched John leave the park. There was a time when he wouldn't have lost sleep over manipulating a friend or thought twice about blackmailing them. 'By all means necessary' had meant exactly that. Huge stakes necessitated huge sacrifices. Ancient cultures understood this. But here he was, somewhat regretful of the bridge he'd just burnt and the insurance he'd taken out to guarantee it'd be John's neck on the line and not his if things went south.

He set his eyes on the empty bench where the traitor had sat and exhaled deeply, releasing all the tension, anxiety and fear that had built up inside him, and finally relaxed his shoulders. For the first time since the pastor's letter had arrived on his desk, he felt powerful. He felt in control. Now that he had the means and the clearance to deal decisively with the situation concerning the Nigerian pastor, he could finally see a way out.

He looked around for the bird that John had been feeding. When they were young men in their twenties, John would often hush everyone to listen to a bird singing, then he would locate it, point it out, and educate everyone on it – its common name, its scientific name, whether it was male or female, and what the particular song was for. He had kept grain in his pockets for as long as Francis had known him.

The blackbird returned as he watched. It searched in the grass where John had tossed the corn. Francis smiled and stood up. It was a cold autumn morning, and the warmth from his morning exercise had long worn off. He patted his pockets and glanced at the bench for anything he might have left behind, then looked at the traitor's seat one more time. The bird flew off again. Francis turned and walked away.

At his office in Clarence House, he shut the door behind him and went to the old Chubb Manifoil MK4 safe in the corner. Twisting the dial to unlock the heavy metal box, he inspected its empty cavity carefully before placing the plastic wallet inside.

Back at his desk, he reclined in the familiar chair, reflecting on the meeting with John. It had gone well. Better than he had anticipated. Maybe too well. He sat back and stared into space, watching their conversation replay in his mind, searching for the source of his discomfort.

The spy catcher had reacted to the letter as Francis had anticipated he would; he had also reacted to Francis' confession in the exact manner that Francis had anticipated, as well as to Francis forcing his hand – with swearing before giving in. Everything had gone according to plan. But things seldom, if ever, go exactly as planned. Something still didn't sit right.

After John had responded to his request by asking to meet in person, Francis had begun to mentally rehearse the different conversations they might have. In the bathtub, alone in his home study, bringing Siobhan's meal up the stairs, he would speak John's words out loud to hear how accurate his anticipations were. While feeding the birds in St James's Park, John had barely strayed from the script – almost as if he too had designed the conversation to go in a similar, predetermined direction. John, after all, trusted no one, and someone could have briefed him on the strangeness of the exercises that Francis made his trainees do. Maybe that was it – the one thing Francis had not anticipated. Maybe John had already known he was up to something and had waited until he came clean. Maybe the conversation had been easy because John had been relieved to learn the true nature of what Francis was up to. Maybe that was it.

Francis' eyes darted back and forth as he double-checked everything: the agents in the park, the traitor's paper, the arrest team, and John's speech. Something still bothered him; he just wasn't sure what it was.

He reached for his phone and dialled a contact.

'Dad?'

'Marcus, how are you?'

'Fine, Dad. Is everything okay?'

'Why wouldn't it be?'

A long pause.

'Dad, did something happen?' Marcus had lowered his voice almost to a whisper. 'Dad? Is it Mum?'

'No. Nothing's happened. I just felt like saying hello.'

'Okay. Hello.'

'Go back to sleep. Say hello to the woman next to you.'

15

Kenny's heart was beating so fast that he couldn't think. He took the loofah from Tashique, and she turned her back to him. He was having the strangest day of his life, stranger even than when he'd first worked out in the dark. But he was in the light now, and he could see what was in front of him.

Water ran down her back, between her buttocks, and down her legs. He had never seen a body so beautiful. Her body was as beautiful as her face. And her voice. Everything about her was beautiful. She was perfect. He knew then that what he felt for her was more than the erection he was pressing against his belly with his hand.

He had been aroused since she'd taken off her clothes while standing in front of him in the bedroom. It did not appear to bother her, but it had shamed him, and on top of that, there was also the physical discomfort from the strain in his groin that he could do nothing about. They were testing him. This was how they would know if he was truly worthy. He wondered how many boys had failed before him. Did they know he had never done it before?

Maybe Abraham had told them. It was unfair that they were testing him this way. Who wouldn't be tempted? He rebuked himself: a person who had adequately prepared his body and his mind to serve God, that's who. The shame and the arousal stared one another down in his spirit, neither stepping back nor gaining ground, so he stayed perfectly still, holding the loofah to her back and, with his other hand, his erection to his belly.

He wanted to apologise for the way his body had betrayed him, but he didn't, and he knew why. He knew he was holding out in case something happened between them. Even though he knew it was a trap, his body still longed for the bait.

'What are you waiting for?' Tashique asked. She glanced at him over her shoulder.

'Sorry.'

'Don't be silly. You didn't do anything wrong.'

He watched the water streaming down her body.

'Whenever you're ready,' she said.

He began to gently rub her back in soft circular motions. He let his eyes wander down to her bum.

This is a test. This is a test.

'Tell me about yourself,' she said.

'Sorry?'

She glanced over her shoulder again. 'What are you sorry for?'

'Sorry. I mean, nothing.'

She giggled. 'You're so cute,' she said. And when he still didn't talk, 'Well?'

'What do you want to know?' he asked.

'Everything, of course. Okay. Let's try this. How about I tell you about myself, then you tell me about yourself? How about that?'

He nodded. He realised she couldn't see it, so he said, 'Yeah.'

'Okay. So, I'm from Golders Green. I'm an only child, but I have a sister and a brother. Okay. I need to explain that. My dad was Jamaican. He died before I was born. He was a radiographer. My mum was half Jamaican, half Trinidadian. People say I look like her, but I think I look more like my father. You know what? I have their picture. I'll show you, and you can tell me who I look like. She was a nurse. She died when I was twelve, and I went to live with my cousins in Edgware for a while, but it didn't work out. Their dad was creepy as hell. Damn. Can you believe this man would . . .'

She fell silent, and Kenny kept circling the same spot on her shoulder.

'You know those old houses where the bathroom has a little window above the door?' she said eventually. 'I shit you not, this grown-ass man would pull a chair up to the door to look at me. His kids were older, so they didn't stay at home, and his wife left early for work, so I would be alone in the house with this man. As soon as he hears me open my door, he comes out into the corridor to catch me in a towel. I was twelve. I was a child. I was his niece.'

She fell silent again. After a while, he felt he should say something, but he didn't know what to say, so he stayed silent with her, and when she was ready, she continued.

'I started changing in the bathroom. Dude, one time

this man tried to open the door. He legit tried to unlock it from the outside. He was very sneaky about it. He waited till I'd turned on the shower, then he used a coin or whatever to open the lock from the other side. I'd heard him come out of his room the minute I shut the door, so I knew he would try something. I shouted, "Who's that?" and this idiot said he didn't know I was in there. Can you imagine? Who did he think locked the door? A ghost? Fucking paedo.

'Anyway. He got done for fraud. When he went to prison, his wife left him, and I ended up with foster parents, and that's how I'm an only child and I have a sister and a brother. They're white. Emily and Giles. Emily is an orthopaedic surgeon. She lives in Scotland now. She moved there to be with her partner, Sasha. I love Sasha. She's Black. Giles works at the UN. We have our own WhatsApp group. They're the only real family I have.

'Isn't that strange? I'm a Black girl but the only sister and brother I've ever had are white. Sadly, Bruce and Dawn, my foster parents, died. Cancer is a bitch.'

She sighed. Kenny continued on her back. He had so many questions. Did she have other foster parents as he did? How come she was living with Pastor D'Don?

'Let's see,' Tashique said after a little while. 'What else, what else? Yeah. Okay. So, I wanted to be a nurse, you know? Like my mum, but anyway. What else? Oh yes. I used to be a model. I was actually trying to be an actress. I have a showreel and all. I'll show you. I did a couple of plays and loads and loads of auditions, then something happened, and long story short, I met D'Don, and now

I work with him.' She turned to him with a small smile. 'Your turn.'

'What happened?' Kenny asked.

'We're done talking about me now,' she replied. 'It's your turn. Tell me about you. And what are you doing? I'm sure my back is clean enough by now.' She giggled. 'Do the rest.'

He lifted the loofah away. His eyes were fixed on the curve of her back. Without intending to and without thinking, he placed the loofah on her bum and squeezed. She swiftly reached back and slapped his hand away. His eyes darted to the bathroom door. Horror filled his heart. There was a sinking feeling in his stomach. He had failed the test.

16

Francis was done for the day. At the door, he patted his pockets and looked around his office. His eyes stopped on the red diary on his desk. He returned, picked it up, placed it in the open safe in the corner, and turned the dial four times to the left.

Leaving the office, he walked from Clarence House to an antique gun shop on Mount Street in Mayfair with 'Dudley & Co.' printed in gold on the window. He waited in the doorway until he was buzzed in. The shopkeeper was standing behind a counter that ran the length of the shop, dressed in a dark suit that blended in with the wall behind him. He said, 'I'll be with you in a moment, sir,' and continued showing a double-barrelled shotgun to an older man in a tweed jacket while Francis busied himself inspecting the contents of the display cases.

Presently, the customer left. Without missing a beat, Francis walked to the far end of the shop, where he lifted the countertop away, swung open the half-door beneath it, and left through the door behind the counter. On a monitor behind the till, the shopkeeper watched him walk down the corridor to a narrow, wrought-iron spiral staircase at the end and begin to descend into the confined space below, where a slender man in his twenties, dressed in a long-sleeved thermal vest, a pair of blue chinos and nubuck boots, was holding open another door.

Francis hung his coat next to a green cardigan on a clothes rack by the door of the windowless room beneath the gun shop. Unlike the casual Mayfair opulence of the floor above, the cellar room was small, taking up a grand footprint of a mere ten by seven feet. The walls were the same colour as their original render – grey and cracked – with fault lines running across the ceiling and down each side. On the left of the cramped space, a woman and a man sat facing their respective screens, surrounded by additional workstations and various monitors. A two-seat sofa stood against the wall on the right, barely a metre away. A water cooler took up the remaining floor area, and a single energy-efficient bulb hung from the low ceiling.

Libby's porcelain fingers and glossy black fingernails hovered above her keyboard as she watched Francis settle down on the sofa. She was dressed all in black – the shiny PVC trench coat hanging from the clothes rack belonged to her – and her white face powder and black lipstick made her look older than her twenty-seven years. Rod, in his early twenties, was next to her at the last workstation in the line, with his own bank of monitors in front of him. He swung around in his swivel chair and clamped his fingers behind his head. Dempsey, who had let Francis in, returned to his seat at the head of the row of computers and sat facing Francis.

'Dempsey?' Francis said.

'I'm afraid I didn't see who my guy was meeting. The station was being evacuated when he got there. I think he might have made me.'

'How so?'

'Evasive manoeuvres after he left St Pancras Hotel. Like he knew he was being followed. Or he expected to be. And he saw me at the station. He may have been searching for the person he was meeting, but I thought it better not to follow him.'

'Good call,' Francis said. 'Libby?'

'I have thirty accounts following her on social media. Oh, and she's finally accepted my friend request.' She turned to her computer and brought up a social media profile on her screen. 'I present to you, racially ambiguous, godly handsome, ovary-stimulating third-year law student, Romeo. I'm giving it a couple of days before he sends her a DM.'

'DM?'

'Direct message.'

Francis turned to the third agent. 'Rod? Settled in?'

Rod was the youngest of the three – a child prodigy whose genius had collided with authority throughout his education – and the shortest of the agents. He wore his red loafers without socks and he rolled his tight jeans three inches above his exposed ankles. He also rolled up the sleeves of his colourful jumper, thus somehow completing the look of an overgrown child actor in a kiddie's detective movie.

'Yeah,' he said. 'They've given me the grand tour.

Nothing new on my guy, so, in the meantime, I've been assisting these two. I helped Libby create Romeo. He's a semi-automated bot programmed to like her posts. An AI built his profile based on her social media interactions.'

'Good,' Francis said. He swept the room, meeting each of their eyes. 'As of today, you all have enhanced access. I want you to look into bank accounts, emails, phone calls, everything. Close associates, too. I want to know who they meet, who they speak to, what they say, where they go, what they do. If you come across anything remotely interesting, you contact me immediately.'

He was standing up to leave when Libby said, 'There's one more thing.'

Francis waited for her to speak.

'Rod thinks he smells mould,' she said.

'Does he now?' Francis said, glancing at the young agent.

He fetched his coat and left.

Francis alighted from his black cab a short distance from Marlborough Gate. He walked into St James's Park and followed a path to the lake. On the Blue Bridge, sightseers snapped photos: Buckingham Palace to the west, Big Ben, Horse Guards Parade, and the London Eye to the east. He stopped mid-bridge, crossing his arms over the railing to watch the water. Beneath him, a family of waterfowl emerged.

Someone set their backpack down next to him. He glanced at the bag, then up at the owner, who was a slim young man with a red beard and a receding hairline.

'What's your speciality?' he asked.

'Accidents,' the man replied.

Francis looked him over. 'Has he briefed you?'

'Yes. And I'm to let you know that I only report to you.'

Francis nodded once. 'It's a house. There are two, maybe three subjects. I'll send you the details.'

'Can I say something?' the man said.

Francis looked at him.

'I just want to say: it's a huge honour, sir.'

'Alex, is it?'

Alex nodded.

Francis lifted himself away from the railing, dusted each elbow of his jacket, turned and walked away.

17

Kenny sat on the edge of Tashique's bed, bathed, towelled, wrapped in her duvet, and mired in shame. Alone in her bedroom, waiting for her to return with borrowed clothes for him or with D'Don to throw him out, he thought of all he had been taught about consent back at the youth centre. She had not once given him consent. They had both been naked, but he had been naked in front of D'Don as well, and that hadn't been sexual, and that was the point. That was the test. Maybe it was normal to be naked as long as you didn't do anything. Adam and Eve were naked before they sinned. He groaned. She'd only been bathing him, as D'Don had asked her to. She hadn't touched his penis. She hadn't even looked at it, even though he had remained erect all the time they'd been in the shower together. Even when she'd washed his legs, she'd manoeuvred around his hands, which had stayed over his groin. One part of him had wanted her to remove his hands and use the loofah on him, but she did no such thing. She did not look at his penis; she did not touch his penis; she did not press her breasts against him; she did not do anything other than bathe him. And she did not give consent for him to touch her the way he did. It was a test, and he had failed. Just a few minutes more and he would have made it through the shower without messing up, but he had failed.

He began to cry. Silently.

He should have known. Anytime things started going well for him, something bad always happened, and this time it was all his fault. He had blown this amazing opportunity all by himself. He was about to lose everything to a moment of madness that he could have avoided. Was she reporting him to D'Don right then? Would they kick him out? What about Abraham? What would he say? Would he take him back? Abraham was the only person who had ever seen any good in Kenny. If he kicked him out as well, he had no idea what he would do with himself.

He hadn't been in trouble since his arrest, or since the lady judge had made him start going to the youth club. It was there that he'd met Abraham, his mentor – a big, muscular man who always wore a suit, unlike the other youth workers who wore tracksuits and trainers and didn't work out.

Abraham was the counsellor for at-risk boys, as the social workers referred to them. He spoke little, but he would often go to a session and watch the boys learn new skills from volunteers who came to teach creative writing, mindfulness, computer skills, or whatever else the charity found someone willing to teach. The workshops had bored Kenny, but sitting through them was better than the prison sentence he'd dodged. On occasion, a rich person would 'come to inspire them' and say things like, 'Look at me now. If I can do it, you can too.' But they were wrong. They didn't know him like that.

They didn't know what he'd been through. They didn't know what it was like to start dealing drugs because it was either that or getting knifed for refusing. They didn't know what it was to have to stop talking to friends, even cousins you'd grown up with, simply because they lived in the wrong postcode. They'd never had to run from the police while throwing kilos away, knowing they were going to have to pay it back to their elder. They didn't know that life, and yet they came and stood in their smart suits and told him they used to be like him. They were not like him. Never had been.

People like him didn't speak like them. People like him didn't get ten-thousand-pound grants from the Prince's Trust to start new businesses. People like him didn't write business plans, pitch to investors, or get bank loans for start-ups. No. People like him were never given a chance by people like them. That was just the way it was. So when they came talking about 'turning your life around' and 'achieving anything in life you put your mind to', he wanted to tell them to fuck off, but he didn't, because being at the youth centre, folding paper hats in the workshops, was what was keeping him out of prison.

Abraham was different. He never told Kenny that he could be anything he wanted to be. Instead, when Kenny had first sat in his office, he'd asked only, 'Have you thought about what you want to do with the rest of your life?'

It was the first time anyone had ever asked him that,

and Abraham had looked like he cared about the answer. Kenny had thought about it while Abraham patiently waited and watched him. In the end, he hadn't known what to say. He had never imagined having a life or making plans for one.

He'd started looking forward to his time with Abraham, when he would talk about things he'd never spoken about and Abraham would listen. Abraham didn't judge him for messing up, getting done, or being another Black kid on his way to prison. With Abraham, he felt that he mattered. As if his life was important to Abraham. As if out of all the boys at the centre, Abraham saw something in Kenny and wanted him to succeed in life, whatever that meant.

Months passed and Kenny stayed out of trouble, largely because his elder had been done and nobody was pressuring him to deal. But then his time at the club was up – they needed space for new boys, and the news terrified Kenny. The centre had protected him from people who wanted him to do bad things. It had also given his life structure. A safe routine. A daily ritual that posed no risk of being shopped, shafted, or shanked. A place where he could learn new stuff – even if he'd scoffed at the workshops at first. A place where he could spend time with people like him – people with the same history, who came from similar neighbourhoods to his. A place that kept him off the streets from morning until evening. Where he was fed daily and didn't have to pay for the food or shoplift it at the corner store. The thought of it all coming to an end filled him with dread.

Abraham himself had broken the news to him and then

watched him deal with the information. Alone with the counsellor, Kenny thought about his time at the youth centre, the friends he'd made, the many nice meals he'd had, the jokes he'd shared, his sessions with Abraham, even the chocolate cake one of the workers had baked and brought to the centre – how it had smelled so delicious, how it had been so moist and creamy, how he had been given a huge slice, how it was the best thing he'd ever tasted in his life – and he began to cry.

That day, Abraham did something he had never done. He stood up, walked around his desk to Kenny, and embraced him as he cried. Then Abraham told him about another place. A special one. This one was funded by a church, and Kenny would never have to leave. He told Kenny where to meet him outside the youth centre so he could tell him more about it. He told Kenny he worked there as well, and he would recommend Kenny, but only if Kenny was ready to do what it took.

Kenny didn't want to take time to think about it, as Abraham suggested, or wait till he'd discussed it with his mum. He wanted to go there right away, but Abraham told him that wasn't how it worked.

'I can only recommend you. You still have to be chosen.'

18

A phone vibrated on a hard surface. It was Tashique's, on the side table where she'd left it. Kenny watched it until it stopped ringing and its lit screen dimmed to black, then the door handle turned and his heart jumped. He looked away to mop his face.

'Here,' Tashique said. Her towel was loosely wound around her body, held in place under one armpit. She tossed a bunch of clothes at him and started to walk towards the bathroom when her phone began to ring again.

'Please pass it,' she said, holding out her hand.

As Kenny passed the ringing phone to her, he saw that it was D'Don calling, and fear overcame him once more. Any time things are going well for him, something bad always happens.

He watched as she pressed the phone to her ear and entered the bathroom. He listened, but she wasn't speaking. After a couple of minutes, she returned and tossed the phone onto the bed.

'He wants to see you,' she said.

'Why?' he asked.

She shrugged, went back into the bathroom, and shut the door behind her.

Alone in her bedroom, Kenny began to mouth the Lord's prayer over and over.

D'Don was on his knees beside his desk. His hands were clasped, and his face was contorted in agony from fervent prayer.

Kenny watched from the open doorway, unable to go further inside. Who was Tashique to D'Don? Why did she live with him? Maybe she was his daughter. Terror renewed its grip on Kenny's heart. He was wearing the white outfit she'd given him. White trousers and a white T-shirt she'd said belonged to him now. He had to confess before D'Don brought it up. But what should he say he'd done? And what could he blame it on? The Devil? Tashique? He should have apologised to her in the shower when it had happened. He should have got on his knees and cried, begged and cursed himself for being so weak. He should have let her know how sorry he was.

D'Don looked up. He had tears on his cheeks. So, she had told him. She must have done; she had been away for far longer than it would take to fetch a pair of trousers and a T-shirt.

'Come,' D'Don said. He stood up and arranged the two guest chairs at his desk so they were facing one another. 'Let's talk.'

He knew.

Each step into the office was suffocating. Kenny felt sick

to his stomach. He prepared himself to beg for forgiveness. He should have begged Tashique's forgiveness first. He cursed himself.

'Please, sit.'

D'Don watched Kenny sit before following suit. 'I'm sorry you are seeing me like this,' he said. 'Do you know what the shortest verse in the Bible is?'

Kenny shook his head. How had he not seen that it was a test? Abraham would be so disappointed. He searched for the right words. I have offended Tashique. I touched Tashique. I am sorry. I have sinned. I failed the test. I messed up.

'John 11:35: "Jesus wept." I just received some bad news. Someone died. Someone I knew. He committed suicide. He jumped in front of a train.'

Kenny stopped holding his breath.

'It's okay,' D'Don said. 'He wasn't my friend. In fact, he was a bad person. A really bad person. I was praying for the people his death would affect. There is no point in praying for the dead; that is a false doctrine. The instant you die, you have received your judgement. Remember, we are already in the rapture. It is the people you leave behind that prayers can help. I was praying for the person his death will affect the most. That is why I want to talk to you. Kenny, what is sin?'

All Kenny's strength drained away from him. Maybe it wasn't too late to confess.

'What makes one thing a sin and another not?' D'Don continued. 'Romans 3:23: "For we have all sinned and come short of the glory." All, not some. All. Psalm 51:5:

"For I was born a sinner – yes, from the moment my mother conceived me." So, if just being born is a sin, what then is a sin? And how can we be absolved of it?

'Did you know that the position of the Catholic Church is that everyone is saved, no matter what? Think about it: Jesus died for your sins. He's already paid the price. You did nothing to deserve it; you were not even born when he was nailed to the cross. It is a free gift, so how can you not be saved no matter what you do? How can you return my gift of grace to me? How?'

It was a feeling that Kenny had never experienced. He was suddenly overcome with remorse so powerful that he began to cry. Tears rushed down his cheeks. He looked down in shame and shook from the force of it, but he didn't cry out.

D'Don took his hands in his. 'Kenny, my grace is sufficient for you. Always remember that. Nothing you can do is a sin. You are covered by grace. You, Tashique, all of my flock, you are all covered by grace. Do not fear for anything. Okay?'

He held on to Kenny's hands until Kenny nodded. 'Kenny, I need a favour from you,' he went on. 'When you were upstairs with Tashique, you were alone for a long time. What did she tell you?'

Fresh tears erupted.

'Listen. Just like you, she was also chosen. She was chosen for you. You were both chosen for each other. Two shall bind together, and they shall become one. You are already bound together, do you understand? She is your helper, and you are hers. I had hoped that in time you would come to realise this yourself, but after what happened today, things have changed. Did she tell you about herself? How I came to be her guardian?'

Kenny shook his head. Something strange was happening. He sensed that he had to really listen.

'Many years ago, I used to be a lawyer. That's how I met her. I was her lawyer. She brought a rather unfortunate case to me and . . . Let's just say, she has been through a lot. She needs you. You have to be there for her. You have to be her rock, do you understand? A time will come when you will be the only person who can protect her. Can you do that? Can you protect her?'

Kenny nodded.

'The man who killed himself today – I don't know how she'll react when she hears the news. The police will come to tell her. I need you to be by her side when that happens. You have to be her rock. He did something bad to her, Kenny. Something really bad.'

Kenny had sufficiently calmed down to notice that D'Don seemed momentarily elsewhere. The pastor stood from his desk and walked to the window, his shoulders tense, as if carrying the weight of the news himself. Kenny watched him, trying to make sense of everything, and was still focused on D'Don's back when the pastor suddenly turned around. Their eyes met, and for a moment, Kenny felt as if he'd been caught.

19

When Dempsey returned, Rod was intermittently singing out fragments of the heavy metal song he was listening to on his extra-large headphones as he worked on his computer. Libby was lying on the sofa, holding her phone above her face with one hand and scrolling through her social media with a thumb. Dempsey pushed the door open with his elbow while balancing three disposable cups of coffee on a paper tray, then paused and shook his head at the other two. 'Tut, tut, tut.'

Libby reached up for her coffee and pouted a kiss at Dempsey.

Rod took off his headphones and swivelled to face the other two. 'The dude just bought some female perfume,' he said as he accepted his cup.

'Pastor Da Duck?'

'Yeah.' Rod turned to his screen. 'Either someone has stolen his bank cards, or he's splurging on expensive gear at Harrods. He bought a Rolex and a whole bunch of clothes from Armani, and now he's just paid nine hundred quid for a hundred-millilitre perfume bottle. Boadicea the Victorious.'

'Nine hundred pounds!' Libby said. 'I'm googling it. Who spends nine hundred pounds on perfume?'

'Someone with a flock of morons to bleed every Sunday,' Dempsey said.

'Does he have a miss?' Rod asked.

'Not that we know of.' Dempsey sat down and swivelled to face the sofa. 'Libs, what do you think?'

'It's for the girl,' Libby said.

'You think they're shagging?' Rod asked.

'Absolutely,' she retorted. 'Have you seen her? I'd do that.'

'Do you have anything that'll excite Black Rod?' Dempsey asked.

'I don't know,' Rod said, then paused. 'Hey, why do you call him Black Rod?'

Libby glanced at him, then at Dempsey.

'It's his nickname from when he was active,' Dempsey said.

'Really? How'd you know that?'

'I asked about him when I got my instructions. I wanted to know why I was assigned to a pensioner. It turns out he's something of a legend.'

'For real? Black Rod. That's got to mean something.'

'It does.'

'Tell me.'

'Need to know,' Dempsey said. He turned to his workstation and set his cup down to tap at the keyboard.

'Libby?' Rod said.

Libby shrugged, clambering off the sofa and returning to her chair.

'I'll ask him,' Rod said.

'I dare you,' Dempsey said.

'Wanna put some money on it?'

Libby extended her arm to Rod, placed her hand on his forearm, and, looking into his eyes, gently shook her head.

'Actually . . .' Rod swivelled to face his monitor. 'We've got enhanced access. I can find out.'

'Don't do that,' Libby said.

'So, tell me.'

She focused on her screen.

'Dempsey?' Rod said.

'Google it.'

'I know what Black Rod is. But what's it got to do with him?'

'What do you think?'

'He's got a huge dick?'

Libby spat out her coffee. 'Dude!'

'What?' Rod held his hands out.

'Okay,' Dempsey said. 'You know about the Black Rod – the ceremonial dude with a sword in the House of Lords – but its origins date way back to the reign of Henry the Eighth. Back then, the job was to maintain order and security at the royal court. Basically, the Black Rod was the head of security.'

'So, it's because he works for the King?'

'For a genius, you're quite unimpressive,' Dempsey said.

Rod gave him the finger.

'Just tell him,' Libby said, her focus still on her screen.

'Okay. Legend has it that our Black Rod was once the only asset on a ragtag mission in a tiny former colony that had just discovered oil. All well and good, but then the country went and elected a socialist who wanted to use the oil to develop his country. He was about to do a deal with the Russians, cutting out British interests. This was wholly unacceptable, as you can imagine, so a cable was dispatched to the mission. Less than twenty-four hours later, the government was overthrown in a particularly bloody coup d'état led by a colonel who happened to have trained at Sandhurst. The colonel executed the president and his cabinet by hanging, after which he elevated himself to the rank of major general and enjoyed a cordial relationship with the West for decades, until he became obsolete.'

'So, they call him the Black Rod because he overthrew the government? He restored order and security?'

'You weren't listening. He had twenty-four hours to complete the task, and he successfully did so. That was his speciality. Regime change. He's responsible for no fewer than eight failed states.'

'You think that's what they're training us for?'

Dempsey laughed. 'Yeah. We're getting ready to overthrow governments by overthrowing a loony pastor. Remind me how you're a genius.'

'Black Rod,' Rod said. He reclined his chair and clasped his fingers behind his head. 'I like that. That's what I want to be called. The Black Rod.'

20

As my Uber pulled away, I looked up to where I knew the waxing moon would be almost full in the sky, catching the last few seconds before it was entirely covered by dark clouds.

I'd had a day. First, it was Roger and the annoyance of having to meet with him and endure his presence just because I'd been afraid of a bad review, then the undercover journalist waylaying me with the unfortunate nickname I'd been given by various officers of the Metropolitan Police, then Roger pulling a no-show just when I did want to see him. What on earth had he done this time, and why had he wanted to see me? I was experiencing that familiar sensation of knowing better than to do what I was about to do, but not being able to stop myself from doing it. Whatever mess he'd got himself into this time, he probably deserved it, and I was probably better off staying well clear of it, but I needed to know.

Roger. I shook my head as I walked up to the main entrance of my block of flats. This was not my paranoia. I wasn't having an episode. What are the chances of an undercover journalist tricking me into meeting the same day Roger asked to meet? As I inserted my key into the lock, I wondered for the millionth time how the journalist had connected him to me. The lock rolled freely as I twisted the key. Not again. I pushed the door, and just as I feared, found it was already open. It was the second time in a week that the lock on the main entrance door had been broken. I swore. The last time, the porter had said that none of the flats had been burgled, and then the management company had sent an email asking all tenants to be vigilant. I'd been tempted to reply, 'How?' I'd spoken to the porter the next day, and his theory had been that someone in the block didn't have a key and had resorted to forcing the front door. Once again, I considered selling up and buying a house.

After I'd left Marylebone, I'd gone for a long walk to clear my head. I should have cancelled my session with Margaret, but I went nonetheless and spent the time talking about everything but the episode I'd had. The last time I'd had one, I'd agreed with her that if it happened again, I would call the therapist she'd recommended. Now it had happened again, but my walk had helped me see that I'd caught it before it had ballooned into a full-blown conspiracy crisis. Also, it wasn't exactly as though I'd made something out of nothing. Roger had been cagey on the phone, the journalist had tricked me into meeting her, then the man in the green cardigan had crossed the road with me before showing up at the station. Yes, that was probably a coincidence, and I wouldn't have noticed him had I not been looking for a tail, but on balance, I wasn't being insane to be suspicious. *Careful*, that's what I was being. While I'd been walking, I came up with the perfect comeback for the journalist too. I should have looked her in the eyes and told her, 'I am not your scandal.'

Roger must be her story. It would make sensational reading for a day or two: 'Cover-up at the Met as Undercover Officer is Accused of Rape.' The Met would have to let him go. Naomi's source had to be a police officer. Someone who knew about me – a former client, perhaps – and someone who knew about Roger. That limited the pool of suspects.

Stop, Bobby. This is not a case.

In the morning, I would inform the Met, prepare a statement for the journalist and have them okay it, and see what I could learn about the trouble Roger was in. Just out of curiosity.

I was mentally composing the statement when I got to my flat. I inserted the key into the first of the two locks, and the door moved from its frame. It hadn't been locked. Panic engulfed me. I checked that I had the right door, then pushed it fully open and reached inside to switch on the light. All the interior doors were open: the guest toilet, the living room and my consultation room. I'd been burgled!

I stood frozen to the spot. My heart pumped frantically, and my skin tingled all over. I tried to think through the ringing in my head. They could still be inside. I could have startled them. I was a big Black bloke; they would attack out of fear. Even if they hadn't brought weapons, a set of knives was on full display on a magnetic board in the kitchen. I was hyperventilating, and I felt light. Weak. I felt like a coward.

I remained still and listened, my pulse fast and erratic. The flat was silent, but whoever was inside could have heard me open the door. I no longer had a service pistol to reach for. Without thinking, I gripped my keys in my fist, even as I tried to calculate which was wiser: quietly backing away before screaming for help or proceeding inside and relying on my mandatory martial arts training. I chose option three instead: waiting and listening. If they were still there, I could envisage us locked in a game of chicken. I imagined that, just like me, they were standing frozen in whatever position they'd been in when I'd arrived. A hooded figure standing perfectly still, mid-stride, with my turntable in their hands, the power cable dangling silently.

But I couldn't stand outside the door forever. The flat was utterly silent. Without intending to, I found myself walking through the door with sharp keys protruding from the bottom of my fist.

'Who's there?' I shouted.

I was breathing so fast, and so much adrenaline was pumping through my system, that my whole body was shaking. Or maybe it was just fear. I proceeded slowly, primed for a desperate scuffle. A little voice kept telling me that I should have backed away and called 999.

I tiptoed through my home, slack-jawed in disbelief. They had pulled down the extractor unit in the guest toilet. It was dangling from a wire. Who does that? What were they searching for in there? Anger replaced fear, even as I realised that the intruders had probably left. I glanced into my consultation room. It was a mess. I flicked the light on. It looked like a tornado had torn through it. My entire bookshelf had been emptied. They had pulled a cabinet away from the wall and its contents lay strewn on the ground. My framed certificates were also smashed on the floor. Violent anger filled my heart. Now I wished I'd caught them in the act.

I continued on to the living room. There I found my records scattered across the rug. My blood boiled. They had moved my turntable from its spot on the credenza, where I stored the records. All of the furniture had been moved.

In the guest bedroom, the mattress was tilted against a wall and the bed frame was on its side. They had gutted the kitchen; its entrails lay splattered all over the ground – cutlery, glasses, pots, saved plastic takeaway containers, and food. Uncooked rice, beans, flour, spices, and spaghetti, all spilled. They'd even emptied my fridge and freezer and left the doors open, before dumping the contents of the waste bags onto the floor. Bastards. Rage built up in me. I just knew my bedroom would be the worst, and I was right. It had been turned inside out. Thoroughly ransacked. Clothes and hangers had been tipped into a pile; shoes and their shoehorns lay where they'd been hurled to opposite ends of the room. I even saw a ripped-out insole curled in the furthest corner. The en-suite bathroom was a mess. The mirror cabinet's doors were wide open, and the contents filled the basin below. They had also emptied the bin. What had they been looking for?

On the ground in the bedroom, I found the contents of the drawer in which I kept my valuables. I sifted through a stack of photos, medicine and envelopes before I found the one I was looking for. It was empty. I swore out loud as I looked around the room. There they were, on the bed. My passports. One blue, one green. They hadn't taken them after all. I picked them up and opened each one – I don't know why. Relief surged through me, but it was short-lived.

I could have gone back through the flat one more time, but instead I sat down heavily on the bed, taking in the mess around me. I already knew the outcome of another search would be the same, and it was a waste of time to pretend otherwise.

Whoever had broken in hadn't taken anything. They'd been searching for something. Something specific. But I had no idea at all what that something might be.

21

As I slumped on my wrecked mattress, my mind racing, a chill rippled through me. My home had been specifically targeted. I felt vulnerable, unsafe, violated and threatened, all at the same time.

The way they'd turned my flat inside out . . . I'd seen it once before. Our home in Nigeria. Shortly after my father had been detained. Soldiers and men in ill-fitting suits had come to our home and spent a good four hours throwing out the contents of every drawer, cutting open the settee, disembowelling mattresses, punching man-sized holes in the ceilings, and pouring the still-steaming pot of beef stew my mother had cooked into the sink and using her spatula to sift through the morsels of meat. They'd even broken through the tiles around the bathtubs and flashed their lights into the hidden plumbing. They'd been searching for something. Incriminating evidence. And that is what they claimed they'd discovered in the pages of a photo album that nobody in the house had opened in years.

My flat had been violated in a similar fashion.

Whoever it was had searched everywhere. What had they been looking for? Did this have to do with Roger and the journalist? I visualised Green Cardigan in the crowd at St Pancras, staring at me. Were they all connected?

It was at that moment that I felt the effects of the adrenaline rushing through me. It felt good. I was still addicted to the thrill, the danger, and the excitement of having a case to solve. I could not afford to have an episode right then. Nobody had been following me earlier, but whoever had broken into my home had been looking for something, and if it was at all connected to Roger, then I realised I might actually know what it was. My coaching notes. Some coaches keep theirs in a fireproof safe – a professional requirement. I kept mine in an encrypted folder on the cloud, and accessing it required two-factor authentication, which in turn required my phone. I'd already read the notes that morning and nothing had jumped out at me. Whatever they thought Roger might have told me wasn't in there. Or was it? I decided I'd go over them immediately after I'd sorted out my home.

I now suspected two things. First, that whatever situation Roger was in, it was bad. Second, that the journalist had nothing to do with the burglary. Breaking into people's phone messages, pretending to be someone else to get close to a source – that was the MO of a journalist, but to burgle a flat? No. Whoever had searched my flat wasn't after a story. But could they be trying to stop one getting out?

In hindsight, it was at this moment that dopamine flooded into my brain unnoticed. The building had CCTV. I had to see the tapes. If the tapes still existed. How many of the intruders were there? How were they dressed? When had they arrived? When had they left? I had to call the police. From working with them, I knew that the chances of an officer coming to take a look were as good as a white Christmas, but I had to act normal. I wouldn't tell them about Roger; I couldn't anyway. Client confidentiality and all that. They had to record the incident as a regular breaking and entering or a burglary. I just hoped that the tapes captured the intruders because this wasn't just a break-in. Whoever had done it had likely done it before, and probably carried weapons and knew how to use them. I wasn't safe until I had what they wanted.

I really had to talk to Roger.

I was about to call him, but I caught myself. What if they could look at my call logs? They would know I'd called him first, before calling the police, and they would wonder why. They would think that I knew whatever they thought he knew, or that I knew something at least.

I will let him call me.

Okay. Maybe I was getting a bit paranoid.

But fucking Roger. Was he in hiding? I dialled 999. I had to act normal.

I paced the flat, taking in the carnage as I answered the questions. I returned to my consultation room. Then, for some unaccountable reason, I decided to go out into the hallway. It was then that I saw two policemen in blue jeans and stab-proof vests walking towards me. I hung up. Their arrival was too quick. Maybe someone else had reported the break-in? Another surge of adrenaline primed my body for fight or flight for the second time that night.

'Mr Fatokun?'

The officer had read my surname off his notebook and murdered it. He introduced himself and his colleague as Inspector Russell and Constable Simon.

'Did you know the lock on the door downstairs is broken?' said Russell.

'Can we go inside to talk?' added Simon.

'What's this about?' I asked. They hadn't come about my flat?

Russell consulted his notebook again. He looked up. Focused on my eyes. 'Do you know a Roger Bainbridge?'

My heart sank. Suddenly, I knew what they were going to tell me.

I nodded.

'When did you last speak to him?'

My mouth had dried up. 'What is this about?' I asked again. I could have been wrong.

'Can we go inside, please?' Simon repeated.

I just wanted them to get to it.

'Come in.' I walked in ahead of them. 'I've just been burgled.'

They looked around as I led them into the living room.

'Have you called nine-nine-nine?' Russell asked.

'Yes.'

'What did they take?' Simon asked.

I turned too swiftly. 'I haven't looked properly,' I said.

I replaced the Egg Chair cushion and sat. They remained standing.

'What is the nature of your relationship with Roger Bainbridge?' Russell asked.

Simon held his notepad ready. I looked at his pencil with distrust.

'You haven't told me what this is about,' I said.

'We're getting to that. Can you please tell me the nature of your relationship with Mr Bainbridge?'

If they'd come to my flat, then they already knew. How else could they have found me?

'I can't. What is this about?'

'When did you last talk to him?'

'Are you going to tell me what this is about?'

'Please answer the question, Mr Fatokun.'

I corrected his pronunciation this time. 'Fa-to-kun.'

'I apologise,' he said. 'When was the last time you spoke to Mr Bainbridge?'

It was clear he wouldn't tell me what was going on until I'd answered their questions. I noticed Simon reading from his notepad. Cross-checking my answers.

'Yesterday,' I said. 'He wanted to meet up.'

'Why?' Russell continued with his questions.

'I don't know. He just said he had to see me.'

'And you didn't ask why?'

'No.'

'How did he sound?'

'Like Roger. Look, what is this about?'

'Was he agitated? Excited? Sad?'

I didn't answer. They waited. Like I would with a client. But it was obvious I would lose this contest.

'He sounded eager to meet,' I said. It was the truth. Though 'eager' could have meant anything.

'Eager like desperate?'

Of course, a police officer would clarify.

'No. Just eager.'

'Do you have any idea what he might have wanted to see you about?'

'No. Is he in trouble?' I asked. I knew he was. I didn't know what it was this time, but I had my suspicions. In that moment, I was not so much distancing myself from him with my economical answers but establishing that I did not know what he'd done, ergo, I was not involved in any way. Even as a professional working for the Met, and a former officer for that matter, talking to the police still put me on edge, as if I'd done something wrong.

'How did you meet?'

'We were introduced by his first-line supervisor–manager.' It was time to set the BS aside. He already knew that, and he knew that I knew. We could get on with it now.

'Why?'

'For professional reasons protected by confidentiality.' I felt I was stretching confidentiality by simply admitting to knowing Roger.

'What do you do?'

'I'm a coach.' He would not ask what kind of coach.

'You currently work with the Metropolitan Police.'

Bingo. He hadn't even bothered making it into a question. He was telling me he knew more about me than I knew about them. Establishing his advantage. Maybe he'd even heard the nickname, 'The Bad Coach'.

'Yes.'

'Was Roger Bainbridge your client?'

'I couldn't answer that if he were.'

'When he contacted you, did you arrange to meet?'

It was starting to feel like an interrogation. Whatever mess Roger was in, I had to think about it in real time and decide how much of it I wanted to make my own. The answer came up as none.

'Yes. Today. At Marylebone Station. At ten twenty this morning. He didn't show up, so I left.'

'Was that strange?'

'That he didn't show up? Yes.'

'So, you were at the station to meet him at twenty past ten?'

'No. Just after ten thirty. I was held up. Look, are you going to tell me what this is about or what? Did something happen to Roger?'

The two of them looked at each other. Their expressions had so transformed that I held my breath for the news.

'I'm afraid it's not good,' Russell said. 'There was an accident at Marylebone Station. Roger is dead.'

'No,' I said. 'He was pushed.'

22

'Pushed?'

I kicked myself. I'd spoken too soon and without thinking first. I'd offered information I should not have had. Not my sudden suspicion that Roger had been murdered, but that he'd died on the tracks. I could just about hear the cogs of their police brains turning. Next, they'd let me dig a bigger hole, and then they'd point out that they hadn't mentioned how he'd died. We've all seen that movie trope. I decided to short-circuit it.

'Outside the station, someone said that a person had jumped onto the tracks, and I figured they'd stopped the trains. I thought that was what had made Roger late. I kept calling his phone. But now you're saying he's the one who fell on the tracks, right? Why would he kill himself? He was coming to see me. We had an appointment. He had a great career ahead of him. There was nothing wrong with him. Why would he jump?'

'He didn't fall, and he wasn't pushed. There were witnesses,' Russell said. 'Their testimonies are consistent with the CCTV footage.'

That changed everything. The entire law enforcement family would treat the death of one of their own as a top priority. They would have spoken to everyone and studied every frame of the CCTV. But why would he ask to meet me and then kill himself? I knew I would become obsessed with finding the red flags I'd missed during our sessions together because I absolutely had not seen this coming.

'You've seen the CCTV?' I asked.

'No, not personally.'

So, he hadn't seen it. Witness testimonies can be unreliable in such an event. No one would have been paying attention to Roger before he ended up on the tracks. Whoever pushed him, if he was pushed, would have waited until no one was watching, and they would have been aware of the cameras. They could have made it look like an accident or a choice. But how? I pictured Roger arriving. Wait.

'He was arriving, not leaving.'

I said it out loud. I hadn't meant to.

'What was that?' Russell said.

How did he end up on the tracks? I imagined that would only be possible if he was standing on a platform waiting for a train to arrive, Marylebone being a terminus. Maybe he changed his mind and decided to leave. Something might have spooked him. My tardiness, maybe. Or he could have spotted his own assassin – if he was pushed.

'He was meeting me there,' I said.

'I understand it's all really hard to take in,' Russell began, but I cut him off.

'No.'

I was still thinking it through, and like my clients do in our sessions, I was thinking and talking. The two are the same, especially when gifted a listener's full and uninterrupted attention. I had two very attentive police officers in front of me.

'He was arriving, not leaving. How could he have jumped onto the tracks?'

'I'm really sorry, Mr . . .' He took his time to get it right. 'Fatokun, but I just need to ask you a few questions.'

So, for whatever reason, he was leaving, and as he waited for the train, someone pushed him. If only I could see the CCTV footage. The killer could have stepped down on his foot, shoved him forward with the side of his knee, and pushed him onto the tracks while pretending to be reaching out to save him. With enough rehearsal, it would look like he was a hero. They. It could be anyone. I had to see that CCTV footage.

'Think about it,' I said. 'Why would he come all the way for an appointment if he planned on killing himself?'

They both stared at me. They must have thought I was in denial. Neither spoke. Out of understanding, I imagined. Pity for the man who just lost a client.

'You were his coach,' Simon said.

'Yes. But listen. Let's say he meant to do it. Why today?'

'You were his coach,' Simon started over. 'Did he say anything? Something that might explain this?'

I felt I was onto something, but I couldn't think with these two standing over me. I returned to the room.

'It was over a year ago,' I said. 'There was nothing to make me suspect he would take his own life.'

It was an investigation. I didn't think I'd be breaking confidentiality by answering.

'He didn't tell you anything?'

'Like what? That he was going to jump in front of a train?'

'Did you take notes? He might have said something.'

I took a good look at Simon. Client records are confidential even in the event of death, unless, of course, foul play is suspected. But they were treating it as a suicide.

'Can I get a copy?' he added.

'I'm afraid that's impossible.'

'Why?'

'Confidentiality.'

'But under the circumstances?'

'Unless a crime has been committed, I can't share any record of client sessions with you.' Even admitting he was a client bothered me, but under the circumstances . . .

'Fair enough.' The two of them exchanged looks. 'Well, since we're here, we might as well take a look around. The robbery.'

'Be my guest,' I said. At this point, I just wanted them to leave.

Russell looked around for somewhere to begin while Simon put away his notepad and started fiddling with his radio.

'What do you think they were after?' he asked.

They were after my coaching notes. It had to be. But I wasn't going to say that.

'Something they can sell for some crack,' I said.

His look called BS. I turned away to admire the mess that they were about to poke through.

'Why did you come looking for me?' I asked.

He hadn't been expecting that. It took a moment before he replied.

'His phone logs.'

That was quick, I thought.

'He called your home seven times,' he added.

I understood. He was kind not to spell it out. Roger was trying to contact me before he ended up on the tracks.

My heart sank.

If only I'd pressed Roger on why he'd wanted to meet. If only I knew what the people who'd ransacked my flat thought he'd told me. I couldn't wait to go over the notes again once the police officers left; there just might be something in there that I'd missed. And then it occurred to me.

I already knew what it was. The fact that Roger had been working undercover – that had to be it. Why else would they be after my notes? And why else would he have contacted me? It was not a new transgression; it was about his time at the church. They wanted to know if he'd revealed anything about his undercover assignment. He hadn't. All I knew was that it was at a church. That was my only lead. I had to find out which church. What was he working on that might have got him killed? Or made him kill himself.

'Maybe he left you a message,' Russell said.

I looked up at him. Again, I understood, yet I contemplated for a moment.

I stood up and I walked over to fetch the handset from behind the TV stand, which the burglars had been kind enough to move out of the way.

They both stood close as I dialled my mailbox on speakerphone: 'Sorry, this mailbox is full; it cannot accept any more messages.'

'It's been full forever,' I said.

At the door, Russell gave me his card. 'Call if you think of anything,' he said.

As I watched him and Simon leave, I already knew I wouldn't.

23

On his back on a bed in his own room in the mansion, Kenny lifted his wrist over his face to admire his new watch. The luminous dials of the Rolex D'Don had bought for him glowed in the dark. At the foot of the bed, bags from their shopping trip to Harrods lay untouched. His life had changed. It felt like a miracle. He had come so close to blowing it all. His heart thumped in his throat at just how close it had been. He felt a sense of panic rise again when he remembered how it had all started. How he had been chosen, like the other girl at the service that day.

The church occupied a former warehouse that once housed crates of pharmaceuticals and high-end electronics bound for Europe. Its white paint and flourishing flower beds made it stand out among the warehouses still in use along the long road.

Inside, almost everything was white or red: the walls and chairs were white, while the rug and the cushions were red. Above, rows of lights and speakers angled toward the congregation hung from the ceiling. At the front, a metal truss frame surrounded the raised platform, holding cameras, screens and spotlights. It looked more like a stage than a pulpit – especially when the house lights dimmed and the stage lights illuminated the preacher's stand.

Kenny had been in the back with the other young girls and boys who had been preparing their bodies and their minds, all of them praying and hoping that their efforts would lead the Holy Spirit to choose them. The congregation had been singing and dancing along with the choir when D'Don walked to the glass pulpit on the raised platform, and applause had drowned out the words of the song. He raised his hand. The band stopped playing. The choir stopped singing. The church fell silent.

'Good morning, church,' he said, and everyone replied, 'Good morning, pastor.'

D'Don opened his giant Bible and lowered his head, remaining still. The congregation waited. Seconds stretched into minutes. Whispered questions rippled through the congregation. Someone clapped, trying to break the silence, but it died almost immediately. Four minutes passed. A senior pastor shifted in her seat. Another rose, taking hesitant steps toward him. Two more followed, exchanging unsure glances.

Then, suddenly, D'Don's body tensed. His arms flung wide, chest and face lifted to heaven, and his whole frame shook as if electrified. The officials jumped back. From the back of the church, a piercing scream cut through the silence. The Spirit released D'Don so he could see her.

Everyone looked at her. She covered her mouth with both hands. Eyes wide with terror.

'What did you see?' D'Don asked, his voice choked and altered by the Holy Spirit's latest possession.

Kenny watched her. He wondered what she'd seen. She shook her head slowly, tears rolling onto her fingers.

'I command you to speak!' D'Don said, glaring at the girl. 'Tell me what you saw.'

A microphone was being passed from person to person along the rows. When it reached the girl, she did not take it, so the church member next to her held it to her mouth, which was still tightly concealed behind her hands.

'Did you see me lifted off the ground?' D'Don asked.

The girl nodded. Vigorously. The church gasped. All eyes turned back to D'Don.

'Who else saw?' D'Don asked. He scanned his flock. 'I know someone else saw it. Who are you? I command you to show yourself!' He searched the faces of his followers. 'You!' He pointed. 'What did you see?'

Everyone turned to Kenny. A spotlight found him. He watched another cone of light stop over the girl who screamed. She was trembling in the hands of a girl beside her. He looked down at his unsteady legs. He was grateful to be seated.

'What is your name?' D'Don asked. His voice had softened and he sounded like himself again.

Another microphone was passed along to Kenny. He stood up. His grip on the microphone stabilised him.

'Kenny,' he answered. His voice boomed over the speakers.

'You saw it, too. Didn't you?'

Kenny opened his mouth, but nothing came out. He felt vulnerable. Exposed.

'Did you see it, too?' the pastor asked.

Kenny's grip on the microphone tightened.

'Do not be afraid. You can tell me. Did you see it?'

Everyone was waiting for Kenny's answer. He felt the weight of their eyes and their expectations. He nodded.

A murmur spread through the church.

'Stop the live transmission,' D'Don said. 'Tech team, delete the recording. Let me know when it's done.'

From the back of the room, a church worker with a headset mic gave a thumbs-up.

'Many are called,' D'Don said, 'but few are chosen.'

The choir began clapping, and soon they were singing while the band played. The entire congregation stood up, dancing with excitement and joy.

Kenny never told anyone the truth, that he had not seen the pastor float off the ground.

24

Roger. The cops. The journalist. My flat. I didn't know what to think. Even when I tried, I was unable to think clearly. I thought of calling my mum and Mimi to tell them what had happened, but I instantly saw how that would play out. Mimi and her partner had a cottage in Oxford, whereas my mum was closer in Golders Green. If I had texted or called, it would have resulted in a three-way video call, during which I would have spent Lord knows how much time reassuring the three women that I was fine and didn't need to stay at either of their places that night. Mimi, in particular, would have insisted. For reasons I've still not fully understood, she grew up with a need to protect me, her older brother. She once punched a kid in the face when he pushed me to win a game of musical chairs. And also, I didn't want to burst their bubbles of safety like had been done to mine.

I walked around for a while, inspecting the mess, but it soon became too punishing. I retired to the sofa, hoping to numb my brain to silence with a mindless TV show, but I couldn't get over the fact that I'd been burgled.

I had never been robbed before. I'd heard stories; I even knew people who'd been mugged, and I'd seen footballer mansions being invaded on the news, but I lived in a block of flats, which gave me a false sense of safety, I now realise. My home was no longer my sanctuary; it had become a crime scene. Malicious strangers had invaded my property, and the police had been as helpful as wet matches at a campfire. Up until that night, the only home invasion I'd experienced was over three thousand miles and two decades away in Nigeria, and that was during the rule of a violent military regime. I was supposed to be safe in London. The moment the burglary had me thinking of that night, I decided that it was time to proactively ignore the mess and try to forget what had happened. At least until the morning. I went to get a pillow and a duvet from the bedroom, placed them on the sofa, got a whisky glass and a bottle of Hennessy, switched off the lights, and aimed the remote at the TV.

I woke up. It was dark outside. The TV was still on, and it was too loud. I'd fallen asleep on the sofa. I sat up. The bottle was empty. I had no memory of draining it. I searched for the remote, but just before I switched off the TV, the image on the screen registered in my brain.

It had to be a commercial. I watched the red bar at the bottom of the screen. It was news, and the ticker said it was live. I hunched forward. The brightness of the TV screen hurt the back of my eyes. A reporter's voice was bringing viewers up to speed. On the screen, I recognised the person in a space suit sans helmet. He was holding the camera up to himself, and he was floating. He was in space. What had I missed? When did he announce he was going up on one of his rockets? Or, knowing who he is, did he simply make the announcement live from space?

He was talking into the camera, but we couldn't hear him. The reporter narrated over the dead silence: 'We are still not getting any sound from Mr Musk. He's broadcasting live from *Falcon Heavy*. We share your confusion, and . . . I've just been informed that we now have sound!'

His voice was clear over the spacecraft's internal sounds. He was his usual self. I shook my head at the screen. And to think I once thought he was cool. I searched for my glass. If there had been any brandy left, I would have raised a toast to him in space. Please don't come back. Then it occurred to me that the bottle had been unopened. I couldn't have polished off a whole bottle of brandy all by myself. I must have knocked it over. Shit.

I bent over to touch the carpet, and I heard what he said: 'So, I decided to do this because, er, the only way to return the planet, Earth, to a stable state so it can continue to host life, is without us.'

What dafuk was he saying?

'It will be painless. It's a cloud. Well, um, more like a gas. It's everywhere. The beauty of it is that, to solve that particular problem, we used what was already there. So, your body is already used to it. You won't feel a thing. You won't know when it's happening. You will just cease to exist in, like, an instant. Everyone. Including yours truly up here alone. The only person with the guts to do what needs to be done. I'm sorry, not sorry. This had to be done. And, er, think about it this way: once it's done, you'll simply be gone. No memory, no pain, no taxes. You know. Like, you know, this was always going to happen anyway. We're not a species built to last. I'm just speeding up the process because, well, we fucked up, and now there's a 99.999 per cent chance we've already fucked it up for all other life forms as well. If our planet is the only one that has evolved life, we must do everything to preserve it, even if it means we go. But, er, like I said, when it happens, you won't feel a thing, and it's happening now. You won't feel anything. You're already breathing it now. It's oxygen. It'll start in ten, nine, eight . . .'

Bastard!

I filled my lungs and held my breath. The fucking bastard! My lungs were burning and bursting, but I had to hold it until it was over. But it was too late. I felt it. It was inside me already. It occurred to me that it would have been painless for me too if I'd not tried to beat it. Now, it was choking me from the inside out. Acidic gas. It was eating my flesh. It was in my lungs. It peppered my chest. It was in my throat. I tried, but I couldn't draw breath. He had sucked out all the oxygen. I was dying a terrible, painful death, and on the screen, I watched the computer animation of dozens of nuclear missiles flying towards his spacecraft. It was the day that humanity ended.

I stood up as I woke, staggering slightly. I was choking on bile. I couldn't draw a breath. I was drowning standing up. I panicked. Was this how I would die? I finally managed a gasp, and after that, I was able to start breathing. My nose was running, and my eyes were full of tears.

I spent a good twenty minutes in the bathroom, bent over the toilet, retching, spitting and snorting out bile. When I'd recovered enough to find the switch, I saw myself in the mirror. Sweat, saliva, tears and fear. For a moment, I thought I wouldn't make it.

I cleaned up only as much as I needed to. My chest burnt. My lungs felt sandpapered from inside. Returning to the living room to gather up the duvet and pillow from the sofa, I realised that the TV hadn't even been on. I headed to the bedroom. I had to write it all down while it was still fresh. I reached for my dream journal on the bedside table, but it wasn't there. I tried to remember if I'd seen it when I'd searched for what had been stolen. I got up and began to look harder for it. It was not in my room. The bastards had taken my dream journal.

I searched again, but my heart wasn't in it. When I finally lay down to sleep, I was too keyed up to rest. Instead, I began to formulate a plan.

25

The next day, I woke up ready to act on the ideas I'd been working on before I'd finally dozed off. Whoever had broken in had my journal. They would not find what they were looking for in it.

I freed my phone from its charger and googled the journalist, Naomi Long-Fuller. She'd done some stories around the Met, but her interests were as varied as the outfits she posed in for her social media followers. She'd studied in Zimbabwe, Spain and America, where she'd got her second degree. She had a much darker sister who looked like a supermodel. She'd once volunteered at a soup kitchen. Her dog looked like a bored ferret.

I called her. She answered on the third ring.

'Hi. Good morning,' she said, sounding like she was already up and at her office desk.

'This is Bobby. Bobby Fatokun.'

'I know. I said hi.'

I got straight to the point. 'I have a proposal.'

She went silent. 'A proposal?'

'Yes.'

'Okay. I'm listening.' She didn't sound convinced.

'I'll tell you what I know if you tell me what you know.'

'On the record?'

'No. Can we meet now?'

'Like, now?

After I hung up, I fetched Russell's card from where I'd put it in the pocket of my phone case. I had to see the CCTV footage of Roger's death myself, and right then, he was my only chance of making that happen. I began to compose a text message. I wanted it to sound urgent without saying as much. I landed on, 'When can we meet today?'

If Russell couldn't or wouldn't facilitate me viewing the footage, I would email Roger's first-line supervisor; perhaps he would have the clout to make it happen.

While the locksmith from the management company replaced the lock on my door, I got dressed to go out. He asked what they'd taken, then made me try each of the three copies of my new key. They all worked. I smiled and said, 'Sorry, I can't tip you. The robbers took all my money.'

'It's all right, mate,' he said and left.

I'd meant it as a joke.

I checked if my cleaner had replied to my message, then grabbed my coat and my laptop case and followed him out.

Downstairs, I looked under my mailbox flap first, and then I checked that the main entrance lock had also been fixed. Stepping out into the bright and chilly morning, my mind was occupied with multiple mental notes as I crossed the road: the cleaner; finding the church where Roger had been undercover; watching the CCTV footage from the train station; what I would reveal to Naomi, and what I would hold back.

I was so preoccupied that I didn't notice anything out of place until I was yanked to the pavement by the strap of my bag. Winded, I looked up, only to see a figure in a black hoodie running away with it.

Righteous anger surged through me like a demonic possession. I scrambled up and ran after him. He was fast, but I was in shape and pumped full of adrenaline. I was catching up. He rounded a corner, and I ran out into the road in case he was hiding against the wall. The bend had slowed him down, and I gunned it towards him, readying myself to lunge once I was close enough.

And then I tripped.

I fell flat on my face. A kick to my ribs came almost before I knew what had happened. I curled into a ball and tucked my head beneath my arms, but the next kick didn't come. Instead, I heard my assailant running away. I looked up and saw two hooded figures on scooters in the distance, waiting for the two who'd attacked me – the first who'd grabbed my bag and the second who'd ambushed me from behind the corner. As I watched, they paired up and drove away.

My bag was gone. My laptop was gone. My latest copy of *Psychologies* magazine was gone. When I got the chance to think about it, I was sure I would realise other replaceable things were gone, but the only real loss was my sense of safety. I had just been mugged for the first time in my life.

26

Kenny woke up yawning and stretching, and for the first few seconds after opening his eyes, he didn't remember where he was. When it came back to him, he felt his wrist for the Rolex, then looked down at the watch on his arm. It hadn't been a dream. He'd decided not to take off the expensive watch because D'Don had told him that wearing it was how it got wound.

Sitting up, he looked around the bedroom. It was a little smaller than Tashique's room down the corridor, but it was still larger than any of the living rooms in the homes he'd lived in. It also had its own bathroom and walk-in closet. And like the rest of the house, it smelled like flowers, but he couldn't find the source.

The bed was the softest thing he'd ever felt; the mattress seemed to hold him. He didn't know he needed four pillows, but they were so ridiculously plush, he found use for all of them, burying himself in their comfort. And the sheets. He ran his hands over them. They were so smooth they felt almost unreal. He felt a sudden rush of emotion as he looked around again. The morning sun shining through the floor-to-ceiling curtains made him well up. This must be what it felt like to sleep in a hotel, he thought.

D'Don himself had taken him up to the room. The pastor had opened the door, stood aside for Kenny to see in, and asked, 'Do you like this one?' Kenny had peered inside and said it was nice, and immediately after he'd said it, he'd realised that he wasn't being asked to appraise the room. He'd looked up at D'Don, who, grinning at him, had simply nodded to confirm what Kenny's stare was checking. He had never had his own bedroom before. A smile had spread across his face before he'd stepped inside.

He was still admiring the room and his luck when someone knocked on the door. He was out of the king-size bed in a flash, throwing on a fresh new T-shirt before opening the door.

Tashique looked cosy in a white bathrobe. He inhaled the sweet smell of hot chocolate steaming from the mugs in her hands, and his belly rumbled.

'Good morning, love,' she said, handing him a mug.

Her smile calmed his worried heart. He stood aside to let her in.

They hadn't spoken about what had happened in the shower. D'Don had taken Kenny out in the Bentley, and when they'd returned, the white Range Rover that had been next to the sports coupé was gone. She still hadn't returned when the dinner D'Don had ordered was delivered, and the two men had eaten together at the breakfast table that extended from the island in the kitchen. When D'Don said goodnight, Kenny wanted to ask about

Tashique, but instead, he went upstairs and stayed there, listening for her car arriving or her door opening. As he lay, waiting for her to return, he oscillated between rehearsing his apology and contemplating denying everything because he was afraid to disturb what felt like a delicate balance. She hadn't yet reported him to D'Don; maybe something he said would tip her into telling on him. He remembered how close he had come to confessing his sin to the pastor, and he shuddered.

Now he placed his mug on the side table to let it cool, while she cradled hers in her hands where she sat with her legs folded up on a chair. He sat on the edge of the bed, watched her purse her lips to take a sip of the hot beverage, and made up his mind.

'I need to tell you something,' he said.

She gently set her mug down next to his, returned her feet to the ground, and shimmied forward towards him, her eyes focused on his.

He hadn't thought of how to say it. The suddenly serious look on her face made it even harder to find the right words. They stared at each other until she said, 'What is it?'

'It's nothing,' he said.

'No. You said you had to tell me something. Tell me. This is a safe space. There is nothing you can't tell me.

Still, he took his time, and she waited, and when he saw that she wasn't going to give up, he asked, 'Were you in church that day?'

'What day? Oh. You mean the day you were chosen? No. But I heard all about it.'

'Were you chosen, too?'

'Not like you. You saw him levitating. You see things other people can't see. It's your gift.'

His conscience heated his face. He shifted in his seat, drawing back as though closeness could expose his secret.

'There was another girl,' he said. 'She also saw him.'

'The girl who screamed? I heard about that.'

'Where is she?'

'I don't know. Why do you ask?'

'I just want to know what happened to her.'

'Happened to her?' Tashique's face scrunched in confusion. 'You say it like she died or something. She was chosen for her own purpose. She's probably on her own path now.'

'Did she also come here?'

'Here? To the house? No. Why would she?'

'No reason.'

She studied his face. 'You said you had to tell me something. What is it?'

'I just wanted to ask about the girl.'

'Do you know why you are here?' Her squinting eyes searched his.

Kenny knew why he was there. It was because he had been chosen. He nodded.

The tension dropped from her shoulders. 'Phew. For a minute there, I thought he hadn't told you.'

She picked up her mug and lifted her legs back onto the chair. 'No more silly questions, mister,' she said. 'Besides, you know things others don't. I'm sure that if you set your mind to it, you will know everything you want to know about that girl.' She blew at the steam rising from the hot chocolate, then took a sip. 'Wait. Are you sure D'Don told you why you're here?'

Kenny nodded, but he was not so sure anymore.

'Then why did you ask if the other girl was brought here?' Tashique said.

'I just thought about her,' Kenny replied.

He sensed her watching him as he reached for his own mug. She knew he had meant to say something else, but now he had decided never to say it to anyone. He could lose everything. The Rolex, his bedroom, the new clothes, his new life, and the one thing that would hurt the most: living in the same house as her.

27

I returned to my flat. My face was bruised, and my jacket was soiled. The gang had been waiting for me. It was probably the same crew that had searched my flat, thinking they'd find my notes on my laptop. They were determined, they were desperate, and they were organised. I was not imagining this.

I went to the guest bathroom to examine the damage. There was a cut right over my cheekbone, and right in the middle, a bruise that extended from above my right eye to my temple. I had nothing to clean it with, and a plaster would simply make the cut worse. I soaked a hand towel in cold water and dabbed my face. It stung, but I would live.

I called Naomi. She answered on the first ring.

'Are you outside?' she asked.

I imagined she was looking out the window of the café she'd suggested in a text message along with the address. I'd replied with a thumbs-up emoji and saved her number.

'No. You have to come to my flat instead,' I said. 'I'm texting you the address now.'

She was a journalist. She was probably used to meeting 'sources' at strange places. And that was what I planned to dangle: me as a source.

But the truth was messier. She'd booked her session under a false name, and then Roger had called asking to meet on the same day I was supposed to see her. After that, she'd waylaid me with my regretful Met nickname, the Bad Coach. Then Roger was killed. My flat was ransacked. And now my laptop had been snatched – obviously for my coaching notes. It was time she started talking. I needed to know what she was working on. I had a feeling she had no idea about the carnage trailing in the wake of her investigation.

'Easy, tiger,' she said, and I could tell she was smiling. 'At least buy me a drink first.'

If only she knew the shitstorm she'd stirred up.

'Like I said, I will tell you what I know if you tell me what you know, but it has to be at my place. I'll send you the address. This is a one-time offer.'

I had no plan B if she called my bluff.

I checked if it was her before I opened the door.

'What happened to your face?' she asked.

'Come in. I'll tell you.'

'You know that people know I'm with you, right?' she said. She stayed in the hallway, her phone ready in her hand.

'Sure,' I said. 'Please, take a picture. Send it to your colleagues. Send your location.'

I waited as she assessed the situation, scrutinising me. I

needed her to come inside. To see for herself what she was messing around with.

Her scowl faded.

'Okay,' she said, and she waved me on. 'After you.'

As she approached, she saw the mess from the door.

'What happened here?' she asked.

'They did this,' I said. I beckoned for her to follow me.

She walked in and stopped at the living room doorway, from where she surveyed the chaos. 'They? Who is *they*?' she asked.

'Whatever your story is,' I said, 'you digging around has scared some very capable people. They followed me after I left you yesterday, and then I came home to this in the evening. And no, they didn't take anything.' She didn't need to know about my dream journal or my weird nightmares. 'What they were looking for was not here. After I spoke to you earlier, I was mugged downstairs, just as I left to meet you. It was a trained, professional, four-man crew. They got my laptop. They still won't find what they're looking for on it, and when they don't, they'll come for me.'

I waited for it to sink in. Her face was blank. I couldn't tell if she didn't believe me or if she was frightened.

'They will come after me,' I said, 'and then they will come after you next.'

She just stared, so I stared back and continued.

'Roger is dead. They killed him. Yesterday. After I met you. I don't care what your story is about; I just don't want to be next. You have to tell me everything you know or else we're both dead.'

'Who is Roger?' Naomi asked, barely louder than a whisper, her voice shaken. I was taken aback. She didn't know about him?

'Roger. Roger Bainbridge. The person you're doing your story on.'

'I don't know who that is.' Her voice cracked. 'My boss got a tip from a source. Someone you coached at the Met. He was pissed off about you. He went on about how it was costing taxpayers two thousand pounds a day for him to talk to you. He sounded racist. I called some contacts and found you. I know you weren't dismissed from the Nigerian police force. I know you're not an ex-convict. I know what you charge is standard. There was no story. There is no story. We . . . Oh my God. You really don't remember me, do you?'

Had I met her before? She didn't look the least bit familiar.

'We matched on the app. A few months ago. You don't remember? We matched, but we didn't message. The next day, you were gone. I didn't know if you'd unmatched me, if you'd quit the app, or if you were banned – I didn't know. I remembered your name when I got the tip and I found your details on your website. I just wanted to meet. Oh my God, they're going to kill me?'

I still didn't recognise her. I'd stopped using the app when I'd realised that I wasn't ready to start dating again. I'd just been waiting for my subscription to run out before deleting it. It must have run out the day after we'd matched. If we'd matched.

If she was telling the truth – and I'd not picked up

anything to indicate otherwise – then she didn't know about Roger. But my flat had been searched and my laptop snatched, and Roger was still dead. I had to see that CCTV footage.

My phone rang. I fetched it and looked at the screen.

'Who is that?' she asked. She sounded panicked. Paranoid.

I heard the fright in her voice. It was also on her face. I now saw the blank look for what it was. Fear. I thought I should say something. But I still had a ringing phone in my hand. I didn't recognise the number. I answered anyway.

'Hello?'

'Hi, it's Inspector Russell.' I hadn't saved his number. 'Is this a good time?'

'Yes. Yes, I can talk.' I realised that I'd been tense. Who did I think was calling? Roger's killer?

I mouthed 'police' to Naomi. She stepped closer to try to listen.

'I just thought you might want to know what was on the CCTV,' Russell said.

My heart leapt. 'You've watched it?'

'Yes.' Russell paused a moment. Then, more quietly, 'He wasn't pushed.'

'Are you sure?' I asked.

'It doesn't look like it.'

'What do you mean it doesn't look like it?'

'The platform was crowded. You can just about make him out. If he didn't jump, then he might have slipped, or maybe he fainted. And we have statements from people standing close to him. Nobody saw exactly what happened, but nobody had the impression he was pushed.'

'Can I see it?' I asked.

'I'm afraid not.'

'Can you describe exactly what you saw?'

He paused. 'Okay. I can do that. Can you meet for coffee, say, this afternoon?' he asked.

I'd expected him to tell me over the phone or simply decline, so I was surprised that he asked to meet.

'Where?' I asked, hoping he didn't change his mind.

I noted the place and hung up.

'What happened?' Naomi asked, eyes wide, missing nothing.

I had told her more than she already knew and more than she needed to know.

'I made a mistake,' I said. 'I was wrong. Roger Bainbridge wasn't pushed. He wasn't murdered.'

I didn't believe that. What are the chances? On the same day he asked to meet because he had something to tell me? I don't think so.

'He's alive?'

'No. He either fell onto the tracks or jumped.'

I couldn't imagine Roger taking his own life.

She was unconvinced. 'Why would he do that?' she asked. She still sounded agitated.

'Why would he commit suicide?' I asked, stupidly.

She'd seen my face when she'd arrived – and the state of my flat – and she'd heard my opening monologue. I'd freaked her out. I wasn't getting off easy. The questions came fast, one after the other, with no space to answer – not that I had all the answers myself. She wanted to know everything. Was Roger in trouble? Did he have enemies? Who were they? Why did I think they'd killed him? What if they had?

I did my best to answer her questions, the ones I could, but nothing I said managed to reassure her. She was really terrified.

'You said they followed you after you left the Hansom,' she said. 'They could have seen us together at the Hansom. They probably know I'm here right now. Oh my God. I live alone. We have to call the police.'

Yeah, I did say that. Careless. I'd been convinced that she was doing a story on Roger. Knowing why she used a fake name explained the suspicious vibe I noticed at the chemistry meeting. And then it occurred to me: she had scheduled her appointment with me two weeks prior – Roger's call the night before our chemistry meeting was just a coincidence. Of course it was. This small detail had escaped my notice. And even if it'd occurred to me earlier, I'd probably have thought up a way that made the two appointments fit in my cloak-and-dagger narrative as I tried to make sense of the situation with Roger.

Unless . . .

Maybe it was Roger who knew that she was meeting me and not the other way around. Maybe he wanted to get ahead of her story, whatever it was, but he couldn't talk over the phone.

Stop, Bobby. This has nothing to do with her.

I had to stop her spiralling. Or deciding to investigate my dead Met client, who she only learnt about from me.

Or calling the police. Not knowing what Roger urgently had to talk to me about, or how he ended up on the tracks, calling the police was the worst possible idea. I hadn't ruled them out.

Looking at her, I saw what I looked like when I joined dots that didn't belong together. I had done this to her.

'Naomi, wait,' I said. 'The thing is . . . I need to tell you . . . What you need to know about me is that I suffer from paranoia. I see connections where there are none. I make up conspiracies in my head. All the time. If I'd known Roger wasn't pushed, I wouldn't have made these connections. It's all in my head. I'm getting help. I am so, so sorry.'

But wait. She herself might have just confirmed that I'd been right all along! None of the police officers that I coached knew what my day rate was. No one. Not even their superiors. I worked through an umbrella company that billed the Met directly. They paid me. After deductions. Whoever had tipped her off wasn't a former Met client; it was someone pretending to be a former client. She wasn't in any danger – unless she started digging around about Roger.

28

'Going to St James's Palace, eh?' the driver of the black cab said as he pulled onto Pall Mall. 'Going to see the King?' He grinned at his passengers in the mirror.

Kenny was in the black suit D'Don had picked out for him. The pastor also had on a black suit, while Tashique wore a red dress.

'Not the King this time,' D'Don said. 'The Prince of Wales.'

'Are you lot like African royalty or something?' the driver asked.

'Yes. Or something,' D'Don said, holding the man's gaze in the mirror until the driver looked away.

The taxi dropped them off on Marlborough Road, where they joined a throng of African guests, almost all dressed in colourful, elaborate outfits of their heritage, drawing tourists' attention as they walked towards Marlborough Gate.

Tashique walked ahead of D'Don and Kenny as they approached Ambassadors' Court, and she held up her phone to record a selfie video.

'A man named Francis will accompany the Prince,' D'Don said to Kenny in a low voice. 'At some point, I will introduce you to him as her boyfriend. You don't need to talk to him, but if he asks you how long the two of you have been together, tell him about two years, okay?'

Kenny nodded. Francis. Francis 666. The antichrist on D'Don's phone. He silently called upon the blood of Jesus.

Palace officials ushered them into a large hall with red walls full of gold-framed paintings. Kenny slowed without meaning to. The space felt too polished, too watched, as though the building itself could tell he did not belong. Here, any mistake would echo for all to see.

They were told where they were to wait in line with the other guests, their black suits standing out in the midst of the beautiful African attire. When Kenny had tried on his Armani suit in the shop and looked at himself in the mirror, he had felt clean. He had felt like a different person and had looked forward to going to church dressed in it. He looked around at the other guests; he imagined that they must all be admiring him and D'Don in their expensive designer suits. He felt the weight of the Rolex on his wrist and looked at D'Don. The pastor appeared handsome and powerful. Kenny looked around. He noticed that he was the only young person. He looked at D'Don again. The pastor was smiling at no one in particular. Kenny also tried to smile slightly, just like D'Don.

The sudden trumpet fanfare caught him unawares.

'Their Royal Highnesses, the Prince and Princess of Wales.'

The crowd fell silent. Everyone faced the entrance to

the room in anticipation. Kenny glanced at D'Don. They had all practised how to behave in front of the royals. He copied the older man and clasped his hands behind his back.

The Prince and Princess of Wales walked in, smiling and talking to the people who accompanied them. The Princess and her escort worked the line on the other side of the hall, while the Prince, escorted by Francis, started with the line that D'Don, Tashique, and Kenny were in.

'This is Dr Dolapo Daniel D'Don,' Francis told the Prince as they reached them. 'He's the founder of WAITRN Church, an African church doing amazing things in the community.'

'Oh, yes?' the Prince said. 'My father's trust does a lot with your church.'

D'Don nodded, his smile occupying the width of his face.

'And you're a doctor,' the Prince added.

'PhD,' D'Don said, an air of importance to his voice.

'In theology, is it?'

'No. Law.'

'That's quite something.'

Tashique was next up. Kenny watched her curtsey just as she had practised before they'd left the mansion that morning, then watched Francis introduce her to the Prince. He noticed something odd about one of Francis' eyes.

'This is the remarkable young woman I was telling you about,' Francis said. 'Miss Tashique Warner. She heads WAITRN Church's Youth in Politics outreach programme. She hopes to represent her constituency in His Majesty's Parliament one day.'

It was his right eye. Kenny watched to see it again. The man's right eye moved slightly slower than the left one, just like the eyes of Mr Spencer, one of his former foster parents. When Amelia, his only daughter, had told Kenny that her father had lost an eye in a fight, Kenny had become obsessed with it, watching Mr Spencer as the overweight magician watched *EastEnders* from his brown recliner in the evenings. Neither D'Don nor Tashique would have noticed the glass eye. Kenny knew something they did not know.

'And this is Kenny Coker, a very talented member of the church.' He snapped to attention as Francis introduced him next.

'Is that so?' The Prince shook hands with Kenny. 'What's your talent?'

Kenny answered without thinking. 'I see things other people don't see.'

He noticed how the woman next to him turned to look his way. He felt stupid. The words had just dropped from his mouth, as his mother would say.

'That could come in handy,' the Prince said with a smile, then he moved on to the woman next in line.

Still embarrassed, Kenny checked on D'Don to gauge how much he'd messed up.

But D'Don was also looking at him. Tashique as well. The pastor seemed to be smiling at him with pride.

Kenny felt a warmth he did not trust spread through his chest. Embarrassment gave way to relief. Even permission.

Perhaps his words had not been a mistake after all. Perhaps God had put them there. He straightened his shoulders, careful not to smile too much. Imagine you're wearing a cape, he reminded himself.

29

After the royals had left, footmen dressed in formal attire – tailored coats, waistcoats, breeches, white gloves, and buckled shoes adorned with the royal insignia – moved discreetly among the guests, serving drinks and canapés. The Prince and the Princess had been representing the King, who had been unable to attend the reception due to a medical concern. The Palace had not elaborated. D'Don was put out. He had been hoping to shake hands with the King.

Tashique, D'Don and Kenny found themselves sharing a tall table with a short, plump, bespectacled man. He introduced himself as Ernest Smith. D'Don asked him, 'The Ernest Smith?'

There were no chairs, so they all stood and spoke over canapés and fruit juice. Ernest Smith and Tashique were soon engrossed in a lively discussion. D'Don and Kenny were on the other side of the table – as Tashique laughed at something, Kenny watched her bend over to recover and hold Ernest's forearm for support. She didn't see Ernest's eyes focus on her cleavage, but Kenny did.

D'Don nudged him. 'Look at Francis,' he said. 'He's about to come and apologise.'

Francis was with a group of people taking turns to talk to him.

'Do you see his horns?' D'Don asked.

Kenny noticed how the older man turned his left ear towards people to listen to them. Maybe he was also deaf in one ear, just like Mr Spencer had been. Francis occasionally glanced at them with his good eye. He made eye contact with Kenny for a moment. Kenny searched for his horns. Maybe D'Don was referring to the patches of white hair on the sides of Francis' head. Or the red birthmark still visible from a distance. Maybe he did not mean actual horns. Or maybe he did, and he could see them, and he expected Kenny to see them too.

'He is a beast that, when it walks, removes people from its path like this.' With pinched fingers, D'Don demonstrated uprooting weeds and setting them aside.

Francis had taken a step away from the group that seemed keen to keep talking to him, keeping his good ear bent towards them even as his body language signalled his intention to leave. He made a final round of handshakes and turned towards their table. Kenny looked up and pretended to admire the decorated ceiling.

'Hi, Don,' Francis said.

'Hi, Francis. How are you?'

The two men shook hands, then, still holding on to D'Don, Francis leant in close and said, 'I'm sorry I said "African church" back there. I know you're particular about it being a place for all people.'

'It's not a problem,' D'Don said. 'Thank you for squeezing Kenny in.'

Francis held out a hand to Kenny. 'I hope I pronounced your name correctly,' he said. 'You are Yoruba? I visited Lagos in the fifties.'

'He's Tashique's boyfriend,' D'Don said.

'Is that so?' Francis responded. 'Where is she?'

They all looked around for Tashique. She was gone, and so was Ernest Smith.

'That business with the policeman,' Francis said. 'I hope it's all settled now.'

'He's dead,' D'Don replied.

'He died?'

'Yesterday. He killed himself. He jumped in front of a train.'

'Oh, dear.'

Francis removed his glasses as if in respect for the departed.

'Yes, indeed,' D'Don said, smiling as he spoke, his gaze steady on Francis. 'God works in mysterious ways. "Touch not my anointed."'

30

Tashique and Ernest Smith had still not returned when the guests began to leave the reception. Kenny searched the crowd for the two as he left the palace with D'Don, who didn't seem to notice that Tashique was missing.

'I can't read your mind, you know?' D'Don said.

Kenny had been feeding his jealousy on images of Ernest Smith and Tashique laughing together. He stared blankly at D'Don.

'I asked if you were still hungry,' D'Don said. 'I am. Are you?'

Where was Tashique? Where had they gone? Kenny continued to search for them in the crowd.

'Are you okay?' D'Don asked.

Kenny nodded.

'Keep up.'

Kenny realised that he'd fallen a step behind as he searched for Tashique.

'Well? Are you hungry?' D'Don asked.

The finger food at the palace had been insufficient and bland, and Kenny hadn't eaten a lot of it because of the way Ernest Smith had been flirting with Tashique and the way she'd allowed him to continue. He thought he saw her red dress amid the crowd.

'I take it you're not hungry,' D'Don said.

'What about Tashique?' Kenny asked.

'What about her?'

Kenny suddenly realised that D'Don probably knew where she was, and that he expected him to as well – the same way he had expected Kenny to see the horns on Francis' head. He should know things that other people didn't. He let the unanswered question remain behind as they joined the queue at a taxi rank.

'I'm hungry,' he said. But as the line moved, he kept searching for her.

In the back of their black cab, D'Don turned to him. 'Everyone is chosen for a purpose,' he said. 'Just like you were chosen to be the man by her side, she was also chosen for a great purpose. That man is expected to run for prime minister one day. It is important that she network with people like him. I noticed that you were watching them. Kenny, no man on this earth has ever met her without liking her. They can't help it. It is a gift. Just like you have your own gift, she has hers. Her gift is going to help her in her calling. She was chosen to be in politics. She is going to be the first Black prime minister of the United Kingdom. Do you want to know how I know?'

Kenny nodded. D'Don was looking at him as he spoke, making him uncomfortable. Kenny felt uncomfortable knowing that the driver would hear them.

'God revealed it to me in a vision as clear as day,' D'Don

said, oblivious to the driver. 'Before I'd even met her. I had been fasting for close to seventy-two hours. Dry fasting. On the night of the third day, the spirit of God descended upon me and occupied my body. He brought her to me at the altar and made her kneel before His glory. He placed this hand upon her head. I looked up, and I saw the host of heaven interceding for her. I was afraid. I did not know what to make of the vision. I consulted the scriptures. I prayed and I waited for Him to tell me what He wanted me to do. On the seventh day of my fasting, I fell into a deep sleep, and God entered my room and sat on my bed. He said, "She will rule over nations. Her helper will be chosen from among the army of God. I will send both of them to you, along with the people through whom it shall all be done."'

Kenny checked on the driver. The man was focused on the road.

'Do you know when her birthday is?' D'Don asked, drawing Kenny's eyes back to him. 'Do you know who else has that birthday? Margaret Thatcher. She was the first female prime minister in this country. Do you see now? This is her destiny. This is not just her destiny, but also yours. She will be this nation's prime minister, and you are the helper that God has chosen to be by her side. Francis and Ernest are just a few of the people that God is using to place both of you at Number Ten. Can you see how important that is? How big her purpose is? You need to ask yourself if you're ready to be the man who will be by her side on that journey. Many are called, but few are chosen, and even among the chosen, few ever live up to their potential.' His voice dropped, slow and deliberate, as though each word had been weighed in prayer. 'How is it going to be with you?'

31

I had shared my mental health condition with Naomi of my own volition, hoping to convince her that whatever I feared, it wasn't something that could touch her. Now that I knew she had only been shooting her shot, albeit in a most stalkerish way, telling her about Roger was like dangling royal scandal meat in front of an investigative journalist bulldog. She wasn't going to let go unless I convinced her there was nothing to see here, for her own good. Using my paranoia as a 'get out of jail free' card was dishonest and maybe even manipulative, and I felt rotten for doing it. But what's that they say about the ends justifying the means? I had freaked her out. I had to unfreak her. From the look on her face – her blank, twitchy stare of understandable fear – I couldn't tell if it had worked. Maybe if I told her about an episode. Holding her gaze, I considered what was safe to share, but before I was ready to speak, she beat me to it.

'We have to call someone,' she said.

It was as if she hadn't heard everything that I'd just said. She was breathing through her mouth – quick, shallow breaths. Her eyes were wide open, soaking in every bit of information. She was on full alert, and she wasn't buying my BS. She sensed the real danger I'd warned her she was in. I caught myself as I was about to say, 'Calm down.' In my experience, those two words always have the exact opposite effect from the intended outcome in any given situation. I had to do better. I owed it to her.

'I suffer from paranoia,' I repeated. 'I make things up in my head. Not intentionally. My brain sees conspiracies where there are none.'

She nodded enthusiastically as I spoke. A good sign. I'd decided which episode to share with her.

'I once imagined I was witnessing a—'

Still nodding, she cut me off.

'I know a guy,' she said. 'He's high up in the Met. He'll know what to do. I'll stay at an Airbnb tonight.' She unlocked her phone. 'If they're watching your flat, they'll see me leaving. I need to change.' She looked up at me. 'Can I borrow some clothes?' she asked.

All the while she'd been nodding, she'd also been thinking – analysing the situation, weighing her options, and planning her escape into hiding. In the space of a few moments, she'd gone from wholly terrified to impressively proactive.

'Seriously, Naomi, no one is coming after you. Or me. I made this all up in my head. I am sick. Do you understand? There is something wrong with me . . .'

'I'll need a cap,' she said, seemingly ignoring my further attempts to allay her fears with lies.

I pictured what was happening in her head. Her reticular activating system – a network of neurones in the brainstem – was sifting out noise so that she could focus on what was most important in the dangerous situation she was in. I was the noise.

She began to pace around, looking down as she picked her way through the mess the burglars had left behind. I was grateful for the way she avoided stepping on my records.

'Do you have a cap? A baseball cap. A pair of jeans and trainers. And a jacket.' She looked up and measured me with her eyes. We were about the same height. She continued in an almost mechanical voice. 'You should come with me. Yes. You should. We'll get different Ubers. Is there a back exit?'

'Naomi. Calm down. You're freaking out.' Shit. I'd said it.

She stopped walking and glared at me. 'Don't you tell me to calm down. Don't you dare!' She jabbed a finger at me. 'Yes, I'm freaking out. The question is, why aren't you? Your client was murdered, your house was raided, and you were mugged. All on the same day.' She was right. 'Don't tell me to calm down. You know what? I'm calling Mark.'

I stepped forward as she brought her phone to her ear, and she stopped me with a try-me look and a warning finger pointed at my face.

She was no longer freaking out; she had full executive function of her mind, while mine was skidding in all directions, and from inside that chaos she struck me as operating at a genius level, seeing through my every bit of bullshit. She could get us out of this mess if only I could trust her with the rest of the things she didn't know. And for a moment – a dangerous one – I almost did. I watched her, sharp and steady, and felt a flicker of something like awe. But I couldn't. No matter how much I wanted to, I couldn't. The less she knew, the better for her.

'Naomi,' I said. 'If I did not make this up, then calling anyone is about the worst thing you could possibly do.'

I meant it. She studied me as she waited for her contact to answer. I knew she was analysing what I'd said. She took the phone away from her ear, crossed her arms over her chest, and waited. I could continue with the lies, or I could come clean. I landed somewhere in between.

'Okay,' I said. 'I agree there's a possibility that it's all connected, and for that to hold true, Roger would have to have been killed. But if he committed suicide, then everything else is a coincidence.'

I waited. She waited. I knew I was in the presence of a superior intellect. I continued.

'I'll know for sure when I meet up with the officer.'

Her blank look was back. Maybe it was her poker face. Maybe I was being played. Who was she, really?

Stop, Bobby. Stop.

'The one who called,' I said. 'He offered to meet to describe the CCTV footage.'

'I'm coming with you,' she said matter-of-factly. She stared back at me.

I shook my head. 'Naomi, he just wants to assure me it was a suicide.'

'I'm coming with you.'

'You're a journalist. He won't talk with you there.'

'When are you meeting him?'

'Today?'

'When?'

'Naomi.'

'Where?'

'He didn't say,' I lied. 'I'll have to call him for details. But you're not coming with me. You are a journalist.' I heard the way I said it, with an accusatory tone. I hadn't meant to.

'I have to know what he tells you,' she said.

'I promise you're the first person I'll call once I've seen him.'

She stood her ground, her arms still crossed. 'Why does he want to meet? Why can't he just tell you over the phone?'

I didn't have an honest answer I could give her. But I'd just been served the perfect hand.

'Maybe he wants to be sure there's no one else listening,' I said. 'He's going to be disclosing confidential information.'

We stood, staring at each other. She didn't trust me, and it was evident on her face.

'Bobby,' she said, her voice calm and measured. 'I know you think you're protecting me. I can't stop you from trying to do that – it's a man thing. I get it. But you are not responsible for me. I am responsible for myself. You understand? You can't invite me to your place to see how it's been searched by professionals – that's what you called them, right? Then tell me that they killed your client – Roger, also right? – and snatched your laptop looking for information, and then expect me to simply wait for you to go see this man and come back to tell me everything is okay. That won't fly. Either I come with you, or you start filling in the blanks. First, let's start with this paranoia of yours. When did it start?'

Calling out my misogyny with clear assertiveness was about the most emotionally intelligent thing I'd witnessed in a long time. In a different situation, I would have been mentally making a note for reflection later in the day and journaling before going to bed. But this was the situation, and she had reached the very core of wounds kept fresh by deep, unforgiving regret.

I was a kid again, on my knees, under the midday sun. My arms were spread out, and my shoulders were starting to ache, so I momentarily forgot the discomfort of my exposed knees on the warm concrete. I would remain like this until my mother said it was enough. It was my disciplinarian father's punishment, which he seemed to think was humane compared to how he described his father stripping him to his underwear before using the cane on him. For me, pain was pain. It was the pain I'd been avoiding that had kept me from expressing my feelings the first time I remembered sensing that something was wrong.

It was the first day of the school holidays. Cousins from Jos and Owerri would soon be arriving, and then, for the next few days, the house would be filled with young children of similar ages, running around charged with sugary soft drinks, inventing new games, sharing tales, and exploring the neighbourhood together. We had the largest home of all the uncles and aunts, so the family congregated at our place.

My mother, Aunty Fatima – who had been my nanny and who had stayed on to become Mimi's nanny as well – Aunty Debbi, the maid, and Mama, the cook, were all busy preparing for the coming mayhem, so no one was paying me any attention. As soon as I heard my father's green Volvo estate leave the compound, I escaped from the dining table, where I'd been pretending to eat my breakfast of boiled yam and spicy scrambled eggs. I slid out of the compound, knowing that Mr Musa, the gatekeeper, would have walked down the road to smoke his cigarettes as soon as my father had left for work. I was going to Femi's house to trade *Archie* comics for the latest copy of *Ikebe Super*, a somewhat adult comic that he'd stolen from his own father. I did not make it across the road, however. Musa was on the other side of the gate, hunched in conversation with a man I hadn't seen before. The two of them stopped talking and looked at me as I stepped out of the gate. Musa, like all the domestic staff, had my father's full permission to punish the stubborn boy. I expected him to exercise that power for my trying to sneak out again, but instead, both he and the strange man just stared at me. I stepped back into the compound and returned to the dining table to finish my breakfast, hoping to store up some points for when Musa outed me later on – something he took delight in doing, even after making me stand in front of the gatehouse with my arms raised above my head.

While waiting for him to wheel me out, I kept thinking

of him and the stranger. I had noticed them talking as if passing secrets and recalled how they had stopped when they saw me – as though I'd caught them out. I began to feel that something was wrong.

Musa did not report me to my mother, so I sat with that terror as I awaited my father's return. Late in the afternoon, when Brother Biodun brought my father back from the factory, Musa still didn't report my failed attempt at disobeying the rules. Anything other than the agony of waiting would have been preferable. I would have even preferred that Musa had used the Koboko he threatened Jehovah's Witnesses with – at least then he wouldn't have been able to report me because he too would have broken one of my father's rules. But the man didn't say a word. It felt strange.

I couldn't get the look on his and the other man's faces out of my mind. Climbing into bed that night, I remembered that Musa still had not reported me, and my heart skipped a beat. I began ruminating over him and the strange man again, seeing how their eyes had darted towards me as I'd pushed the gate open and how they'd stood so close together, their heads bent in secret talks, as if they were up to something. It felt as if that was the reason Musa had not reported me to my parents. I became convinced that I had caught him and the strange man plotting something really bad, and that they really, really didn't want me to tell my parents about it, which meant I should have told them. But to do so would have been to expose my own disobedience. Still, I had a nagging feeling that I had to say something to my parents, even if I was wrong. Even if it was merely my active imagination, as a teacher had once noted on my report card.

The following day, Brother Biodun drove my father to work, and they never returned. That same day, Musa also abandoned his post and I never saw him again. I never told anyone about how I'd caught him talking to a stranger who looked like a soldier just a day before my father and his driver had been abducted, but the memory of it has haunted me ever since. Maybe if I'd trusted my instincts and said something, we would all have escaped to England together as a family. Every time I remember the episode, my body perceives it as a punishment. It was both my earliest memory of sensing that something was wrong and my first failure to act upon the suspicion. It was a lifelong regret that I carried with me.

Not this time.

Naomi was still waiting for me to say something, but I wouldn't share this.

'Since I was a child,' I said, answering her question shortly. 'I had a very active imagination. And I guess being a policeman didn't help. You always have to come up with theories simply by looking at the evidence.

'Have you ever been right? I mean, about your paranoia?' she asked.

I hadn't seen that one coming. 'Yes,' I admitted. 'Sometimes.'

'How often?'

She hadn't come to play. I thought of the times I'd been wrong, and as I did so, an undeniable truth slowly made itself clear. I realised, for the first time – and because of the powerful question she had gifted me – what I had been doing. I'd trained myself to focus only on the times I'd been wrong. I'd created my own confirmation bias. But simply by looking past my doomsaying, I saw what I hadn't noticed before: that I was more often right than I was wrong. Far more often. I just hadn't been aware of it until that moment.

The thought was both intoxicating and terrifying – a rush of vindication followed by the cold certainty that if I was right more often than I admitted, then I could never fully trust myself to know when I wasn't.

The realisation left me ambivalent. I was sick, but not all the time. Like seeing dead people, except that some of them are still alive.

'Quite often,' I admitted, as much to myself as to her.

'So, it's intuition,' Naomi said, looking at me as if she dared me to contradict her. I couldn't. She had blown my mind again. Maybe I wasn't mad after all.

32

Naomi was on my mind all the way to my meeting with Russell. Her emotionless stare bleached blank by fear; her freaked-out face; her swift transition from terror to analysis; her plan to wear my clothes as a disguise and then sneak out through the rear exit and run away into hiding. Her dress, her perfume, the playfulness in her voice when she'd said, 'Easy Tiger. Buy me a drink first.'

I smiled.

She was the most amazing woman I'd ever met. And to think that she'd liked me back on the dating app. I still didn't remember clicking on her profile, but I must have been feeling very confident that day. A part of me was proud of myself for daring to reach, while another part said to me, 'Yes, but she's still out of your league. Like, way out.'

I remembered how frightened she'd been. I squirmed. I remembered that she'd asked me to call her after meeting the police officer. I smiled. I felt the chemical signature of giddiness in my chest. I liked her. I longed to talk to her again. After calling to tell her about the meeting with Roger, maybe I could call again about the coroner's report. Maybe we could even meet somewhere to talk. Perhaps at the restaurant she'd picked to meet at earlier in the morning. She would definitely want to know what else I'd learnt, and I would get to see her again.

Really, Bobby? Using your client's death to see her again? Really? That's a new low.

I continued thinking of Naomi all the way to the pub where Russell had asked to meet. It was called the Black Friar, in the area of the same name. I almost missed it but for the model of an actual Black Friar that looked like a black Buddha gazing down from the art deco building at the tip of a triangle-shaped block. I looked around as I made my way to the back, where he'd said he would be.

I can pick out Met officers in a crowd, even when they're in plain clothes. It's something about the way they sit or stand with their backs straight. They're all invariably in shape, and they all have conservative hairstyles, wear nothing-out-of-the-ordinary outfits and maintain perpetually neutral expressions. In many sessions, while exploring deeply personal or otherwise emotive issues, I often marvelled at how little emotion made it to their faces. Often, none at all. They sat rigid through every conversation, which was often a problem for me as I attempted to mirror their body posture. I always wished they would be relaxed like Nigerian police officers.

I spotted Russell easily. We were the only police officers in there. It wasn't a typical police hangout, and I suspected he didn't want to be seen talking to me. I sat opposite him and his fizzing glass of Coke and lemon. The small bottle stood empty on the table. His back was as straight as a ballerina's.

Still not certain why he'd asked to meet, I fantasised that perhaps he had chosen a pub away from the curious eyes of other officers so he could show me the footage. Maybe I should have sat next to him. I'd noticed this about my tendency to fantasise. Maybe it was an extension of my paranoia. I really wouldn't know until I saw the therapist Margaret had recommended – something I'd been putting off.

We got our greetings out of the way, and I waited for him to say something, as I hadn't thought of an opening. I got the feeling he was waiting on me as well, and for the same reason. Maybe he just wasn't sure how to do this. My guess was that it wasn't every day he met a civilian to discuss the death of a mutual acquaintance. And just like that, I had my opening.

'How well did you know Roger?' I asked. I watched for Russell's reaction.

'I didn't.'

I had not expected that.

'How well did you know him?' he asked. From the way he looked at me, I knew he was also watching for my reaction.

'As well as one can know a client, I guess.'

'You thought he was pushed.'

I often asked my clients non-question questions, just as he was doing. They're powerful tools. They force you to think differently as you grapple with the intended confusion, and there's no telling how you'll respond. Often, a client would answer a question other than the one that had been asked – one that I wouldn't have known to ask – and it would reveal something new and important. In my case, Russell's non-question question took me back to the events of the past twenty-four hours, starting with the chemistry meeting with Naomi and ending with my bag being snatched outside my building. And as I reflected, it dawned on me that this wasn't about the footage after all. He had seen it, and he was convinced it wasn't murder. He hadn't asked to meet because he wanted to describe the content to me; he had asked to meet because he wanted to know what made me suspect that a former client of mine had been murdered.

For a moment, I had thought we might be working together, two professionals piecing a case together. But it quickly became clear that this meeting was more official than I'd suspected.

Maybe he'd tricked me into talking before reading me my rights. Maybe I'd been framed for Roger's death.

The thoughts multiplied. Maybe it wasn't Roger on the phone the night before. Maybe someone had called him, too, pretending to be me.

Maybe I was having an episode.

He wasn't inviting collaboration; he was probing me like a suspect, testing what I knew and why I suspected what I did. He held the silence just like a coach would, waiting for me to implicate myself. I had walked into a trap. I chose my next words carefully.

'Maybe I'm a little worried that I missed something he mentioned in our sessions together,' I said. 'Something that, in hindsight and in light of what has happened, might have signalled thoughts of self-harm.'

'Maybe?'

He was good. It was an interrogation. I remembered my own training in interrogation techniques years ago. I would have asked the same probing questions using the very same words.

'Yeah. Maybe he said something that I missed at the time.'

Russell held the silence until it was obvious I was done talking. Then he did what I would have done.

'So, when you learnt that Roger had died,' he said, 'you thought he might have said something to you that you'd missed at the time. Something that could have indicated a possibility that he would harm himself?' He was summarising what I'd said.

I nodded. Something was unsettling about the way he'd worded it, but I didn't have time to probe it; all my focus was on not making it easy for him to read me. I kept silent until he spoke again.

'So, you think he committed suicide and you missed the signs?'

Unsettledness turned to confusion. Something was causing me angst, but I couldn't show it. Russell waited. He maintained eye contact, just like I would. It hit me too late that the time to shut up had been long before I'd started talking.

'But you thought he was pushed. Now you claim you thought he was suicidal.'

Claim. He might as well have said, 'I put it to you,' but

I had figured out what had caused my discombobulation. It was when I'd answered his non-question question. I had indeed answered a question he had not asked, but one that was revealing for me all the same.

Right there in that pub in Blackfriars, it dawned on me that I was, in fact, worried that Roger might have said something a year ago during our sessions that I'd missed. Something that should have warned me that he was at risk of suicide. Something I missed because I was prejudiced. I felt sick.

I realised that the fear had been with me since Russell himself had informed me of Roger being the accident at Marylebone Station.

Could it be that my choice to believe that Roger had been killed was just that? A choice? Rather than confronting the fear that I might have missed a chance to save a client's life, I'd gone straight to a conspiracy that absolved me of blame. It was the standard response to trauma, a self-preservation mechanism. My stomach turned. My lip twitched as I suppressed a groan.

The silence stretched. I felt it in my chest, a tightness I hadn't noticed before, and became aware of how long it was taking me to probe and process this sudden realisation – and of the fact that Russell was watching me all the while, like I would a client in deep thought.

'I might have missed something,' I said. More to myself than to him. It was a sobering realisation. I might have missed something.

I looked up. On his steady face, I saw a slight hint of what I took to be pity.

'Do you still want me to describe the video?' he asked.

'Yes,' I said.

This time, I was listening differently.

33

Francis walked from his office in Clarence House to the gun shop on Mount Street. The shopkeeper was alone in the store. Without speaking, Francis went behind the counter and into the corridor beyond.

In the cramped room beneath the shop, Dempsey noticed movement in one of the squares on the CCTV monitor to the left of his own screens.

'Heads up. Black Rod,' he said. The agents watched as Francis moved down the narrow corridor, past two unmarked doors, and descended the spiral stairwell that led to the hidden operations room. They turned in their swivel chairs to face the sofa on which he would sit to receive his briefings.

Rod lifted his nose and sniffed. 'You really don't smell that?' he asked. Libby and Dempsey ignored him.

Francis entered the room and frowned at the CCTV monitor. His eyes landed on a man in a blue blazer lingering in the shop.

'Turn up the volume,' he said.

Dempsey adjusted the controls.

Francis studied the man on the screen for a moment, then, satisfied he'd seen enough, he turned and left the room.

The three agents crowded around the monitor, listening intently.

Upstairs, the shopkeeper asked from behind his counter, 'May I help you, sir?'

'Oh, hi. I could have sworn I saw my old pal walk in here. Do you have a back door?' the man said, eyes darting around.

'No, sir, we do not have a back door. Is there anything else I can assist you with?'

Francis emerged from the door behind the counter and walked onto the shop floor.

The man in the blue blazer turned to the shopkeeper. 'I thought you said he had already left.'

'He said no such thing,' Francis said evenly, shoulders relaxed. 'His instructions are to say nothing if a situation like this were ever to occur.'

The man's jaw tightened. 'You're not denying it, then?'

'Denying what, Rufus?' Francis replied, voice calm.

'That you're running some kind of off-the-books operation?'

'I'm just visiting friends. But what about you? What are you doing here?'

The man grinned. 'Sir Francis,' he said, 'help me to understand something. How come no one who could have given you approval knows anything about whatever it is you're up to? What's going on, Francis? What are you up to?'

Francis sighed. 'Rufus,' he said. 'If this is about what

happened back then . . . If that is why you followed me, you know I will have to raise my concerns.'

'You're threatening me,' Rufus said. 'You're scared.' His grin grew wider.

'If you're not buying something,' Francis said, 'the gentleman will have to ask you to leave.'

'What are you doing, old man?' Rufus persisted. 'Still chasing Nazi ghosts? Spying on your mistress? Going senile?'

'Pick one,' Francis said, his voice cold.

The shopkeeper cleared his throat. 'If you don't mind,' he said. He held his hand out to the door.

Rufus looked at the shopkeeper, then at Francis.

Francis raised his eyebrows, turned around and stepped back behind the counter without another word.

Down below, Libby, Dempsey and Rod scampered from the monitor back to their chairs and sat facing Francis' sofa, quiet and immobile, like schoolchildren playing innocent after pulling off a prank.

After a few moments, Francis entered the room again. He paused first at the door, looked at the monitor behind Dempsey, then sat down heavily on the sofa.

'No doubt you all witnessed that unfortunate incident,' he said. 'And I'm sure you all listened to our little conversation. If at this juncture any one of you wishes to leave, I have to let you know that it is already too late.'

He gazed levelly at the eyes staring back at him.

'That's a joke,' he said.

Libby was the first to exhale, her rigid body deflating with relief.

'Well,' Francis said. 'I guess I should tell you all that I am sane, I do not have a mistress, and this is neither a personal vendetta of any kind nor some training exercise to relive the adventures of my field days. Nor, for that matter, is it something likely to stain your records. At least not while I'm still alive.'

He looked at the agents in turn.

'That was another joke. All right, that's enough fun for one day. What do you have for me?' He leant back in the sofa. 'Dempsey.'

Dempsey gave his update. 'I've gone over the documents on my guy's laptop,' he said. 'Nothing interesting there. I looked at his web history, too: no red flags. He's careful. He watches porn in privacy mode. Empties his bin. He's into straight sex – no spanking, no trans, no role play, no threesomes, foursomes, or gang bangs.'

'Heterosexual cis male,' Libby sniggered.

Dempsey continued. 'He averages about five minutes per clip. Nothing interesting there.'

'A record for some,' Libby said, and Dempsey glared at her.

'Anything else?' Francis asked.

'I'm going through his pictures,' Dempsey continued. 'Checking the geotags, maybe we'll come across something to cross-reference. The only interesting thing so far is that he hasn't tried to wipe the computer since we grabbed it. You'd think that by now he'd have done that. We've cloned the hard drive anyway, but all the same, I think that's interesting.'

'Why?'

'Without a profile, I can't be sure, but I'd say he's a trained operative. Maybe he wants us to see what's on the laptop.'

'Thank you,' Francis said. 'Libby?'

Libby grinned. 'My girl left with your favourite paedo minister. Right now, they're having pre-coital small talk. Want to see? I bet these two that he'll take her to his place in Fulham. Want in on the action?'

Francis turned to Rod. 'What about you? Anything less disappointing?'

'I might have something. Nothing yet on my guy, so Dempsey has me looking at the other stuff. I wrote a bot to monitor the church's accounts and my script flagged an out-of-pattern transaction today. It might have something to do with the chatter we've been seeing on social media. His followers have been at it all day and it's still going on now. Looks like something big is happening tonight. There have been more than twenty attempts at a hashtag, but none of them has taken off. I'm following them all. The most promising one is #thegathering.'

'What is the unusual transaction?'

'They've ordered a huge amount of fresh sardines to be delivered to the house tonight. I'm guessing that's where this gathering is happening, whatever it is.'

'Sardines?'

'Yup. And bread.'

'How much?'

'Five hundred pounds, and that's just the sardines.'

'Weight or money?'

'Money. I can find out how much fish that is. I'm guessing he plans to feed a huge crowd.'

'How huge?'

'I don't know. A hundred? Two hundred? I could try to work it out if it's interesting.'

'Stay on it.'

'It would really help if we knew what we were looking for,' Dempsey said.

'You'll know when you find it,' Francis said. He stood up from the sofa and turned to Rod. 'Five loaves and two fishes. Google it.'

34

Francis hailed a black cab outside Dudley & Co. and told the driver, '67 Pall Mall'.

The receptionist at the private members' club recognised him as he walked in. Francis muttered, 'Just meeting someone,' and wandered into the dining area.

Tashique was at a table with Ernest Smith, a decanted burgundy breathing next to two glasses on the tablecloth. She spotted Francis and waved. Ernest looked up to see who had captured her attention, getting to his feet as Francis approached and bumping the table with his leg as he did so.

'Francis,' he said, extending a handshake. 'Are you dining?'

Francis took his hand and didn't let go. 'I'm meeting someone,' he said. He glanced at Tashique. She smiled and looked away. 'I didn't mean to interrupt,' he said to Ernest.

'Oh, no. Not at all. It's, er . . . She's, er . . .'

Francis drew him close. 'How old is she?' he asked.

'Oh. Umm, it's not what you're thinking, you old dog.' With his free hand, he patted Francis on the arm.

'You look flustered,' Francis noted Ernest's face turning red.

'Do I?'

'It's none of my business,' Francis went on, 'but one might wonder what a married junior minister is doing with a young lady in a private gentleman's club. Is that one of the bottles you have cellared here? Must be quite expensive.'

Ernest's cheeks flushed still redder. 'It's really not what it looks like.'

'May I recommend the private booths at the restaurant in the Blue Boar Hotel in Westminster to avoid the possibility of anyone getting the wrong idea? Are you familiar with the place? A few of your colleagues find it rather conducive for private discussions.'

'Who did you say you were meeting?'

'I didn't say. Anyway, seeing as I've found you here, there's a matter I'd like to discuss. I suggest you get her a taxi to take her home. Now.'

35

'Busted!' Libby flicked her fingers at her screen as she reclined in her chair.

Dempsey and Rod rolled over just in time to see Tashique going for a hug and Ernest extending a handshake instead. Francis' back was to the CCTV camera Libby had hacked into.

'He actually went there,' Dempsey said.

'Oh, God, please tell me we're not going to have to start watching this guy, too,' Rod said.

'No,' Libby said. 'She's the subject; he's just noise. But I wouldn't mind watching him.'

'You're too old for him,' Dempsey said.

She flipped him off without looking his way. 'You know that's not what I meant.'

'What are we doing here, anyway?' Rod asked. The other two stared at him. 'Come on, guys. Tell me you don't also think this stinks.'

There was a pause.

'Do you need a cigarette break?' Dempsey asked.

'What?'

'Take a cigarette break. Get some fresh air.'

'I'll come with you,' Libby said. She pulled her black rucksack with steel studs from under the table and rummaged inside for a lighter and her packet of tobacco. She stood up and headed for the door, but Rod was still sitting, looking confused. 'Come on. Let's go.'

The young agents exited the gun shop and crossed the road; Rod hunched against the cold and rubbed his ungloved hands together while Libby constructed her roll-up.

Watching her lick the edge of the rolling paper, Rod said, 'You know I don't smoke, don't you?'

Libby inspected the roll-up before inserting it between her lips and lighting it. She tilted her head up to exhale.

'He didn't ask me where they were,' she said.

It took Rod a moment to understand. 'He saw your screen?' he suggested.

Libby shook her head. She blew a thin jet of smoke upward. 'It wasn't up.'

'How did he know?'

'How do you think?'

They were both facing the gun shop. She looked at him from the corner of her eye as she took another drag.

'Think about it,' she said. 'We don't have a clear objective. We were never briefed – just given names and no profiles. We're just to report anything interesting, and we're not the first team on it.'

'We're not?'

'Nope. Dempsey was here before me. The girl you replaced was here before him. The team she joined was here before her. He keeps one person on to pass on gathered intel to the new team, and it's all verbal – nothing ever gets written down, just like the stand-ups. We've been here for, what, four months? We know of two previous teams, so that's at least twelve months this operation has been active.'

'Any idea what it's all about?'

'Nope. No one stays on long enough to figure it out.'

Rod shuffled his feet. 'Maybe it's training? He's old-school. One of the best, I hear.'

'Nope. This is real. He's after something, and only he knows what.'

'But if we don't know what we're looking for, how are we going to find it?'

Libby blew out another stream of smoke and looked him in the eye. 'Dempsey and I think he's got other teams going at the same time, each working on separate pieces of the puzzle. That way, no one ever sees the whole picture. No one finds out what it's about. No one knows anything but him and whoever is handling him.'

'You don't think he's doing this alone?'

'One team, maybe. But multiple teams, each of them on rotation? That level of resourcing, no. It's not a solo operation.'

The driver in an idling white van waved down an approaching black cab. The two men spoke briefly through the windows of their vehicles, temporarily blocking the agents' view of Dudley & Co. Both Libby and Rod watched the small disruption, each of them aware how easily a simple move could obscure the bigger picture.

'He's a cut-out, then,' Rod said, his eyes on the idling vehicles.

'Nope. A firewall. Think deniability.' Libby took a slow drag from her roll-up and let the smoke curl up into the cold. 'Whatever this is, it's big. And it's happening on home soil. If it all goes south, it stops with him. He becomes the cranky old spy gone rogue, and us? Well, it never happened, and we're all shipped off to different stations and kept apart till they figure out what to do with us.'

She threw the cigarette down and ground it beneath her foot. 'So, you see, even if you think this stinks or that this whole setup is some sort of bullshit, you've got to keep that shit to yourself. We might be watching those people, but I bet you, he has other people watching us as well.'

The white van and the black cab pulled away in opposite directions.

36

Russell moved the items on the table to one side. He inspected the clutter he'd made on his left and picked out two knives. Placing them parallel to each other on the table, he looked up and said, 'These are the tracks.'

Next, he picked up the salt and pepper shakers and placed them an inch apart. Pointing at the salt, he said, 'This is Roger.' Then he leant over and reached out for the pepper shaker on the empty table beside us, which he placed on the other side of the salt.

'It wasn't rush hour, so the platform wasn't too busy. Those two are the closest to him.'

He searched again and chose a spoon, which he placed between the knives.

'The train is arriving.' He slid the spoon over the table.

'A group of kids run onto the platform.' He tapped his fingers on the table to illustrate passengers rushing up behind Roger.

'These two turn around.' He turned the pepper shakers on both sides of Roger, and then, as he slid the spoon along, he tipped the salt shaker with his little finger, sending it falling across the tracks in the path of the train.

'We've spoken to him.' Russell sat back, pointing to the scene as he spoke. 'To the driver. I haven't seen it, but I understand there's a video from the train, which basically shows the same thing. We've spoken to everyone who was on the platform that day. Either Roger killed himself or he fell. Maybe he fainted or he had a heart attack. Who knows.' He looked me in the eye. 'But he wasn't pushed.'

I stepped out of the Black Friar and zipped my jacket all the way to the top.

I hadn't thought of a camera on the train itself. Maybe the driver had a GoPro. The driver. Only then did the anguish they must be going through occur to me. The total anguish. I imagined it would never end. They would forever be guilty of being the person driving the train that day. I'd never once considered them. It might not even have been their first. Poor driver.

And Roger. What an awful, awful way to die. In all the time I'd been convinced he was murdered, I'd never once thought about his family. I knew he had a wife. He'd talked about her in our sessions. At the time, I'd thought he was just trying to show me how much he loved her.

I had to talk to his first-line supervisor–manager.

I took out my phone. I stared at it in my hands. One life had ended, but the violence of his passing would forever alter the lives of so many still living, including mine.

I inhaled slowly. Deeply. As I exhaled, scenes from our sessions flashed by. I needed two more cycles. I remained still and silent, out of respect. I had never liked the man nor trusted him. But he was a person I knew – and knew somewhat intimately. And now he was gone. And maybe I could have stopped it.

The feelings hit all at once: regret, fear, sinking helplessness, and a painful awareness of my own prejudice, delivered like a gut punch. I had failed him. I had failed my client. I failed Roger.

I wrote a message: *I was informed of Roger's death. Please accept my condolences. I would like to attend the funeral to pay my respects. Please advise.*

I had to go to the funeral. I felt I owed it to him. He hadn't been pushed – I had made it all up in my head.

I didn't know what to do.

I began to walk on autopilot. I crossed the Hungerford Bridge to the South Bank. I turned left and continued walking. I couldn't stop myself from mentally revisiting my sessions with Roger. I knew that I was panicking. Possibly catastrophising. Even though I did not know for sure that I'd missed something, my brain was behaving as if I had. My client had killed himself, and my body was experiencing it as an existential threat: I would lose my job. I would lose my practice. I would lose everything.

I came up to the Book Market under Waterloo Bridge, between the National Theatre and Queen Elizabeth Hall, and realised where I was. I had subconsciously come to the South Bank because it was close and because it was one of my favourite places in London, and I particularly liked the Book Market. I'd bought a 1963 reprint of Ian Fleming's *Moonraker* there. I stopped by the rows of tables with old books packed spine-up and briefly scanned the titles before continuing on. But just as I did so, something caught my attention. I turned right back to the books, searching the rows until I found it again. A green, faded, cloth-covered hardback. Printed on the spine, in gold letters: 'Francis Conford – Mountains and Molehills.'

It smacked me in the face. I had made one big mountain of conspiracy out of nothing.

It wasn't just another episode. I had unconsciously strung together a bunch of unrelated events to fit into a narrative that absolved me of guilt. If I applied Occam's razor, my home was burgled because the lock on the front door to the building was broken – maybe even by the very thieves who'd ransacked the flat. They could have been looking for drugs. Maybe that's why they'd gone through the medicine cabinet. My bag had been snatched because I'd been preoccupied with my thoughts and hadn't noticed the opportunistic scooter gang, who would have overlooked me if they'd known I would see them coming. Roger had not been pushed onto the tracks. Could he have asked me to meet him at the station because he had wanted to kill himself, and he wanted me to know that it was my fault?

Don't make this about yourself, Bobby.

He called me because he needed help and he believed I could help him. That I would help him. My spirit groaned. I became aware that I was still actively avoiding that inconvenient truth.

This was unlike any episode I'd had before. I'd made this one up to protect myself. Not only had I acted on it, but it had gone on for too long, and I'd failed to stop myself until a police officer had started asking questions about my practice. I was the one who needed help.

I fetched the therapist's card from my phone case and dialled the number. But after two rings, I ended the call.

What was I thinking? What if they referred me to a psychiatrist? What if I were diagnosed with something? Would I still be able to coach? Would I have to inform the Met? Would I be culpable for Roger's death?

I crumpled up the card. My fist tightened around it as I walked away without consciously choosing a direction or a destination. Perhaps I was walking away from myself – my guilt, my life – before it was prised from my hands.

37

Francis and Alex met on the Blue Bridge over the lake in St James's Park. They leant over the railing, watched the water, and spoke without looking at each other. The conversation was brief and measured. When it ended, Alex walked back towards Whitehall, Francis towards the Mall, and within seconds it was as though the meeting had never taken place.

Sunlight slanted through the shop window, catching the fish laid out on ice and turning them briefly silver. A tiny crab inched across the display, trying to escape.

'Hello, Sunny Daily Fish. How can I help you?'

The fishmonger wedged the handset between his ear and shoulder and continued filleting the halibut on the counter as his watchful customer waited.

'Hello,' the caller said. 'I'm calling about the order of sardines you're delivering at ten p.m. tonight.'

'What about it, mate?'

'We'll be picking it up instead.'

'Okay by me.'

'Our driver is on his way to you now. Is that okay?'

'Yeah, it's all here.' The fishmonger checked the time. Six p.m. 'I'll add some ice.'

The headlamps of Alex's white van swept over the SUVs and supercars parked on the country road leading up to the mansion and on both sides of its circular driveway. He stopped just outside the front door and checked his watch. Ten thirty. He pressed the bell and waited, looking down at his outfit. White trainers, a pair of white skinny jeans, white storekeeper's overalls, and, under the overalls, a white jumper.

He was about to ring the bell again when he heard the lock turn. He recognised Tashique, dressed in a flowing white gown, as she opened the door. She was either exhausted or sad. He couldn't tell.

'Hi. I've come to deliver the fish.'

The large hallway was empty behind her. The house was quiet. There was no sign of the people who had arrived in the cars.

She stared blankly at him, then her face lit up with understanding.

'I'm going to need some help,' he added.

Together, they fetched two heavy cooler boxes from the back of the van and carried them into the kitchen, where packs of paper plates and cups crammed the island and stacked boxes of wine and champagne obscured the tiled marble floor.

'I'm going to need a signature for this,' Alex said. He held out the Sunny Daily Fish invoice he had printed.

He looked around while she searched a drawer for something to write with. The pictures he had been given were up to date.

'Can I wash my hands, please?' he asked.

'Of course,' Tashique said. She handed him the signed invoice and motioned for him to follow her to the sink. She let the water run, testing the temperature with a finger, then she squeezed washing liquid into his cupped hands.

'You've got a beautiful home,' Alex said as he washed. 'My entire flat would fit in here. Are you having a party?'

They both turned at the sound of someone walking into the kitchen behind them. Alex recognised Kenny. Out of the corner of his eye, he caught Tashique rolling her eyes at the younger man.

'Can we talk?' Kenny said. He stood on the other side of the island from them.

'Yes, we're having a party,' Tashique replied to Alex.

'Yeah? I thought so. All those cars outside – where is everybody? Why do you need so much fish? What are you going to do with it?' He dried his hands on his coat and pretended to admire the kitchen.

'Tashique?' Kenny said.

'Eat it?' Tashique replied. A smile broke the stern look on her face.

'Are you done?' Kenny asked.

Alex turned to him. 'Me?' he asked, pointing at the middle of his chest.

'Yes. If you're done, you can leave now.' Kenny sounded as hard as his angry glare.

'Once I get those boxes,' Alex said, pointing at the fish.

'Come back for them tomorrow. We'll pay you.'

Tashique swung around. 'How dare you talk to him like that?' she shouted.

'Like what?' Kenny asked.

'Who do you think you are?'

'Tashique,' he said. He began to walk towards her.

She halted him with a hand. 'Do not say my name. I do not ever want to hear my name come out of your mouth again. Ever.'

Alex watched.

'Can we go upstairs?' Kenny asked.

'To do what? You want to ask if I'm sleeping with him, too?'

'Tashique!'

'Fuck you.' She turned to Alex. 'What's your name?'

'Bruno.'

She held out a hand. 'Hi, Bruno. I'm Tashique. Yes, we're having a party, and you're invited. I want you to stay.'

'For real? I mean, I do need to take the boxes.'

'You'll be my guest. Come, I'll take you.'

She put her arm through his and led him out the back door.

38

In the darkness, Francis stood in the door frame and watched Siobhan lie still in bed. Between her illness and the medication, there was little left of her sparkle and wit. The Irish girl who trained dragons in her novels now found herself engulfed in the fiery breath of one – the burning fatigue, the constant pain, the fever that made even breathing a chore. A gardener now tended her beloved peonies, her writing desk was collecting dust in the shed, and her sharp sense of humour, beloved by her fans, was fading into the past. He missed her. Every day, he missed her.

He gently closed the door. His hand slid along the bannister as he made his way downstairs. He stopped at the open door to his study and stood there, neither going inside nor turning back. In the end, he turned around and went in search of the liquor cabinet in the dining room – another pastime lost to the vicious disease. While he'd encouraged Siobhan to pay attention to the delicateness of fine wine, she had introduced him to strong spirits after dinner in front of a crackling fire, their child in bed and his parents free to be who they were when they first met.

He grabbed a bottle of bourbon and a glass and returned to his study, where he left the light off, shut the door behind him, and drew the curtains. He settled down at his desk and switched on his laptop, his face glowing in the light of the screen. He inserted earbuds into his ears so that he could hear what Alex heard, just as he could now see what Alex saw. Without taking his eyes off the screen, he reached for the bottle of bourbon on the desk, twisted the cap open, and then, eyes still on the screen, reached for the glass and poured himself a full drink. He glanced up to where Siobhan would be lying in dreamless sleep and raised a toast to his memories of them, before sipping his first taste of the golden liquor in months. He turned back to the screen and watched what Alex's camera captured for him.

Brown paper-bag lanterns cast a warm glow along a paved path, like a runway stretching from the back of the mansion, across the lawn, to a gigantic round marquee that blazed orange in the moonless night.

Young people in white outfits lingered around the marquee. Some queued at grill stations tended by uniformed cooks. The gentle breeze carried the smell of barbecue and the chatter of excited conversations.

Inside, yet more people sat on straw mats arranged in a loose circle beneath the towering central peak of the marquee, the canvas rising three storeys above them to a central point. Beneath, in the clear space in the middle, stood a large harp in front of an empty stool. All around, people ate, drank and talked. Some had white blankets wrapped around them to keep warm. A handful sat alone or lay on their sides on cushions. A couple sharing a blanket shared a pillow as well. One person sat in the lotus position, their eyes closed as if in meditation. Another wore their blanket draped over their bowed head. One more swayed from side to side on his knees, humming to himself.

Tashique took Alex's hand and led him to a mat bearing two cushions and a man in a white suit.

'No way,' Alex said. The man stood to greet him. 'You're RIMIX, innit?'

The superstar pulled Alex in for a hug. Sitting between them, Tashique introduced the men to each other. She leant against Alex to whisper into his ear, and with her eyes, she directed his gaze to the other superstars sitting close by.

Alex reacted with stifled shock, then they both leant into a fit of conspiratorial giggles. Tashique gave up more stars and celebrities. Alex surreptitiously turned to find them. His eyes swept over Kenny, standing at the entrance, watching them.

The lights dimmed, leaving only the space in the middle illuminated.

'It's about to start,' RIMIX whispered.

All around, people hushed.

A woman in a long dress walked barefoot to the centre of the marquee and began to sing the chorus to Leonard Cohen's 'Hallelujah'. Her voice was clear and unadorned, carrying easily through the tent. For a moment, she sang alone. Then someone near the edge joined in, then another. One by one, those inside stood, lifting their voices cautiously at first, as if testing the sound.

Alex joined in, the word 'hallelujah' rising and falling with the others, the familiar melody taking on a strange, communal power.

The tent filled as those outside came in, drawn by the singing. The song that had started with a single voice swelled into a chorus that spilled out into the night.

The person with their blanket over their head was the last to stand up. He rose slowly, as if in step with the music, then he removed the covering and let it fall to the ground. The light caught the white tunic he wore, simple and loose, the fabric glowing as he walked to the middle, his face calm, almost serene. A ripple went through the crowd, igniting a chain reaction of whistling, clapping and cheering. Phones were above heads to capture the moment.

D'Don stood barefoot before his flock. He raised his hands and turned in a circle, and as he did, the people fell quiet, as if he had spread a spirit of silence over them.

For a moment, the chirping of crickets could be heard. Intrigued cooks watched from the entrance to the marquee.

Alex focused on the man before him.

'When Jesus fed the five thousand with five loaves and two fish, do you think he did it to demonstrate his powers, or did he do it because the people needed to be fed?'

After a brief pause, the sound of clicking fingers followed.

Turning on the spot as he spoke, he said, 'Have you learnt not to question God? Have you learnt to hear them? Do you know that we have been living in the End Times since the term was first coined?'

Finger clicks accompanied each question he asked.

'Who is God?'

A solitary click died in the silence that resisted it.

D'Don held his hands out and looked at his feet. 'There is life beneath my feet. Under whose feet do I exist?'

He looked up, making eye contact with as many people as he could, and slowly turned again.

'Luke 11:11: "Which of you parents, if your child asks for a fish, will give them a snake instead?"'

He searched their faces.

'Who among you has requested assistance only to have it denied? Who has asked me for advice but not received it? Which of you has said to me, "I am behind on my rent," and I have not shown you how to own your own home? Which of you has asked me for any lawful assistance, and I have not given it without hesitation?'

His voice was calm, yet it easily carried across the marquee.

'If I, your spiritual father on earth, am ready to give you everything you ask for that is within my power, why wouldn't our heavenly parent give us all that we ask of them? Why can't we ask of them, "Heal all the sick," and it would be done? "Stop all wars," and it would be done. "No more famines," and there would be no more famines.'

He paused, letting the questions settle.

'We ask. We pray. And yet, the world remains broken.

We know why. We understand why those who have all the power cannot intervene.'

His voice dropped.

'Because WAITRN. We Are In The Rapture Now.'

A ripple passed through the crowd.

'Do not run to miracle workers or charlatans asking for your tithes and offerings. People will tell you, "Here he is!" or "There he is!" Do not go running after them. There will be signs in the sun, moon and stars. On earth, nations will be in anguish and perplexity at the roaring and tossing of the sea. Do we not see all these signs, already? We are in the rapture now, and our destinies are firmly in our own hands.'

He looked around, and the people clicked their fingers.

'Let us sit,' he said.

Everyone obeyed at once. Except for a barefooted, freckled young man with red hair, lithe in his white dashiki. He walked through the crowd, eyes fixed ahead. He sat behind the harp and pulled it back to rest on his shoulder. He lifted his hands to the strings and paused. He struck the strings. He played 'Hallelujah' on the harp.

D'Don sat on the ground nearby. He reached between his legs, plucked a blade of grass and held it up.

'A blade of grass emerges from the soil. How beautiful is it to absorb the sun's energy and transform it into nourishment? How beautiful is that? And you – look at you. My wonderful children, look at yourselves. See how beautiful you are. Turn to your neighbours and tell them, "You are beautiful!"'

The crowd did as commanded, their faces full of awe, tears and hugs flowing freely until his voice rounded up the herd once more.

'The same beauty in you and in this blade of grass is in the birds of the sky, the fish of the oceans, the jungle animals, and the crawling and flying insects.

'Insects do not see humans. The ant does not think, "That is a human being approaching; I better move away from its path lest it unknowingly stamp on me." When we spray our insecticide, the ants do not think, "It is those humans doing this to us." Just as the ant lives its life without knowing about us, so too does the amoeba remain unaware of the ant's existence. Yet we all exist side by side, sharing space.

'You only know about that over which you have dominion. Famines, pandemics, wars and pestilence – all are in the hands of that which sees us but we cannot see. When they watch you, what do they see?

'Do they see you helping your sister but not your neighbour?'

He scanned his flock. Everywhere he looked, they were looking straight at him.

'I will tell you what they want to see. They want to see their beauty in you. They want you to treat yourself and everything they created – animals, plants, humans – kindly, even those who behave badly. They want you to be like them so they can be the God who grants your requests.'

He rose to his feet and held out his hand for the crowd to remain seated.

'Luke 11:11. From now on, your spirit will draw your attention to that number whenever it appears around you.'

He looked around the marquee.

'You will see it everywhere.'

Alex glanced at his watch.

Eleven minutes past eleven.

In his study, Francis brought his wrist over the keyboard, leant forward, and turned his watch towards the light on the screen. Eleven minutes past eleven.

He sat back and watched the awed crowd turn and beam at one another, clapping and hugging, celebrating with one another their pastor's latest miracle. He shook his head at the screen. He leant forward and held down a key on the laptop.

'Go and take a look in the boy's room,' he said, before reclining back in his chair and locking his fingers behind his neck.

Tashique turned to Alex with outstretched arms. Her tear-streaked face was as beautiful as when she told him he was beautiful and he replied that she was beautiful, too. He realised he might be the only one under the marquee whose cheeks were still dry. All around them, joyful young people lingered in long, embracing hugs.

D'Don's calm, powerful voice broke their embrace. 'Whenever you see the number, remember this: God is watching you to see if the beauty they invested in you when they created the universe still lives in you.'

D'Don's eyes slowly swept over his elated and

mesmerised flock. Faces glistened with tears, smiles beamed, and laughter bubbled quietly among them. The harpist continued playing.

'Please stand,' he said.

The people stood. D'Don introduced the harpist, and Alex clapped along as the crowd applauded, all the while aware of Francis listening and watching through the hidden earphone in his ear and camera in his glasses.

He looked sideways at Tashique. She was transfixed. Still clapping, he leant towards her ear and said, 'I'll be back.'

'What?'

'I said, I'll be back.'

'Where are you going?'

'Bathroom.'

'Know where it is?'

'Inside?'

'No. Portable loos. Behind.' She gestured with her hand.

'Cool. Thanks.'

Alex shouldered his way through the crowd. Fuck. Whoever had missed the tent had also missed the portable toilets. He didn't have a good reason to go into the house to find the boy's room, as Francis had instructed.

39

Kenny watched Alex leave the tent. He checked his new Rolex. Something about the fish deliveryman had irked him, but he didn't know what.

He looked at Tashique. She was focused on D'Don, as was everyone else. All except Kenny, who couldn't stop feeling upset about the fish deliveryman.

Nobody noticed Alex walking up to the mansion because everyone was in the marquee listening intently to the pastor's stirring sermon.

Francis watched the shaky video on his screen. His ears hurt when Alex shouted 'Hello' in the empty kitchen. It was the only room downstairs where the lights had been left on.

Francis' screen grew dark as Alex ascended the staircase. Other agents had been in the mansion before. They had spent hours combing through the building. They'd looked in the safe in the pastor's office, found the one hidden in the wall behind the painting over his bed, and gone through every inch of the young woman's bedroom, but their search had not produced any old mobile phones. Alex attending the event as an invited guest was the perfect opportunity to find out more about the timid young man called Kenny. Alex already knew which were the pastor's and Tashique's bedrooms. The only other room with personal effects was the one with windows looking out onto the front of the building.

Francis' screen brightened once more when Alex switched on his torch. He watched the agent's hand probe through shopping bags of clothes, shoes and other personal effects. The drawers and the wardrobes were empty.

He leant forward and held down a key on his laptop.

'Go to his office,' he said.

As Alex exited the room, he noticed light in the stairwell. He quickly switched off his torch, then stepped backwards into the bedroom, gently shut the door behind him, and slid under the bed.

He listened as doors were opened and closed and lights flicked on and off along the hallway. The door to the room he was in opened, and the light came on. Alex recognised Kenny's shoes. The young man hesitated at the door before walking to the en suite and flicking on the light in there. After a moment, he switched it back off and returned to the room, pausing at the window. Then he left, switching off the bedroom lights and shutting the door behind him. Alex stayed under the bed and listened to Kenny's footsteps moving away. He waited a few minutes before crawling out from under the bed. The teenager must have seen him leaving the tent. He was obviously searching for him. He was smart, after all.

Kenny had also switched off the lights downstairs, including the one in the kitchen. Alex crept down the staircase and across to the front door, gently easing it open. At his van, he pulled off his shopkeeper's coat and tossed it into the back, then leant against the driver's door and lit a cigarette in full view of the doorbell camera.

When he returned to the building, the lights were still off. He gave his eyes a few seconds to readjust. The door to the pastor's office was wide open. He went inside and did a 360-degree sweep with his torch, illuminating what the camera in his glasses captured.

'What are you doing?'

Alex swung around. Kenny was in the doorway.

'I smelled gas,' Alex said. He sniffed the air. 'Can't you smell it? I think it's coming from here.' He beamed the torch at the stained oak radiator cover by the window, tucked his other hand into his pocket, and held down the pusher on his lighter.

'I don't smell anything. Why are you in here?'

'I told you, man. I smelled gas.' Alex slid the torch into his pocket as he walked up to Kenny by the door. He brought out both hands to smooth his hair. 'You really don't smell that?'

Kenny searched for the whiff he'd detected. 'You are not allowed in here,' he said.

'I told you, bro. I smelled gas. I went out to smoke, and when I came back in, I smelled gas. You guys should have it checked out.'

'Why are you wearing white?'

Alex inspected his own outfit. He tugged at his white jumper and jeans. 'These? You always wear white in the trade, bro. That way, if you get blood on you, you can just bleach it out.' He looked into Kenny's eyes. 'In my line of work, you always get blood on you.'

'I think you should leave.'

'Leave? It looks like the party's just starting.'

'Go home.'

'You're kicking me out? It's because of your lady, innit? I guess I won't be telling you what she said about you, then.'

He waited for Kenny to react. Nothing.

'Okay.' Alex shrugged and shouldered past the teenager. 'I'm done listening to your crazy guru anyway. Where are my boxes? Be a nice lad and go fetch them, will you? I'll be out by my van.'

40

I couldn't sleep. I lay in bed, staring at the ceiling, unable to silence my brain. My flat was still a mess, and my mind was in worse shape. Not only had I had a serious episode, I had even infected someone else with it. Naomi. What must she think of me? A nutcase playing coach to police officers. If she wasn't after a story before, now she had one. I groaned. Surely, this was the end of me. The end of my career, the end of my contract with the Met, the end of any hope of ever earning another penny as a bona fide coach. I was done. I would lose my practice and my home, just like I was already losing my mind. I turned onto my side, pulled a pillow to my chest, and curled into the foetal position. I buried my face in the pillow and felt the back of my eyes burn with tears. The pillow muffled my scream of deathly agony.

I was catastrophising. Of course I was. I was aware of it, but I couldn't stop myself. The episodes were getting worse. My ability to detect and stop them before acting on them was getting weaker. I was descending into madness, but one thing I knew for sure was that I wasn't going to see a shrink. Another thing I knew for sure was that I should probably see a shrink.

All of this because I had missed something in my sessions with Roger. I could have done something.

I could have referred him to someone. I could have spoken to his bosses.

I could have done something.

I lay there in anguish, alternating between thoughts of losing my mind and my practice and what I'd missed about Roger. I had to read the notes again. I knew I did. But was I really ready to find out what I'd missed?

He had asked me to meet him at the place where he planned to take his own life. Why? One possible answer was as simple as it was punishing: he wanted me to be there so I would know it was my fault. That I had failed him.

I groaned. I had to find out what it was I'd missed that could have kept him alive. I went over everything again, lingering on his unexpected call and the way he'd sounded on the phone. I had assumed he'd asked to meet at the station because he didn't want to be seen coming to me. When he hadn't shown up, my mind had concocted an entire conspiracy, and upon learning of his death, that conspiracy had only seemed more real. Naomi. The stranger in a green cardigan. The burglary. My laptop. From the way my flat had been ransacked, I'd convinced myself that unseen operatives were after my coaching notes. Though I didn't know for sure that they hadn't taken something else entirely.

Tears welled up and I began to shudder. Just as I was

about to go all in and start full-blown wailing, my phone vibrated.

It was Naomi. I let it ring out. I hadn't called her after my meeting with Russell like I'd promised. That was insensitive of me. She must be losing her mind by now. Damn you, Bobby.

I composed myself and answered when she called back a few minutes later.

'Hello.'

'Bobby, I was worried.'

It sounded as if she meant she was worried for me and not for herself.

'I'm fine,' I said.

'Bobby, are you okay?'

'Yeah. I'm sorry, I should have called you or sent a message.'

'How did it go?'

I paused. I saw Roger's face in my mind.

'He killed himself,' I said.

She fell silent. I imagined she was taking a moment out of respect, or she was letting the relief permeate. I had sufficiently frightened her in the morning, after all.

'You watched the video?' she asked.

'No. He described it to me.'

'What did he say?'

At that point, I remembered I was talking to an investigative journalist, and I had already told her too much.

'There's nothing to it,' I said. 'He wasn't pushed. He either fainted and slumped, or he just let himself fall onto the tracks.'

She went silent again. I hoped she wasn't taking notes. Or worse, recording the conversation.

'Bobby?'

I realised in that moment that I liked the way she said my name.

'Yeah?'

'Listen, I know you're probably thinking, "What the hell am I doing talking to a journalist?" But I assure you, I am not doing a story. I just need to know that you're sure the dude wasn't killed and that I'm safe. I know it sounds selfish, but look, I'm not even in my house right now. I just need to know if you're sure. Describe the video. What happened? Was anything odd or out of place?'

Fair enough. I visualised the video the way Russell had described it. But what if she'd lied when she said she wasn't doing a story?

'Naomi, I'm really sorry about earlier. I told you that I suffer from paranoia. No one pushed Roger; no one followed me; my flat was just a robbery. I made everything up in my head. I'm getting help.' I grimaced at yet another lie. It felt like a significant one, too.

'You said they didn't take anything,' she said.

'From my flat? Yeah, but that's probably because I haven't found out what they took yet.'

'What do you think they were looking for?'

'I don't know. I mean, maybe they weren't looking for anything. Or nothing specific. It was just a robbery.'

'You're lying. You take notes, don't you? You think that's why they snatched your laptop?'

It sank in just how much I'd told her.

'That's what I thought too, but I was wrong. I read the notes. There's nothing there. He didn't tell me anything he shouldn't have, as far as I know. Nothing out of the ordinary. We mostly talked about him. You know, his relationship with himself, with the situation he was in, stuff like that.'

'What if that wasn't what they were after?' she said.

That threw me. I couldn't think of anything else they might have been after. She waited for me to respond, but I had nothing, so I waited for her to continue. I was keen to know what she was thinking. My gut told me to listen to her. To trust her.

Helplessness, maybe. Ceding responsibility.

'What if they did take something?' she said. 'What if Roger hid something in your flat? What if that's what they were after?'

My brain tingled. I felt the surge. A rousing excitement radiated through my body.

No, Bobby. Not today.

I took a deep breath. 'No, Naomi. I promise you; he wasn't killed. The whole conspiracy plot I made up only makes sense if he was killed, and he wasn't.'

'But you did not watch the video yourself,' she countered.

I realised I had to describe the video to her. I owed it to her. I had done this to her.

She interrupted me when I got to the two men on either side of Roger turning at the same time.

'Why did they turn?' she asked.

'I don't know. It could have been an announcement.'

'So, why didn't he turn as well?' she asked.

'I don't know that he didn't turn,' I said. I tried to remember exactly what Russell had illustrated. I visualised the scene, searching for an answer to her question. She had a point. 'I'm sure it was then that he jumped. Or fell.'

'Yes, but why did he jump at that very moment?'

'Maybe someone called out to them?' I suggested.

'You mean, like, someone they both knew?'

'Yes. Or maybe they were waiting for someone, so they both looked back to search for them when the train arrived.'

I stopped to consider it myself. She was silent. Maybe she was considering it as well.

I had filled my lungs to continue when she spoke. She said, with a pensive voice, 'Maybe. Yes. That makes sense.'

'Yes.' I agreed with her agreeing with me. 'Yes, that explains it.' I pictured the two people anxiously searching for their friend as the train arrived. 'It makes sense.' I nodded at myself. I considered how previously I would have been obsessed with the two men turning at the same time. I would have invented a reason that fit my narrative. I would have drawn them into my conspiracy. I took a deep breath, as if breathing was a workable alternative to therapy.

'Thanks,' Naomi said.

'For what?' I asked.

'For letting me know,' she said. 'I was worried.'

'I'm really sorry,' I said. We remained on the phone.

Silent. I was thinking of the two men on the platform. God knows what she was thinking.

She was the first to speak. She asked, 'Are you going to be okay?'

There was no way she could know just how much that meant to me or how much I was not okay. 'I'm fine,' I said, lying yet again. 'I'll call you in the morning.'

'Okay. Sweet dreams.'

We hung up, and I felt a flutter. Without thinking, I'd said I'd call her, and she'd said, 'Okay', and then she'd said, 'Sweet dreams.'

I have come to realise that, just as I make up conspiracies where there are none, I read meaning into every word spoken or held back by women I like. Unlike my paranoid episodes, however, with women everything stays in my mind as a fantasy – I never give in to the impetus to act. The root of my self-sabotage. 'Sweet dreams' could mean nothing. It might just be what she said to everyone. Or it could mean something. Maybe right then, she was cringing at saying it, wondering if I'd noticed how she'd slipped and revealed something of her intentions towards me.

I was overthinking, as usual. But then again, we had matched on a dating app. Naomi had seen my profile and seen that I'd liked hers, and she'd liked me back. I smiled, but it didn't last long. I had still lost a client. Did negligence apply to coaching? If I missed something during our sessions, could I be found negligent for that – for not preventing harm?

I didn't have too long to dwell on that because my brain

jumped straight back to her. I recalled our conversation. That last bit of it when she'd said, 'Sweet dreams.'

It was no use. I was wide awake. I inserted my charger back into my phone, but I couldn't go to sleep. I got out of bed and stood in the darkness. What was I thinking of doing? I could start tidying up. I could try to figure out what the burglars took, if anything. My mind kept bouncing from thought to thought, subject to subject, and worry to worry.

Bobby, what made you get out of bed?

I placed my fists on my hips, my mind abuzz, and I said out loud, 'Why did they turn at the same time?'

My body flooded with adrenaline, and this time I didn't try to fight it. What if Roger did hide something in my consultation room? It wasn't my paranoia; it was an investigative journalist's hunch, and it had merit. I hadn't thought of it myself, but it tied everything together. This wasn't an episode.

I went to my consultation room and took everything in from the door. What could Roger have hidden in there? It would have had to be something small. Like a memory stick. A SIM card, maybe. Or a note on a piece of paper. What could it be? And where could he have hidden it? He could have slipped something somewhere any of the times I'd left him alone to use the bathroom or answer the doorbell, hoping it would be safe in my home.

I knew that I was once again giving in to the seduction of something being afoot, but what if Roger had indeed been killed? What if, like Naomi suggested, he'd really hidden something in my consultation room? What if he didn't want to come to mine because he knew he was being watched – by the people who wanted what he hid – and he didn't want to lead them to it?

I began a detailed search, going through the pages of every book, searching behind every drawer, under my printer, beneath the faux leather mat on my desk, and through the contents of drawers left scattered on the ground by the intruders.

Middle of the night or not, paranoia or not – if there was the slightest chance that Roger had planted something there, I wasn't going to rest until I'd ruled that possibility out.

41

The caterers were the last to leave. D'Don and Tashique thanked them at the door, handing out fifty pound notes as tips, while Kenny lingered behind in the entrance hall.

D'Don set the alarm, and Tashique bade him goodnight with a hug. Then she turned around, rolled her eyes at Kenny, and brushed past him as she went upstairs.

'What did you do to upset her?' D'Don asked with a smirk on his face.

They both gazed up the staircase after Tashique.

'I asked her where she went with the politician,' Kenny said.

D'Don sucked air through his teeth and shook his head. 'Oh dear. And what did she say?'

'She said it was none of my business.'

'I told you she was networking.' He put his arm around Kenny's shoulder. 'Come with me.'

In his office, he opened a drinks cabinet and poured two glasses from a brandy decanter.

'The thing with women is that they want exactly the same thing that men want: to be respected. You disrespected her by questioning her. You shouldn't have done that. Especially when I had already told you what she was doing.'

They sat on opposite sides of the desk. Kenny put his untouched glass down and listened.

'Give her time. She'll learn to trust you, and you'll learn to trust her, but you must show her that you respect her at all times. Do you understand?'

Kenny nodded.

'You just have to play your cards right. Hey, what did you think about the Gathering?' D'Don held his glass up.

'It was nice,' Kenny said. He raised his glass to the pastor's before setting it back down.

'"Nice"? That's all you've got?' D'Don chuckled. 'It was transcendental. Do you know what that means?'

Kenny wasn't sure. He was beginning to feel the panic that creeps upon his spirit whenever he remembered his new good fortune and how precariously it rested on a miracle that hadn't happened. D'Don was a powerful man. Kenny was a liar. He hid himself in silence.

'It's just the beginning,' D'Don continued. 'The plan is to make it a monthly thing. It's going to become a movement. People will talk about it. It's going to change lives.'

He took a sip and studied Kenny over the top of his glass.

'You're afraid to drink?'

Kenny looked at the glass and shook his head.

'No? Have you had a drink before?'

Kenny nodded.

'Then why aren't you drinking? Cheer up, man. It's

not the end of the world. Hey, have you ever been drunk before?'

Kenny's head snapped up, a look of alarm on his face. He shook his head, suspicious of the question.

'Oh, have I got a great story for you,' D'Don said.

He threw his head back to laugh and shook his head at the memory of his own story. Then he emptied his glass, poured another shot, and began.

'It was a long time ago, in Ghana. My mother is Ghanaian. We were in the family house in Aburi. In the hills. I was sixteen, I think. One night, my older cousins took me to a party in Osu. That's in Accra. Bro, one thing you should know is that Ghanaian women are beautiful. My God. And I'm not just saying so because I'm half Ghanaian – they are the most beautiful women in the world. Their glowing black skin, the way they walk, their intelligence, their big bum-bums, and their accent. Try to imagine a sixteen-year-old boy from Nigeria at a night party in Ghana full of young, beautiful Ghanaian women drinking, smoking, talking about revolution, and dancing. It was a lot.

'As soon as we arrived, I saw a girl chatting with a group of people, and my heart just started going jigi-jigi-jigi-jigi. To this day, she is the most beautiful woman I have ever seen in my entire life. She looked like a doll. Like what people Photoshop their pictures to look like. She was phenomenally beautiful. Breathtakingly beautiful. Wow. I couldn't stop looking at her. When someone blocked my view, I would use style to move so I could still see her. When she went somewhere, I would follow her with my eyes and strategically place myself where I could continue to watch her. I was mesmerised. I just kept following her and hoping she did not notice me watching her. I should have walked up and said hello. I knew I would regret not talking to her when we left, but, bro, my liver failed me that day. I was paralysed. The mere thought of talking to her made my palpitations worse.

'I didn't know anybody else at the party other than my cousins, and, you know how boys are, they had abandoned me soon after we arrived. Then, somebody tapped my shoulder from behind. It was Kojo, my eldest cousin. He asked me if I liked her. He said he had noticed me looking at her. Man, the fear that cut through my heart. I was like, "Did other people notice?" He just started laughing. He said he knew her and that he could introduce us. Kenny, right there, I knew I couldn't talk to her. I had to confess to him that, with the way I was feeling, I didn't think I could stand straight in front of her and have actual words come out of my mouth. He just laughed at me, and just like that, he shouted her name and waved her over. My heart was going dum, dum, dum.

'He introduced us and said he was going to the bathroom. Bro, my heart was beating so fast, I couldn't talk. It was so awkward. After like ten seconds of saying nothing, I told her I also had to go to the bathroom. I locked myself in the toilet, and I just started crying. I'd just walked away from her. I don't even think she heard me excuse myself. I hid in the restroom until someone knocked, and I didn't even open the door. But it was Kojo, and he began shouting my name. I opened the door, and he took me outside to talk, and I told him how I'd messed up. He laughed, eh? He said I should just drink enough alcohol to calm myself down until I was no longer afraid to talk to her.

'I don't know how he convinced me, but he found me a full bottle of Remy Martin V.S.O.P. That's what we're drinking now. I drained the entire bottle, but oh boy, my heart was still not cooperating. I was still too nervous, so Kojo got me another bottle. I do not remember getting into my aunt's car to return to the house. They woke me up when we arrived. I was so drunk that I had no idea where I was. My cousins made me go in first. My mum, my aunties, my siblings, and all the younger cousins were all in the sitting room watching TV. Kenny, I walked in, and I started going around shaking hands with each person and introducing myself. I shook hands with my mother and said, "Good evening. My name is Dolapo." Can you imagine that? I was so drunk – I introduced myself to my own mother!'

Kenny was smiling. He waited until the pastor recovered from his laughter, then he asked, 'What happened?'

'I slept it off. I had the most fantastic hangover the next day.'

'I meant with the girl,' Kenny said.

'Ah, I know. Nana. That was her name. She had the most beautiful voice in the world.' D'Don paused as he reminisced. 'Anyway. So, I had the mother of all hangovers. When I finally came out for breakfast, everybody started cheering and clapping.' He stopped to laugh. 'My mother gave me painkillers, and then, after scolding me for getting drunk, she asked me, "Who is this girl that made my fine bobo feel this way?"'

'Kojo had told everyone what had happened. When we were alone in her room, I told my mother everything: how I was stunned the moment I saw Nana, how I just walked away from her and went to hide in the toilet, how my heart was beating so fast that I couldn't string together a coherent set of words. While I was telling her, I started to remember that I had actually talked to Nana again and that I'd just been talking rubbish. I couldn't even remember what I'd been saying, but I knew I'd made no sense at all. She'd just looked at me, listening, and smiling as if to say, "Look at this one that can't even talk to a woman." Kojo later told me that I'd been telling her how I could run very fast, how I liked Waakye, how I'd had four different dogs, and how I could do this and do that. He said I was just running my mouth at a hundred kilometres per hour.

'I poured out my heart, and God bless my mum, she just listened. When I was done, the first thing she said was, "She will understand." She said it was normal. She said that I had experienced love at first sight. It took my mother, another woman, saying those words to me for me to stop beating myself up for the way I had behaved. Till then, I was afraid to ever see Nana again. I was convinced that if I did, I still wouldn't be able to talk like a normal human being, and she would think I was mad. But I was lovestruck, and my mother said she would understand.'

He leant forward over his desk.

'You're falling in love with her. You were jealous. She will understand.'

42

Kenny tossed and turned, but in whichever position he tried to lay his worries to rest, he kept thinking of Tashique, and his heart kept skipping at what D'Don had said. He was happy, excited, and anxious all at the same time. He hadn't put it into words himself, but the pastor was right; he was in love with her. And just like D'Don's heart had been unable to stop beating fast for Nana, his own heart was also refusing to calm down. He could hear her voice. He could see her eyes. He could see her naked. He had to make things right between them.

Kenny settled on his back and opened his eyes to the darkness. He checked the time. It was almost three a.m. He flipped the duvet off his body and sat on the edge of the bed, his face in his palms. His clothes were on the chair by his side. He got up and pulled on his shirt and trousers. In the end, it was the need to be in close proximity to her that got him.

Via the dark hallway, he made his way to Tashique's room. He was about to knock when he looked back down the hall again. D'Don might hear. The older man had advised him to give Tashique space until she was ready. Kenny bit his lip, but then tapped softly on the door, and waited. Nothing. He tried the handle, and the door opened.

He gently tiptoed inside, then closed the door behind him and stood with his back to it. He took one step towards her bed and stopped at the sound of the sheets ruffling.

'D'Don, is that you?' Tashique whispered in the dark.

Kenny stood frozen in place.

She switched on the bedside lamp.

'Oh, it's you,' she said, sinking her head back into her pillow and rolling away from him, her back to the door.

'Why did you think it was him?' Kenny asked.

'Oh, no. Not this again!'

She kicked away her duvet, sat against the headboard, and crossed her arms over her chest. 'Are you going to accuse me of sleeping with him as well?'

'No. Not at all. I'm sorry.'

'For what? Tell me. What are you sorry for? What, Kenny? You saw me on the phone, and you asked me, "Is that the man you went to sleep with?"'

He looked at the floor. 'I'm sorry. I know nothing happened.'

She shook her head. 'The way you say it: "I know nothing happened." Like, what could have happened? What did you expect would happen?'

'Nothing, I swear. I knew nothing was going to happen. I mean—'

'Do you even hear yourself?' Tashique snorted in

disgust. 'Do you even realise how problematic that sounds? Okay. Let me humour you. If you knew nothing was going to happen,' she said, forming air quotes with her fingers, 'then why did you say what you said? And that delivery guy, too. Did you also know nothing would've happened with him?'

'Tashique, I—' He hung his head.

'What?'

'I was jealous,' he muttered at the floor. 'I am sorry. I said it to hurt you.'

'You wanted to hurt me. Congratulations. You succeeded. Now tell me, why? Why did you want to hurt me?'

He couldn't look at her. 'Because I love you.'

'Because you love me?' Tashique's voice was incredulous. 'Really? That's your excuse?'

'I really love you.'

'You do?'

'Yeah.'

'And so, because you think you love me, you think it's okay for you to accuse me of going off and sleeping with someone I just met at an event?'

'You don't understand, Tashique. I'm in love with you. And I don't just think that I am – I know I am. I feel it. I know it's real.'

'Yeah? Okay. You know how you're feeling now, yeah? The way you say you love me, yeah? If someone else loved me like that and I loved them too, would you be okay with that?'

'I don't understand.' Kenny shifted uncomfortably.

'Yeah, I didn't think so. You'll get there.'

He looked up at her. 'Tashique, when a man loves a woman, he does stupid things.'

'Like what? List the stupid things you have done so far.'

'Tashique, I'm really sorry.'

'What for? Tell me.'

'For everything.'

'Be specific.'

'For saying what I said.'

She folded her arms more tightly. 'For calling me a slapper. That's one. What else?'

'I didn't call you a slapper.'

'You didn't? So, what do you call someone who sleeps with random men they just met?'

'I'm sorry. Like I said, I only said it to hurt you because I'm in love with you.'

'Are you even listening to yourself? Tell me, what makes you think it is acceptable behaviour to hurt the people you love?'

They stared at each other. Then tears erupted from her eyes, and she buried her face in her palms.

Kenny crossed the room cautiously and climbed onto the bed. He held her, drawing her into his embrace and letting her cry into his chest. He rocked her and looked around the room. He had no idea what he was looking for. She pushed herself away from his arms and rested against the headboard. Her face was wet with tears.

'And if you must know,' she said, 'Didi saw me crying, so I thought he'd come to check on me.'

'Didi?'

'D'Don.'

'Oh.'

Tashique sniffled and blinked her tears away.

'You hurt me, Kenny.'

'I'm sorry.'

'What really hurts is that I know you're better than this. The way you behaved today was really bad. It was ugly. And not just what you said to me. The way you treated that guy, the delivery guy, was uncalled for, Kenny. So uncalled for. You were not just rude; you were arrogant. I didn't like seeing you that way.'

Kenny stiffened. 'That was different. I wasn't being rude on purpose. I just wanted him to leave. I felt something about him. I can't explain it, but there was something about him. I saw it.'

'You saw it?'

'Yes.'

'Like a vision?'

'No. It was the way he looked at me.'

'The way he looked at you.' Tashique sounded sceptical.

'Yes.'

'Explain it.'

'I can't.'

'Are you making this up?'

'No, no. I've seen the look before.'

He tried to pull her back into his embrace, but she pushed him away, watched and waited.

'Kenny, you have to explain it to me. If you want me to believe you, if you want me to forgive you.'

'Okay. Okay. It's, er . . . It happened a long time ago. Remember when I told you I had many foster parents?

Okay, so I had just been moved to another foster family. I was young. I was ten. On that same night, the husband and wife got into a loud quarrel in their room. They had other children with them. Foster children. There were five of us. The woman was screaming and yelling. We all heard them. They were knocking things around. We thought they were having a fight. We were frightened. It went on and on, and then the husband came out with a suitcase and a guitar. He went around picking up his things, and she followed him around, screaming at him. He just smoked and ignored her. He tossed his keys onto the sofa just before he left the house, and then he looked at me. He just looked at me. It was so weird. She was screaming at him, the other kids were crying, and he just looked at me. Like he was sorry for me, you know. Like his eyes were saying, you don't know what you're in for.

'The next day, she just kept screaming and yelling and throwing things. She said terrible things to us. She said she would kill all of us if we said anything to anyone. Before bed, she held Dora's head in the bathwater. We thought she was going to die.

'When I fell asleep, I dreamed about how her husband was looking at me and smoking his cigarette. I woke up and smelled smoke. Thick smoke. I woke up the other kids. I went to her room. She wasn't there. The neighbours called nine-nine-nine. They found her body in the kitchen.'

Kenny paused. 'It was the way her husband looked at me before he left – like he knew something terrible was about to happen, and he was trying to warn me. The delivery guy had the same look.'

He and Tashique stared at each other in silence. Kenny was the first to look away. He looked down at the duvet, but he could still feel her eyes on him.

43

Francis was returning from his morning swim in the pool at Buckingham Palace. The cool, crisp autumn air filled his exercised lungs with a freshness that was both sweet and exhilarating. Walking past Lancaster House, he realised that for the first time in a long time, he had done his laps with nothing but the most mundane thoughts flitting through his mind: a mental note to send flowers to a former colleague's widow; a banquet invitation to respond to; and an upcoming dental appointment to reschedule. And now, as he noticed the changing colours of autumn, the serenity of his morning walk to work, and the sombre beauty of the gentle sun in the grey sky, he became aware of the agility of his limbs, the clarity of his thinking, and the calmness of his mind. Until that moment, he had not realised just how heavily the uncertainty of the mission he had dutifully taken on alone had weighed on his soul. Now there was a clear path to resolving the issue once and for all. He wished he had been at the lunatic house to experience the Gathering himself. He imagined how he could have engineered an invitation had he had more time to plot, and he smiled at the fantasy.

His phone vibrated. He turned his face to the rising sun as he stopped to fish the device from his pocket. It was a message: 'Meet in ten.'

He frowned at the screen. He dropped his hand to his side and looked around. He turned and headed to the park.

John was waiting on the bench, tossing grain onto the grass. Francis set his duffel bag down and stood over his friend. Apprehension had built up in him with each step he had taken towards the unsolicited and unexpected meeting. As far as he could tell, John was alone, and he didn't know what to make of that.

'Go on, sit down,' John said. He continued tossing his grain and searching for birds.

A moment of hesitation passed, and then Francis sat, his bag between them. He waited for John to reveal the purpose of the meeting.

John watched a blackbird land just beyond the perimeter of the grain he'd spread into the grass. 'I understand you had a visitor,' he said.

'This is about Rufus?' Francis said.

'Any idea how he got wind of your little project?'

'He followed me into a shop.'

'I see.'

'Did he report it up the chain?'

'No. Not yet. And please, don't ask.'

Francis narrowed his eyes. 'Don't ask what?'

'You want to know how I know about him. You know better than to ask.'

'What's this about, John?'

'I gather you and he have history?'

'Rufus? Yes. I was asked for my opinion on him, and I gave it.'

John nodded. 'And he hasn't forgiven you for your honesty.'

'I guess not.'

'Are you worried?'

'No. Are you?'

'He's just an annoying brown-noser,' John said, 'but, with what's at stake, I think precautions are necessary.'

It was Francis' turn to nod. 'I'll move the team.'

'No, that won't be enough, I'm afraid. It's over. You've got to shut it down. All of it.'

Francis twisted to face him. 'John.'

'I know, I know. But if this gets out, it's not just you who'll be burnt. All your agents will be out as well.'

'John, you know what's at stake.'

'I do. And I regret that this has happened, but you must understand. A cover-up will only make it worse.'

'I could bring him in,' Francis said.

'Who, Rufus? Oh, dear God, no. I'm having him sent to Niger. An opportunity has opened up in what remains of the mission there.'

'Then why are you shutting me down now?'

'There's no gentle way to say this, but Rufus found you, and he's a buffoon. The entire thing is compromised. Shut it down. Maybe that pervert should face his judgement. Maybe it's the right thing.'

Francis buried his face in his palms. He felt John's hand on his back, and he looked up.

'Give me a little more time,' Francis said. 'I'm close.'

'You know, Francis, something has always bugged me about this. Did you ever wonder if the pastor specifically selected you because of who you are?'

They stared at each other the way they always did when they were both trying to read the other's thoughts and intentions. John shook his head.

John threw the remaining grains in his hand at the feeding birds, who scattered at the sudden movement and flew to safety. He stood up, dusted his palms off on his coat, and patted Francis' resigned shoulders.

'Two days,' he said.

Francis watched him walk away.

44

The cleaner had left just in time for my first client, a police officer I'd worked with previously. The Met wasn't paying for her sessions this time, and I knew how much she earned, so when she'd called and asked how much I'd charge her as a private client, I'd offered to take her on pro bono. It would be the first time I'd seen her in over a year, and I was very much looking forward to seeing how she'd progressed since then.

Normally, I'd have gone through the coaching notes from our previous sessions, but after staying up till well past three a.m. doing a detailed search of my consultation room, I'd spent the morning, after the alarm had woken me up, going over my notes from Roger's sessions one more time. As I'd expected, no red flags had jumped out at me. I had sent an email to his superior expressing my condolences and requesting information about the funeral. They hadn't responded, so I decided to compose a text message specifically indicating my desire to pay my respects in person. Maybe I could get some answers that way.

As I went to write the text, I saw unread message notifications from Naomi, and my heart fluttered as a smile caressed my face. I considered saving them for later, after my session, but I knew they would be on my mind throughout and that would be a disservice to my client. I sent the message and opened our thread. The notifications were gone. The conversation was empty. Panic. When had she deleted them? Why? I should have read them immediately. It felt like a punch to the gut. Maybe she thought I was ignoring her. I felt a profound sense of loss, not only because I would never get to know the content of the messages but also because I was certain that I'd lost something between us. I groaned. I didn't know what to do.

The bell rang. My client was on time, as always. I buzzed her up and continued to wonder what to make of Naomi's deleted messages. They totalled eight lines. That was a lot of messages. What could they have been? I could send an apology, but what exactly would I say? If she replied, by the time she did, I might already be in the middle of my session, and then I would appear to be ignoring her messages again. Was that really why she'd deleted them? Time constraints prevented me from overanalysing the situation. I hurriedly composed a message, hit Send, and grimaced. I'd just realised that 'Meet for lunch?' could come across as the most chauvinistic thing possible after I'd failed to read her messages and she'd deleted them. I wouldn't blame her if she already thought of me as some sort of tragic case, and now, after sending that text, she was probably glad I hadn't talked to her on the dating app.

Well done, Bobby. You just took your self-sabotaging ways to a new level.

A gentle knock on the door interrupted my self-flagellation.

When I let my client in, the first thing I noticed was her baby bump, but I hesitated to congratulate her until I saw her cradling it and I knew I wouldn't be committing a faux pas. She was six months pregnant and expecting a girl. I learnt this from our warm-up chit-chat before we contracted for the session, as well as hearing about her promotion and her new job heading a small station in an 'idyllic village', and then I asked her what she wanted to talk about.

'It's a case I'm working on,' she said. 'I'm a bit stuck. You might have seen it on the news – "Murder in the Countryside", they're calling it. A farmer, her husband, and their teenage twin daughters were gunned down in their beds with a shotgun the family owned. The paddock gates were left open and the family Labrador was missing.'

Sometimes I struggle to maintain interest in what my clients are talking about, but this made me sit up. She was effectively asking me to coach her through solving multiple murders. This was not exactly new territory, but that's a story for another time.

'There's just something wrong with the picture, but I can't seem to figure out what it is,' she said.

I listened with undivided attention. I asked open questions. I held the silence and let her fill it. When she became quiet, I watched her agonised face as she searched for the thing that eluded her, and I waited.

I got the idea to do a constellation. She was already familiar with the exercise from our previous engagement, so I got out my Lego box and invited her to use any space on the desk. Without having to stop to think, she began to recreate her murder scene with the Lego pieces, just like Russell had used salt and pepper shakers and cutlery to depict the circumstances of Roger's death on the train station platform. She placed Lego people flat on the table. The victims. After taking a moment to inspect her handiwork, she began to talk me through the scene, but I was no longer listening. I'd had an idea of my own. I did my best to hide it, and the session ended with homework for her and a date for the next session, but the instant I shut the door, I rushed back to my desk, swept her murder scene away, and began to recreate the scene on the platform myself.

I laid down Lego tracks and placed pieces to represent Roger and the two men on either side of him. I didn't bother with the train. I turned the two men outwards like Russell had shown me with the shakers, and I asked them, 'What made you turn?'

45

'Pay up, lads.'

Libby held out her palms to her colleagues. On her screen, the video clip she'd just received was still playing. Dempsey and Rod reluctantly handed over ten-pound notes. She playfully held the polymer notes up to inspect them.

'I told you he had people there,' she said. 'I should have gone for twenty.'

Rod was still peering at her monitor. 'Wait, pause it. Go back. Stop.'

'What are we looking at?' Dempsey asked.

Rod pointed. Libby's face lit up with recognition and she whistled in admiration.

'That's RIMIX with my girl,' she said.

'Who's he?' Dempsey asked.

'Just the biggest homegrown superstar,' Libby said. 'You've heard his stuff.'

Dempsey shook his head.

'I assure you,' Libby said, 'you have. He's done an Afrobeats remix of every hit for the past two years.'

'He's a star for remixing other people's hits?'

'No,' Rod said. 'He makes them into hits when he remixes them.' He pointed at the screen. 'Look. That's Viper. And that's Lady G. And that's Afua. Holy shit, that's Uncle L.' He kept pointing people out. 'She won a Grammy. She's big in Ghana. And that's Decent. Amapiano. And those are the Protesters. Damn. It's like a gathering of all the cool artists.'

'African artists,' Dempsey said.

'Not just,' Rod replied. 'May I?'

Libby let him have her keyboard. He scrolled back through the frames beneath the paused video. 'That dude on the harp – that's Mike Timbers. He's American. He's like the greatest harpist of this generation. And . . .' He scrolled back further. 'Tell me you recognise her.'

Dempsey moved closer and squinted at the woman singing in the middle of the Gathering. He shook his head.

'Old School,' Libby said.

'Old School? She looks younger than Rod,' Dempsey said. The other two laughed and he stood up straighter. 'Okay,' he said. 'So he had someone at the party. You called it.' He checked his watch. 'He'll be here in a bit. We better find something for him before he arrives.'

'I might already have something,' Rod said.

His colleagues turned to him. He waved them over to his screen.

'I've been looking at the church accounts. The closing balance as of today is north of eight hundred thousand.'

'Easy, with all those stars,' Libby said.

'That's the takings from last Sunday alone,' Rod said.

'What?' Dempsey exclaimed.

'I think I just found Jesus,' Libby said.

Rod continued. 'We always assumed he was bilking the church, like every other evangelical out there, but get this: he hasn't been benefiting financially from it. You know how churches are registered as charities? Even the Church of England is a registered charity – that way, they're exempt from paying taxes and can claim them back on donations. Well, this church is not registered as a charity: it's a co-op. They pay corporation taxes. And get this: every member who pays tithes has that amount registered in their name. The pot is invested in stocks, and each person makes a little profit. They are basically investing a tenth of their monthly income, and it looks to be doing well.'

'So, money laundering?' Dempsey asked.

'Nope. It looks clean,' Rod said.

'Okay. That is interesting. But is it interesting enough for Francis?'

'Aha. So, we spent so much time looking at the church, not knowing what we were looking for, but with the enhanced access, I dug a bit deeper into the pastor himself. Get this. The same week he registered the church, he quit his job at a law firm.'

'So?' Dempsey asked.

'So, he took his equity payout before he quit.'

'Yeah?'

'Guess how much.'

Dempsey shrugged.

'Six fucking million.'

'What?!' Libby exclaimed.

'No shit!' Dempsey said.

'Fuck me!' Libby added.

'Six million, five hundred and forty-seven thousand, five hundred and sixty-six,' Rod said. 'That was his share. He'd had a particularly good year.'

'Fuck me!' Libby said again.

'It gets better. The church building, the studios, the blocks of flats, and the youth centre he's building were all paid for from his own pocket.'

Libby clasped her hands over her head and whistled.

'He's practically given his money away for free,' Dempsey said. 'What a fucking lunatic! This just keeps getting stranger.'

'Yup,' Rod said. He stood up from his computer and leant against the desk. 'What the fuck is this?' he asked. 'I mean, do you think Francis already knew? He probably did. You've been digging around on this guy for, what, months? Before I joined? And we've come up with nothing. What exactly are we looking for? It looks to me like a fucking waste of time. Why are we scrutinising this poor guy's life? Okay, not poor, but heck, all we've discovered is that he helps his community, he pays his fucking taxes, and he's spending his legit millions on the church. What are we looking for? What are we doing here? I don't know about you guys, but unless this is some sort of training exercise, I'm not comfortable with it.'

Dempsey looked at him. 'Your job is not to be comfortable. Your job is to do your job.'

'You guys might be okay with this,' Rod said, 'but I'm

not. We're fucking breaking laws here. This is on fucking home soil, people.'

Libby shook her head at him and turned to her own computer. Dempsey returned to his as well.

'Guys,' Rod said, looking at their turned backs. 'Guys.'

But they continued to ignore him.

46

I was in the lobby waiting for my cab. I looked out the glass door with suspicion. I registered every face I saw. I was going to be taking a lot of cabs for a while.

The messages Naomi deleted had been on my mind since she deleted them. After my client left, I'd been constantly checking my phone and, almost as often, opening up our deleted exchange to stare at the ghost of what she might have sent.

I felt I should respond in some way. I didn't want to ask her about it because, as per one of the tangents of the overthinking I'd done, I was afraid that to ask was to question her agency. She wanted to delete what she sent and so she did. She didn't have to explain herself.

But I couldn't just pretend it didn't happen. I mean, she knew that I knew she sent the messages and then deleted them.

I had no idea what she could have sent. I'd said I'd call her in the morning; it was still morning, and I still didn't know what to say when I called. If I called. I'd not been thinking when I said it the night before. What exactly would I say? Ask if she slept well, like in some Nollywood movie? Or if she'd eaten? Another Nigerian love language. I shook my head, trying to stop the overthinking.

I checked the app to see how close my driver was. The cab was still stuck in the same spot, and the app still claimed they were five minutes away. Since I was still holding my phone, I messaged Naomi something designed to sidestep the awkwardness of her deleted messages. I texted, 'After all that's happened, may I buy you coffee, lunch, dinner?' I hit send. Immediately, a knot twisted in my belly.

Ten minutes later, she hadn't replied, my cab hadn't arrived, and I wanted to delete my message.

I'd researched a replacement laptop and called the Apple Store on Regent Street to see if they had the one that I wanted. Then I'd booked the cab. An hour later, I was finally sitting at a white oak table upstairs in the store, waiting for my new computer, rueful that I'd sent that unanswered text to Naomi – when a message from her arrived.

My heart skipped a beat.

I was filled with trepidation as I opened it, but it was just one word: 'Date?'

I exhaled, relieved. I had expected her to read the message and not reply, and that would be the last time we communicated. Why had I expected the worst? I'd not thought it through when I'd asked to meet. I wanted to see her again, to hear her voice again, but . . .

I read it again: Date? A familiar warmth spread through me, and I found myself smiling at the screen.

Wait, Bobby. What if she's asking if it's a date? Was she? Yes. Yes, of course. My heart soared, and for the first time in hours, I felt light.

I replied, 'Of course. Six?' I then held my breath, staring at the screen, waiting for her to reply. Was this really happening? She replied. I beamed at the screen. I looked around. I wanted to share the moment with someone.

A few exchanges later, and Naomi and I had made plans to meet at Demon, Wise & Partners, a basement cocktail bar on Throgmorton Road in Bank that I'd suggested. I would have cancelled all my plans for the day if I could, but I had clients to see and places to go before I was free. My next client was not until three.

The lady helping me with my purchase was sorry I'd been mugged and surprised I hadn't used the Find My tool. In the craziness of the past day, I'd forgotten about the feature. I remembered setting it up for the laptop two years ago when I'd bought it. She waited while I opened up the app, but the laptop showed up as 'No location found'.

'You have the option to mark it as lost or remotely erase it,' she informed me.

'How?'

She had me click on the icon for the laptop, explaining that I might want to mark it as lost if I thought there was a chance of finding it, but as I was buying a new one, she thought I might want to erase it.

'Can I tell if it's been accessed?' I asked, though it was wishful thinking.

In the end I chose the option to 'Erase this device'. The button was unresponsive when I clicked on it, and also when I tried again. The Apple employee asked if she could try, and I handed her the phone. A few taps later, it finally worked.

'That's odd,' she said as she returned my phone to me.

'Has that ever happened before?' I asked.

'It's probably just a network thing,' she replied.

As she helped with setting up the new computer from my last cloud backup, I wondered who could have the resources to interfere with remotely erasing my stolen computer.

I'd brought an old backpack with me for the new laptop and kept it securely fastened to my back when I left. I was alert from the time I stepped out of the store, through my brisk walk to Charing Cross Station and when I got onto the Bakerloo line for a five-stop journey to Marylebone. I paid attention to everyone. I stared. If I made people uncomfortable, I didn't care. I found myself imagining that the delay with the erase button had set off some alarm somewhere. I was being paranoid, and I was aware of it. But it's better to be careful and wrong than careless and sorry.

As I got off at Marylebone, my eyes went up in search of cameras. There were a lot. I walked the length of the platform, searching, and stood with my back to the passengers as they left. I checked behind me before stepping past the yellow line, then inspected the tracks, looked up to find more cameras and noted their locations. The next arrival was in one minute. Commuters were already arriving, and I was suddenly nervous about people being behind me. I stepped away from the edge and stood sideways as the platform filled up. The tracks squealed with the approaching train and I continued to monitor my immediate surroundings as it approached. Spotting a man about Roger's height, I got as close as I could to him, then, as the train arrived, I turned around like the men standing next to Roger had, from Russell's description. As I watched the passengers walking up to catch the train, I stepped away to let those arriving on it get off and looked up at the cameras again. I repeated my experiment at the other exits, then joined the commuters leaving the platform.

On the opposite platform for travel in the other direction, I stood behind the crowd until the most recent train had left. As I began my inspection, a morbid thought entered my mind: by the time I was done, I would have seen the exact length of the tracks upon which Roger had died. I shrugged the thought away and continued. I wasn't sure what I was looking for, but I hoped to find something. When the next train was delayed, I looked around with suspicion. As it became due, I stayed well back and watched the three people I'd noticed standing together nearby. I kept my eyes on them till they stepped aside for an arriving passenger and they got onto the train. Next, I joined the passengers leaving, but stopped in the passage until it was empty and waited for the next train.

'Everything okay?'

I jumped, startled. When I turned around to see a British Transport Police officer, I wished I hadn't flinched. I was immediately aware of the camera on her stab vest. I averted my body from its lens.

'I'm good,' I said, and I began to walk away.

She followed me onto the platform and stood a few

paces away. I pretended that her presence didn't bother me and, as the platform filled, I noticed that the next train was overdue. The officer calmly strolled towards me, and as I turned, I became aware of two of her colleagues circling me from the other direction.

'Can I ask you to step this way, sir?' the first officer asked, holding her hand away from the edge of the platform.

I complied and her male colleagues completed a triangle around me. Other passengers stared. I chose to remain silent.

'Are you okay?' the officer asked.

'Yup.'

'Are you lost?'

'Nope. What's this about?' I asked. I turned and eyed the two men.

'We noticed you walking the platforms,' she said. 'Is anything the matter?'

'Like what?' I asked.

'Do you need any help? Maybe you need to talk to someone?'

'No, I'm fine.'

'We have someone you can talk to,' she said. 'They're on their way.'

I got it. Someone keeping vigil on the monitors had noticed my suspicious behaviour. They thought I was contemplating jumping. I considered telling them what I was up to but swiftly decided against it. I still didn't know who or what I was up against.

'I think I lost my Oyster card,' I said. I patted my

pockets for effect. I noticed one of the first officer's colleagues lean over to scan the tracks.

'When was that, sir?' she asked.

'Earlier today,' I said.

'You were looking up at the cameras,' she said.

'Yeah. I was wondering if someone would have seen me drop it.'

I knew they weren't buying any of it, but I also knew they couldn't keep me. The speakers crackled with a TfL staffer apologising for the delayed train and promising updates as soon as she got some. It occurred to me that I might be the reason the train was delayed, and I felt a sudden rush of guilt. I checked my time and puffed as if dismayed.

'I'm sorry I bothered you all,' I said. 'I'm running late.'

I ignored her suggestion to check in the office to see if someone had found my Oyster card. Outside, still with the uncomfortable feeling that I was being watched, I went in search of a black cab. I gave the driver my address, and then I checked my messages. There was still no response from the Met, but when I checked my email, I had a new message.

My heart leapt. My fingers hesitated before opening it. Roger returned to my mind in force, and a heaviness settled on my chest. What a way to go. What a way to go.

47

'Can I change the destination?' I asked the cab driver.

'Course you can,' he said, without looking back.

'New Scotland Yard,' I said. He took his eyes off the road then to glance over his shoulder at me.

Roger's first-line supervisor–manager had invited me in for a meeting. With any luck, I would make the appointment. If I had seen the email before I'd left the station, I would have walked to Bond Street and caught the Jubilee line to Westminster; instead, I was in the back of a black cab, checking the time, getting nervous and fighting the urge to ask the driver to go faster. I made a show of grimacing at my watch, but he only looked at me in his mirror and kept to the speed limit. Google Maps showing the same journey time by car or public transport did nothing to ease my discomfort. What was I so anxious about? Even if I was too late, the meeting could always be rescheduled. That wasn't it. I dug deeper.

As we moved from red light to red light, weaving through West End traffic at well below the twenty-miles-per-hour speed limit, I realised what it was. I was afraid that I was about to lose my contract with the Met. Why else would Roger's supervisor have invited me to a meeting rather than simply informing me of the arrangements for his burial?

I knew why.

My client, whom they sent to me, had committed suicide. I was no good. They were letting me go.

Bobby, stop. You are catastrophising. Stop.

I tried to pay attention to my breathing, inhaling deeper and exhaling for longer. I was attempting to retake control of my brain's executive functions after delirious emotions had taken over. This was not an existential threat. I did not know that I was being fired; it occurred to me now that terminating my employment would have been better done via email, not a meeting. It must be about Roger. It could be about my request; it could be standard procedure; they might even want to check that I was okay – you know, since my client had taken his own life. I would not find out what it was about until I got there. There was nothing I could do until then, and it was pointless to suffer now for a future event that might or might not even occur. Breathe in. Breathe out.

The first time I had met Roger's first-line supervisor–manager was when she'd emailed to introduce herself and asked if I could come in to discuss an officer who she'd wanted to send to me. Maybe face-to-face meetings were her thing. All my previous meetings at the Met had been in dedicated meeting rooms, but she'd collected me downstairs and taken me up to her office.

It was small, but it was still hers alone. This time, a sergeant picked me up when the black cab dropped me off and escorted me further and deeper inside the building than I had ever been. He left me in a waiting room all by myself, and my terrible thoughts found me again there.

They let me stew in there for fifteen minutes. I knew exactly how long it was because, for the entire time, as the precariousness of my situation grew clearer, my eyes darted between the door and my watch. My thoughts spiralled: What is it about the imminence of death that fills me with the need to know the time? But you are not dying, Bobby. They wouldn't murder you at the Met. This may be bad, but it is not as bad as you think it is. It is not the end of your life. Breathe.

No matter what I told myself, I still couldn't breathe. I couldn't calm myself down. I couldn't rein in my fears. How had I missed it? Who could have put a tail on me, raided my flat and snatched my bag? The police, of course. Who stood to gain from Roger's death? Very likely them as well. I had foolishly made myself a loose end in the cover-up of whatever they had got Roger involved in. I had walked into the proverbial lion's den.

Just when I thought I couldn't take it any longer, the sergeant returned to take me further still down endless corridors and up another floor, and when he finally got permission to let me into the room he'd taken me to, I found five of them sat across the top of a U formation. There was a single seat in the centre.

Roger's supervisor was in the middle, in her uniform. Simon and Russell were to her right, and two commanders who were also in uniform sat to her left. It felt like I was walking the gauntlet when they invited me to sit.

She introduced everyone, noting that we'd met before, and I had already met Simon and Russell, and then she went straight to the point, reading from a printout in front of her.

'First of all, Mr Fatokun, please accept my apologies for not reaching out to you sooner. I can only imagine how difficult this dreadful affair must be for you. I received your request to attend the funeral. Do you really mean to go?'

She peered over her glasses at me. I'd first felt the cut of her laser eyes when I'd met her in her office to discuss Roger. She had the calm, assured, steely disposition of someone who knows that nothing ever gets by them.

I had no idea what was going on. Was this a preamble to my punishment? Compassion for the condemned? Or was this about finding out how much I knew? They all watched me. Each pair of judging eyes was telepathically communicating what I already knew: you are fucked.

'Yes,' I said. 'I would love to pay my respects in person.'

'May I ask why?'

I had to take a moment. 'Roger was my client. We spent a lot of time together.'

I could hear how defensive I sounded.

'You do not think it was your fault in any way, do you? Because if you do, if you want to speak to someone who is a professional, we have people you can talk to. Highly capable and highly recommended, like yourself. Do you want me to make an introduction?'

'I'm fine, Mary. I would just like to pay my respects.'

She studied me. She waited. It sounded like a genuine offer, and I was confused.

'Did you take any notes while you were working with him?'

There it was – why we were really here: one last attempt to locate my notes. I could finally breathe. Relief and excitement surged through me. I'd been right all along. Someone was after my coaching notes. Maybe they knew it, too. Maybe it was them.

There was little point in lying.

'Yes,' I said, admitting my guilt, as it were. I inhaled deeply, accepting my fate. So, this was how it ended.

'Under the circumstances,' Mary said, 'would you be comfortable letting the investigating officer see them?'

'There's an investigation? I thought . . . I thought the evidence was conclusive.'

'An inquiry. It's standard protocol if an officer dies on active duty.'

'Oh. Oh, I see. Okay. My notes? Sure. I'll just need a formal request.'

Mary looked at her colleagues. 'I take it then, Mr Fatokun, that you are not wholly comfortable sharing your confidential notes with the investigator. And you do not have to.'

Again, she made eye contact with her colleagues. What was that about?

'May I ask you a couple of questions regarding the contents of those notes?' she asked further, still in the same steady voice. 'If you can answer them, great; if you can't, fine. Just say so. It's to help with the investigation. I want to say it's nothing serious, but a man did take his own life. It'll only be a few questions. Three. Exactly three. Is that all right? I don't expect you to break client confidentiality.'

'Okay.'

She read from her printout before talking. I sensed she was paraphrasing.

'Did your client at any point indicate, or give you reason to suspect, that he might be at risk of self-harm, was currently self-harming or had self-harmed in the past?'

'No to all. That was three questions.'

'I did say three.' Mary placed the printout face down and crossed her arms over it. There was a brief pause as she seemed to gather herself. 'As to your request, I personally spoke to the widow. Unfortunately, you cannot go to the funeral.'

It was the wording. There was something not being said. I felt her studying my reaction before she continued. 'However, she will meet with you today.' She paused again. 'Mr Fatokun, there's a reasonable chance that Roger's widow may not be aware of the circumstances under which he came to be a client of yours. There is no need to bother her with any of it. You understand.'

'I understand.'

'Besides, it is all confidential,' she added, and I felt it was for the sake of her colleagues. 'If there's nothing else, Russell and Simon can take you to her now.'

And that ended our meeting. No NDAs to sign; no subtle or outright threats; no backdoor exit under a hood and in handcuffs. There had been nothing to raise my suspicions, and the question of my notes had been dropped without a second glance. It all felt almost pro forma.

They hadn't killed Roger, and they weren't out to kill me. I almost smiled at how I'd anticipated the end of my life as I knew it, only to realise that all that angst I'd felt was self-inflicted.

The problem with emotions is that they are real. Even though I knew I wasn't in trouble and wasn't losing my contract, my practice, or all my money, the chemical surge still lingered in my body.

As I followed Russell and Simon out of the room, I sent a message to my client, telling them how sorry I was to have to cancel our session. There was someone else I had to meet instead.

48

Neither Simon, Russell nor I spoke a single word during my long ride in the back of an unmarked police car – a black BMW that I would have picked out as a cop car any day. They took me to an old pub that looked lively inside as we approached, escorting me, one in front and one behind, through the throngs of nosy partygoers. As they led me through, I was conscious of the attention we were getting. They took me up to the first floor to a private room, where they shut the door behind me.

She was in the second-to-last chair at the end of a long dining table that I estimated could seat twenty. Roger's widow. The wood-clad walls behind her were partly lit by soft sunshine from the windows opposite her, but the slice of light started a foot above her head. She was alone in a dark room, in its only shadow, bearing her grief in solitude but looking tranquil, as if the dimness had bathed her in peace. Maybe I shouldn't have come.

I noticed that she was slight and frail – the kind of frailty that comes with new grief, altering the face and leaving its mark in grooves that soon become part of a new self, as the person that existed before gives way to who they become after. I felt sorry for her.

I walked over and sat down in a chair opposite. Her eyes followed me all the way.

I used my coaching voice. 'My name is Bobby,' I said. 'I don't know if Roger mentioned me, but we . . .'

'I know who you are. You're the therapist they made him see.'

I nodded as if I were guilty as charged, and indeed, it felt like an accusation. Her eyes, looking at me sideways from behind their grief, hinted at discussions she'd had with her late husband. Difficult conversations in which I'd come up. I decided not to correct her.

'He didn't do it, you know?' she said, looking me straight in the eyes, with absolutely no doubt.

I was taken aback. It was the last thing I could have expected her to say to someone she wouldn't allow to attend her late husband's funeral.

Did she know something?

'You know how I know?'

Wait a minute. I sat up straighter, a tingle of excitement moving down my spine. She might know something I didn't. I just knew there was something wrong with the platform scene.

'Because she's Black.'

Hold on. What?

In that moment, several things that I had seen and experienced but had not noticed properly all fell into place. Russell and Simon hadn't talked to me the entire way over. The tinted glass in the back of the car had made it unpleasant to watch the road, so I'd been lost in my own thoughts and had not paid attention to where they were taking me. The people in the pub downstairs had all looked at me like I shouldn't be in there. With hostility. My head began ringing. They were all white.

'It's not like we're racists or anything like that,' Roger's widow said. 'It's just that people shouldn't be forced to live with people that aren't like them. I mean, they keep coming here and doing crimes, you know? They get all the benefits, all the housing. They take all the jobs. They're just no good for anyone, really. Not like you. You know what I mean. We just keep taking them in, and now the country is all full up. They're coming here for the free stuff, taking advantage of us, and people like to call us all sorts of names, saying we're racists and Nazis, but we're just ordinary people who want to remain English, you know? We want to protect our culture – what's wrong with that? And if it makes us racists, I don't know what to say to that. I just don't know. And Roger, he would never have anything to do with a girl like her. Never. Never, never, never.

'Talking to you really helped him. He was able to bear it all. They stuck him behind a desk, but he was a fighter, my Roger. A real survivor. They thought they could break his spirit and make him quit, but he was doing just fine. He had put it all behind him, kept his head down and carried on, but then he saw that African preacher on the news talking about building some stuff for the kids, and the King was going to visit, and it just got him all worked up again.

'He called you that night. He said he had to see you. I guess seeing that man was just too much for him. He just couldn't take it anymore. They ruined him, the two of them. They ruined him. They framed him and they took everything from him. Everything. You know what it does to a detective when you stick him behind a desk, when he could be out there solving crimes, getting the bad guys? It's like putting a tiger in a cage. They go crazy or they die.'

She paused for a breath, eyes wild, staring deep into mine. 'Those two, they killed him. That preacher and his little whore. They've got his blood on their hands.'

49

I needed air. I had to get away from that room, from the pub, from Russell and Simon, and, most urgently, from the neighbourhood.

As I descended the stairs, I felt all eyes on me again. How did it come to be that the skin that protected one's flesh could also put one in such danger? I felt deeply unsafe.

Russell and Simon followed me out. On the walk to their car, I noticed the flags hanging from the pub's windows that I'd missed when we'd driven down. The two officers offered to take me to a station, but I called an Uber instead and asked if they would wait until it arrived. They did. I could see they felt bad, and I felt bad for them too. I suspected they would have warned me if they could have. But how do you find the right words to say something like that?

Before too long, the Prius pulled up behind us. The driver was Somali and I don't remember ever being so relieved to see another brown face. In the safety of the back seat of his car, I began to breathe again. Yasir looked at me in his mirror, and in the split second that our eyes locked, we communicated volumes that reached back to the first foreign ships that landed on African shores.

'Do you work around here?' he asked. He kept his eyes on me in his mirror while driving at the edge of the speed limit.

'No.'

'It's a bad area, brother. Not nice for people like us.'

I nodded and tested my seatbelt.

'I pick one customer here. She spit when she get down. She slam my door. She not even bother hide it. I give her one star.' He held up a finger and grinned at me in the mirror. He had a gold tooth and it gleamed in his mouth.

I smiled back. To be fair, the spitting might have had something to do with the various coloured Christmas-tree air fresheners hanging from his mirror. It was intense. I wished he would keep his eyes on the road while I went back to searching for what was alive inside me. What was I feeling? I wanted to label the emotion so I could gain control over it, short-circuit the hardwired response and bring my prefrontal cortex back into play. Regain self-management.

I found anger.

I was angry at myself for not seeing it. A lot of things from the time Roger and I had spent together were beginning to make sense in the new light of who he was beyond being a police officer. At the time, I had never been able to decipher his looks. His micro-expressions, which I ignored as soon as I'd detected them; his microaggressions, which

I'd dismissed as projections – I am no Truth Wizard, but I can usually tell when a client is holding back or bullshitting. With Roger, I could never tell what was true and what wasn't. I'd thought that the lies I picked up on were because of his undercover work; the most memorable thing he'd ever told me about that was when he'd said, 'It's not what it seems.' At the time, at least, I'd thought it was a reference to his mission, but now I wondered what he'd meant by it. What wasn't what it seemed to be? And in what way or ways?

'You all right, brother?'

I looked up at Yasir. 'Yeah. I'm good.'

In spite of all that had happened, I was good. The trip had not been a waste of time. Far from it. I now had an important piece of information.

Until I'd sat across from Roger's widow, all I'd known about Roger's undercover work was that it had been at a church and that his cover had been a security manager, whatever that meant. I had immediately assumed, and continued to assume, that it was a parish of the Church of England. A white church. That was a bias on my part. I now knew that it was an African pastor and, most likely, an African church. That narrowed it down a bit. He had been careful to keep that detail from me.

I also knew that the pastor of the church had been on the news the night Roger called me, and that meant that I could find him. I could get online and search the schedules of all the TV stations on that day. I would start with the major ones and work my way down. It could take a few minutes or a whole day. It would be painstaking, but

I knew who would have the superpower to get it done superfast. A journalist.

'Hey,' Naomi answered. She sounded cheerful. 'You better not be cancelling on me.'

'I need a favour,' I said.

'What is it?'

I checked on Yasir.

'An African pastor was on TV two nights ago, on the news. That's all I've got. I need his name.'

'Does it have to do with . . .?'

'Yes.'

'Can you talk? Are you alone?'

'No.'

'Where are you? Can you come meet me at Waterloo? I'm meeting a source.'

I gave Yasir the new address, and he showed me how to change the destination on the app. Then I settled back and considered how much I was willing to tell Naomi.

50

When my cab approached Blackfriars Bridge, memories of my pub meeting with Russell came flooding back. Naomi was waiting for me in front of the two arches of the Blackfriars Railway Bridge that housed the Burrell Street Sexual Health Centre. She was stunning. She looked completely at ease, her hands in the pockets of her long coat, her face glistening in the low autumn sun, with a smile that made me smile. I still couldn't believe my luck to be going on a date with her later that evening. But then again, we had already matched on that app. She already saw something in me; I just had to be careful not to ruin it.

As he parked, I noticed Yasir looking at her, smiling at me. As I crossed the road towards Naomi, he spoke to me out of his window.

'I give you five stars,' he called.

He was grinning and showing me his five fingers. There was no way he could have known that it was a rude gesture in Nigeria. 'Your mother,' to be precise.

'Sexual health clinic, eh?' I said as I approached Naomi, nodding at the clinic.

She accepted my attempt at humour, grinning widely before feigning shock and indignation. 'I told you I was meeting a source,' she said, as she spread her arms, inviting me into a hug.

As we embraced, I inhaled as much of her fragrance as possible. Our bodies pressed together felt like home. The feel of her arms around my neck made me want to cry. I hated that I had to be dishonest, but she was a journalist, no matter what I felt for her. In the back of the cab, I had perfected my lie. I wasn't going to be a source for her.

'I've just been to meet Roger's widow,' I explained. 'She mentioned an African pastor had been on television the night before Roger killed himself. Something about it upset him. I'm curious to know what it could be.'

I couldn't tell if she believed me or not.

'Anything else?' she asked.

'The man was talking about the King visiting a youth facility he's building.'

'That's easy, then. We can look at the King's itinerary. It'll be there unless it was a private meeting.'

'Sorry. I meant that the King would be visiting the place. The man boasted that the King would be visiting.'

'Oh.'

Inside, the centre felt more like a space for creatives than a clinic. There was art everywhere, and art in the design of the place itself. The waiting area held a long, padded bench that ran the length of the glass front of one of the arches. In front of that, there was a table that would have been right at home in the Apple Store I'd visited to get my new laptop and, on the other side of the table, a sitting space at the top of a double-perforated white wall punctured with grey circles. Above us, delicate wire sculptures and slow-turning and brightly coloured sculptures were suspended from the ceiling.

It did not feel like any NHS clinic I'd ever been to, and I wondered who Naomi was meeting there. A patient or an employee? There were other people in the waiting room, all respecting the unspoken rule of silence in such places. I wondered what they had.

'Are you okay?' she whispered as we sat down.

I had drifted. I gave her a thumbs up.

'How was she?' Naomi continued.

'Who?'

'Your friend's widow.'

He wasn't my friend. 'In mourning,' I said.

'He saw the pastor on TV?'

'Yes. They both did and, according to her, he called me right after.'

'Do you remember what day that was?'

'The day I met you.'

She looked at me. For a moment, we just stared into each other's eyes before she broke the connection to reach into her bag. I watched her set her Sony notebook on her lap.

'And he's African,' I said. 'The pastor.'

'Yeah, you said.'

'I mean, it's a Pentecostal church.'

'Did she say that?'

I couldn't remember if she had. I was going by my gut. 'Yes.'

I watched Naomi's fingers hover over her keyboard – long, slim and delicately beautiful. I remembered shaking hands with her at the Hansom.

She noticed me staring and gave me a look.

'Sorry,' I said, and I quickly looked away so she could type in her password.

I felt stupid. I hoped she didn't think I was trying to spy on her. Or worse still, caught a hint as to what I *was* thinking.

I turned my attention elsewhere. I wondered what would have happened if I'd seen that we'd matched on that app. Would we have left it at 'hello' and 'hi' or whatever creative derivations of it we came up with? Would we have exchanged numbers? Met for coffee, maybe even at the café she'd wanted to meet at the other day? Would we have started dating?

I looked at her again. She was focused on her computer.

She was my type of good-looking. It made sense that I had clicked on her profile. I had definitely liked her first, but she must have seen something in my profile that had attracted her enough to make her like me back. But why couldn't I remember spotting her? Maybe she looked different in her pictures. Younger, perhaps. Different hair?

We'd been sitting in silence for a while as she searched for my pastor. I instinctively checked on her progress and then quickly snapped my gaze away from her screen. I turned to the artwork dangling from the ceiling, and only then did I realise that it depicted sexual organs and blown-up molecules responsible for STDs. Hanging from near-invisible strings, the sculptures dangled from both ends of long, thin poles that swayed softly in the enclosed, windless space. I noticed what looked like a tiny mechanism attached to the base of one of them, which must have created the motion. I kept staring.

When I did a walking session with a client, I would ask them to pay attention to their surroundings as we walked and talked, and to say when they saw anything that caught their attention. We would then stop to look at the object, and I would ask them to tell me how it related to what we'd been discussing. The idea was that their brain – while probing a thought, seeking an answer or working towards a resolution – would be drawn to external representations of their internal situation. A musician client once said of a tree in Battersea Park, 'The branches are my records, and the leaves are my fans. I may lose some fans, but new leaves and branches will grow too. I am the tree, and my roots are deep.' She had recently been cancelled for posting an opinion contrary to popular sentiments.

I wondered what the suspended art said about Naomi and me. We were floating in space. Suspended in fatal bad timing?

'Found him,' Naomi said.

She was still bent over her laptop and typing away. After a few seconds, she sat up straighter and tilted her screen towards me. The picture on it had an AP watermark and showed a bespectacled man in a suit and a blue hard hat. His smile was carefully neutral; it looked rehearsed, the kind worn by men used to cameras. He was shaking hands with the Mayor of London. Next to them was a smiling young woman holding her hands behind her back, her face turned to the pastor. She also wore a hard hat. I scanned the overview text next to the picture. Amid the jargon of information, I found their names: 'Pastor Dolapo Daniel D'Don, WAITRN Church, and Tashique Warner, WAITRN Church, at the groundbreaking ceremony for a new community youth centre.'

Got you.

51

Naomi had found several news segments that had featured the pastor. It must have been a slow news day, as all the main channels had covered the progress of the youth facility their church was building. I took the laptop from her, moved it onto my lap and stared at the pastor and the young woman.

'What's going to happen now?' Naomi asked.

I desperately wanted to go home so that I could get on my new laptop and learn everything I could about Dolapo Daniel D'Don and his church. For the first time since the entire affair had started, I sensed that I was approaching a significant milestone. Knowing myself, I would likely stay up late, glued to my computer, searching for clues. Then I remembered – we were going out on a date.

'I'll watch the video when I get home,' I said.

I was particularly interested in the young lady in the picture. Could she be the one who had made the accusation against Roger?

'Are you okay?' she asked.

Again, she had a look of concern that would have been

cute were it not for the fact that she'd seen me freaking out and I'd had to tell her about my paranoia to calm her down. By asking, 'Are you okay?' she was definitely referring to my mental health. My intrusive thoughts took over. What if we were only going on a date because she felt sorry for me? Or did she hope to get a story out of me? Come to think of it, in a way, she was the one who had asked *me* out.

'I'm fine,' I assured her, and told myself, Stop it, Bobby.

I looked around the waiting room. A handful of people had come and gone since we'd arrived. 'When is your source coming?' I asked.

'I already saw him,' she said, with a smile that seemed mischievous and made me a little uncomfortable. 'Do you still want to go out tonight?'

Now I had a new dilemma. Of course I did, but to be truly honest, I was increasingly tempted to take a rain check so I could get onto my computer. She must have read it in my face.

'Why?' I asked, stalling.

'You look like you just want to go home and watch the video.'

She had me. It is not a superpower of mine to be aware, in the moment, that I am about to self-sabotage and thus have the opportunity to stop myself from doing so. I knew exactly how this would play out: I would plead with her to please understand, and she would say that it was okay. Only it wouldn't be.

'It's okay,' she said.

I hadn't even said anything!

'No!'

People looked at us.

'No,' I repeated, nearly whispering. I took her hands in mine. 'It can wait.'

'It's okay,' she said. 'I understand.' She squeezed my hands back to stop me from protesting. 'You know, I've been researching your thing.'

'My thing?'

'Your paranoia. I think you might have ADHD. It explains everything: your hypervigilance – which is why you notice things in the first place – your strong intuition and your goofiness.'

'You think I'm goofy?'

'Yes. It's cute.'

I blushed under my black skin.

She looked around. 'Tell me what you see now,' she said.

I took in our surroundings. I understood the game she was playing. I found myself drawn to a slender man stooping over a novel. I'd tried to read the title on the cover when we'd sat down, suspecting that he was trying to listen to us. It would only have been harmless eavesdropping. We must have looked like an interesting couple, and we were the only ones talking in the waiting area, almost whispering. I looked up at the hanging artwork that had previously caught my attention instead. As much as I wanted to play along, I was getting nothing.

'It doesn't work like that,' I said.

'Like how?'

'Well, I don't just make up conspiracy theories.

Something has to jump out at me.' My eyes rolled over the suspended sculptures. I was sure they were telling me something about us.

She followed my gaze. 'They're STIs,' she said.

I wasn't sure if she was trying to make me laugh. I was afraid she would infer something negative about us, and nothing good could come out of that.

'You know,' she said. 'The CIA invented the term "conspiracy theory" to discredit anyone speaking out against anything they were doing.'

'That's a conspiracy theory,' I said.

'Precisely,' she replied.

Later on, as I walked towards the South Bank alone, I kept thinking of the way we'd parted. I'd waited with her until her taxi had arrived, and then, careful not to breach her bodily autonomy as if we were already a couple, I'd awkwardly kept my arms by my side until she'd lifted hers. But she hadn't hugged me. Instead, she'd placed her lips on mine and held my face in her palms. It wasn't a full-on kiss, but it could have been one. I still couldn't believe my luck. It felt too good to be real. Maybe she just wanted to explore what could have been following our initial match. Stop, Bobby.

Eventually I began to beat myself up for accepting her offer to postpone the date until tomorrow so that I could go home and do the work my mind was desperate to get on with. She'd said it was hyperfixation, which she and the internet had identified as another symptom of my ADHD. As I walked, I smiled despite myself. There are two times when London is beautiful: when it's summer and when I'm in love. And I was in love. People looked at me as we passed each other, my full-blown smile startling them. I didn't care. I was going over mine and Naomi's time together – every word we'd spoken, every look we'd shared. I visualised the suspended artworks again, and I wondered how they were symbolic of our relationship – the sex organs and nasty molecules that had swayed above our heads.

The other thing on my mind was what Naomi had found about the pastor, and in the end I couldn't wait until I got home. I stopped on the South Bank, got a coffee, fired up my new laptop in the main foyer of the Royal Festival Hall and began my search for anything I could find on Pastor Dolapo Daniel D'Don and Tashique Warner, both of WAITRN Church.

I found the church's website, the pastor's Facebook page and the church's YouTube channel, among others. They were both very active on social media, and I enlarged a selfie from Tashique's Instagram. She was a stunningly attractive woman. There were loads of videos of the pastor talking about everything from meditation to taxation. I'd been expecting lots of Bible quoting, staged healings and that sort of thing, but in the clips, he talked calmly and sounded intelligent. He was always so composed – you could even say he was sort of charming – but there was definitely something off about him, too. It's one thing to be charismatic, and it's quite another to be the charismatic leader of a religious sect, which was the vibe I was getting from his church.

It was the things he said. The kind of intelligent-sounding bullshit that, upon examination, really makes no sense. And the way he spoke. His voice had a hypnotic quality to it, like he was brainwashing his followers. Maybe that was what Roger had been investigating. Some of the things the guy said were quite weird. Like this one video in which he talked about not being afraid to die because 'we are all dead once we are born'. In another video, he also claimed that the so-called Rapture the Bible predicted had already happened.

I turned to the church's X account. The latest posts on the page all ended with the hashtag #thegathering. I scrolled down and kept seeing the same ominous hashtag. Some of the posts had been liked and reposted thousands of times. My curiosity grew.

From what I could glean, there had been some sort of gathering of the church members a day ago. Pictures and clips, along with quotes from the event, were still being shared and re-shared.

I clicked on one of the most liked and reposted videos. It had been recorded at night on someone's mobile. The camera swept over crowds of people hanging out against the backdrop of a giant white marquee. All young. All in white outfits. Some held red disposable cups. I found the contrast interesting.

I found another video of the inside of the marquee. There had to be at least a few hundred people at the event, which had apparently been held in the dark in what looked like the middle of a barren field. I wondered where it was, then focused on reading the posts. I came across posts like, 'For real, we are in the rapture now!' And 'If you are not here, you are in the wrong place,' and 'Fishes and bread, yo!', along with a slew of other accidental ciphers and vacuous texts, all preceded by the viral hashtag, #thegathering.

The pastor himself was quoted a lot: 'D'Don: There is no true social revolution without the liberation of women.' 'May my eyes never see and my feet never take me to a society where half the people are held in silence. I hear the roar of women's silence. Pastor DD.'

I doubted whether the people attributing the quotes to their leader knew who Thomas Sankara was.

With each direct quote, occasional plagiarism aside, my view of the man began to shift. I began to nod along to some of his sayings as I mentally agreed with the ideas he seemed to be proposing. It was as if I was being sucked into the lure of his spell. But that all ended when I came across a quote attributed to him: 'A blade of grass equals all of humanity.' With that single gem of a post, his hypnotic spell lifted, and I saw him for what he really was: a person who spoke mostly in motivational stickers. His followers, too, were nothing more than the kinds of people who spent their lives searching for someone to tell them what to think, what to do, who to love, and who to hate.

He would have remained, in my mind, nothing but a harmless charlatan of a conman, deftly picking his followers' pockets, but then I turned to posts not quoting him, and my body registered alarm. A sort of excitement mixed with fear. I read, 'We came alone. We leave together. #thegathering.' 'I am not afraid to follow you to the end. #DDon #thegathering.' 'I am ready to transcend to the spiritual realm tonight. #thegathering.'

Granted, I'd started off thinking the least of the man, but in those posts, I sensed an encrypted rallying call to a zombified flock. Surely, someone from the appropriate authority must have seen this – if they were looking out for such red flags. If he was on their radar.

The more I read, the more WAITRN Church felt like a cult, and the reposted quotes like a call to mass action. It bothered me a lot. I went over the posts to make sure I wasn't overacting. This one seemed to confirm my fears, and forcefully too: 'At the right time, we will walk together into eternal glory #DDon #thegathering.'

I wondered how far his message was reaching.

The church's social media accounts had two million followers altogether. The website boasted of a congregation of 'over one million members worldwide'. One million. That was a lot of flock. I guessed crazy had its own followers. Perhaps there was more to the unease I was beginning to feel about the man, D'Don, and his church. Perhaps Roger's undercover investigation had been looking into whatever that was.

When I finally looked up, hours had passed. Naomi was right; I did get hyperfixated on things. The other night, I'd stayed up searching through my home because she'd suggested that Roger might have hidden something there, and now I'd been totally blind to the time I'd spent in the festival hall foyer. She seemed to possess an uncanny ability to see me. The more I thought about her, the more I discovered new things that I loved about her. How come I didn't remember her from the app? I must have been swiping right without looking. Shameful. Another reason I'd deleted it.

I reluctantly packed up my laptop and made my way back home. As I walked to the station, I kept thinking of Naomi, resisting the urge to call her and hoping she would call me or send a message.

'Having a good day?' someone said.

I turned to look at them as they walked past me, not sure if they'd been talking to me. The young man was also looking back at me, smiling.

'Yes,' I said, beaming from my heart, which was filled with the warm, fuzzy joy that they had seen on my face.

I strolled on, carefree, my mind filled only with thoughts of Naomi. I still couldn't believe how lucky I was.

I had planned to wait until the morning before continuing my research on WAITRN so that I would have a rested, clear perspective, as well as to convince myself that I could control my hyperfixation. But my attempts to stay away from the church only left me fixating on Naomi. I so desperately wanted to call her, but we had agreed to go on our date the next day, and I didn't want to do anything to mess that up – a call could be just that thing. I decided to keep myself busy with the church, so I sat at the dining table with my laptop and settled in.

I went over the posts again. There were dozens of new ones, still focused on the so-called gathering, whatever that was. I googled the pastor once more. There was surprisingly little information about his personal life on the web, and it appeared as though a paid promoter had written his Wikipedia page. I brought Tashique Warner's social media pages back up and expanded her pictures. She was really beautiful. Roger had described his accuser as being pretty and seductive; could it be her? Nah. I could see him lusting after her, but I couldn't see her noticing him in a room. Still, I stared at the images in the silence of the night until I noticed the time in the corner of the screen.

I got into bed and immediately started to think of Naomi. I decided it was okay to send her a text. I started to compose a message: 'Hiya. I just want to thank you for earlier today . . .' I didn't know where to go with it. In the darkness, with the light from the screen causing a slight ache in my eyes, I paused and tried to come up with the rest of the message. I hit the backspace button until I'd deleted the whole thing, then I plugged the phone into its charger, lay on my back and worried that she might have already seen that I was typing a message to her. Stop it, Bobby. You are overthinking again.

As I lay still, I tried to empty my mind of thoughts, but the neurones in my brain began to fire in all directions from all the information dumps. I saw the posts, I saw the pastor's face, and I saw the pretty young woman, Tashique. I didn't want to think of any of that until I'd had some rest. I closed my eyes and gave in to thinking about Naomi. I saw her head bent over her laptop, helping me find the pastor I was looking for. I saw the suspended art installation in the waiting room of the Burrell Street Sexual Health Centre. My eyes shot open.

I knew why the two men had turned on the platform the way they had. Roger had been murdered.

52

Francis tossed and turned, sweating his worries onto the sheets and turning his pillow over and over again as it got too warm. He kept asking himself how he could have been so careless. He had chosen the agents, the shop and what everyone knew with care, but Rufus was the one person he hadn't expected to see on Mount Street. At first, he wondered who else knew about the plan. Whoever it was, they must have told Rufus about it, for surely Rufus could not have found him alone. But no matter what scenario he played in his mind, he kept coming back to the fact that no one else, apart from John, knew what he was up to. There was simply no trail to follow. It became clear that Rufus had indeed simply stumbled upon him. The one person from Francis' entire career who had a reason to still hold a grudge.

He turned around, away from Siobhan, now comatose from the trazodone she took for the insomnia caused by the donepezil that made her sleepy during the day. He turned the damp pillow around and fluffed it again, then laid his head back down, his one eye darting around in the dark. He went over each word of the short dialogue he'd had with Rufus at the gun shop. Had he revealed anything after the other agent had followed him inside?

Francis lifted his head off the pillow and propped himself up on one elbow. 'Why didn't he stop me in the street?' he asked the darkness.

Rufus had stumbled upon him, but it wasn't on the day he had come into the gun shop and asked the shopkeeper about Francis.

Francis lay back down and sucked in his regret. If only he had been more careful. He imagined how it must have happened. First, Rufus randomly spotted him. Perhaps he saw Francis enter the gun shop. Perhaps he'd followed him for no reason other than his grudge. He must have noted the place and time and returned to see if his old boss came back. Then he would have researched the gun shop and found it to be a legitimate business under royal warrant and still run by the same family who had originally founded it. He would have seen Francis' agents arriving and departing. If he had kept digging, he would have found that they apparently worked for a tech start-up renting space below the shop, and then he would have asked himself, 'What is Francis doing visiting a start-up?'

Rufus was stupid, but even he was not that stupid. He knew that Francis was retired. But he also knew that Francis was running a team. He'd walked into the gun shop to confirm his suspicions.

Francis berated himself. How could he have been so careless? A dimwit now threatened months of meticulous planning, plotting, planting and pruning. A dimwit.

Had D'Don been aware of it all, he would have called it a miracle. However, it was just an unfortunate coincidence – albeit one that now threatened to derail everything. Francis pictured the pastor's grinning face. Now he might have to endure that fraud of a preacher for much longer – the whimsical requests for invitations, the self-serving demands for introductions, the microaggressions, the condescension, the random late-night text messages. The constant reminder that he, D'Don, owned Francis.

Francis groaned. Too much was at stake. For him and for others. Too much. Failure was not an option, and Rufus, that idiot, embodied failure. The only real option he could think of was to bring Rufus in, but bringing him in was also the most dangerous thing he could do. It was Rufus, after all.

He slipped out of the duvet and sat on the edge of the bed, holding his bowed head in his palms. Standing up, he left the room, left Siobhan, and went to his study, where he sat in the darkness and poured himself a full glass of bourbon.

53

Francis had hardly slept, yet he was up at six a.m. The sky was still bruised purple as he arrived at Buckingham Palace. The corridors were still quiet, save for his footsteps, marching like a ghost through the palace dawn. By seven thirty, he was at the pool, attacking the water with clean slices and powerful strokes, propelling him faster and further as his mind cut into the obstacles in his path. The junior minister who had taken a shine to Tashique had seemed to pose a significant challenge with his unbridled libido. Francis' mind had latched on to this potential threat, carefully weighing and assessing it, before Rufus had turned up. Rufus. Rufus. What to do about Rufus? It would all be over soon. The endgame was so close. Francis had not planned on an extensive clean-up, and even with meticulous planning, some messes would always remain uncleanable. He was so close. So close. Bloody Rufus.

He rotated in the water and saw a figure walking along the pool's edge. Francis always swam at the same time – maybe that was a mistake, but it was when he could have the pool to himself. The man was keeping pace with him. White, blond, late thirties and six feet tall, with a swimmer's body, blue-black speedos and no goggles. Francis stopped at the end of the lap and looked up at the intruder.

'That must be a record,' the man said, an effusive smile on his face and his fists resting on his hips.

Francis noticed the hard 'r'. The stranger had managed not to devoice the last consonants, at the expense of flatness. His swimwear did not appear to conceal any weapons, but he could have been hiding something in his fists.

'Who sent you?' Francis asked, ready to take his chances in the water if it came to it.

'No one. I always come after you. You have completed more than fifty laps today.'

'Are you watching me?'

'Oh, no. I am Alexei Mikhailovich Sokolov.' The man got down on one knee and stretched out a hand to Francis. 'I'm a guest of the palace. The pool guy told me there is a gentleman who swims fifty laps every day. Did you know that he doesn't let anyone in until you've finished?'

Francis kept both the hand and the crouched body in sight. 'I didn't know that,' he said. 'Sorry for hogging the pool.'

He pushed himself off to get out at the other end.

For the first time, Francis took a different route from his office at Clarence House to the antique gun shop on Mount Street. As he walked, he berated himself for not taking this precaution earlier. He would live the rest of the few good months he had left with the pastor's strings still hooked into his flesh.

When he arrived in the basement, he sat down and spread his arms over the back of the sofa.

'Tell me what you've got,' he said.

The other two agents looked at Libby; a grin had pushed up the corners of her lips. 'He's been anonymously supporting local hospices, care homes and youth centres,' she said.

'Anything interesting?' Francis cut in.

The agents exchanged looks.

'Like what?' Libby asked.

'Anything unusual.'

'I think this whole thing is unusual. I mean him. Not us, of course. Not this.'

'Of course,' Francis said.

She continued, 'I mean, we've been digging, and we haven't found anything worth pursuing.'

'How would you know when you find something worth pursuing?' Francis asked.

Libby looked at the agents. 'Actionable intel,' she said.

'Like?'

'Like, association with known terrorists.'

'What else?'

'Any involvement in plans to carry out acts of terrorism.'

'Good. So, have you got anything for me?'

'Nothing.' Libby shrugged.

'Nothing, *yet*. Keep digging.'

Dempsey leant forward. 'What about the Nigerian coach?' he said.

'What about him?' Francis asked.

'Rod is still on him and the young guy. We could use his time on other things.'

Francis turned to Rod. 'What do you think? Should we stay on the coach?'

'We have ... I have done a full check on him. I've explored his known contacts and ... Maybe if I knew how he's related to the primary subjects, I ...'

'That's not important. What I want to hear from you is, "I think I should stay with the coach," or, "I think the coach is a dead end." Which is it?'

Rod glanced at Dempsey.

'I want your opinion, not his,' Francis said.

'I think it's a dead end,' Rod said.

'All right then, forget the coach.' Francis looked at each of the young agents in turn. 'What did you find in the video?'

'Nothing,' Libby said.

'Not really nothing,' Dempsey interjected. 'We think your asset was made by the young guy.'

'Anything else?'

Once again, the agents exchanged looks.

'Well?' Francis prompted.

Libby and Rod left it to Dempsey to respond.

'Without knowing what we're looking for, we can't say that we found anything.'

'Damn it!' Francis banged his fist on the armrest and rose to his feet. 'You're telling me you don't find that video disturbing? All those kids dressed in white? All that cryptic nonsense? Did you watch it? Did you watch all of it?

That man is up to something, and it's up to you to figure it out. Was anyone there on any watch lists? Was he passing secret messages? Were there communists in the tent? For God's sake, find me something!'

He left them sitting in stunned silence. When the door shut behind him, he stood for a minute with his back against it. His lips were tight over his teeth, and as he held out his hand, he saw it shake. Slowly, he formed a fist and unfurled it, then, after several deep breaths, he turned back to the door and grasped the handle tight. A long moment passed, then he let go and continued on his way out of the basement beneath the gun shop.

54

I woke up feeling excited. I stayed in bed for a while, searching my brain for what it was that I was excited about. It had to be something. I felt it in my belly and in my chest – an energetic eagerness, a compulsion to act – but try as I might, I couldn't put my finger on it. What had I been thinking of before I went to bed? What seemed so important that it dragged me out of sleep with so much energy?

I sat up against the headboard and racked my brain, but it felt like trying to see through heavy fog. I cast my eyes across the bedroom, searching for a clue, and my gaze fell on the treadmill. The only item the intruders had not touched or moved, I guessed because it was too heavy. I could do with a good run to get my brain working, but I felt like I could do with some scenery as well, so I fetched my running shoes and dressed for an early morning autumn run.

It was chilly outside. Cold, actually. And dark. Grey and cloudy, with fat, overlapping clouds standing still in the sky like a painted backdrop. My breath turned to steam even before I finished stretching outside the main entrance downstairs. I should have worn jogging tights, and a long-sleeved vest, for that matter. As it was, my wristband was ultimately pointless, as I already knew I'd be back much sooner than I'd planned – earlier than it'd take to work up a sweat. I exhaled into my palms and set off, proud of myself for even trying. I scanned around for would-be assailants, my hypervigilance even stronger than usual at six in the morning.

As I began pounding the pavement, I returned to racking my brain to try to remember what it was that had woken me with such a dose of adrenaline. It must have had something to do with the investigation. Investigation? It was only then that I became aware that, in my mind, it was an investigation. I had fully regressed to being a police officer – a detective trying to solve the murder of his former client. But was that it? Was that what had woken me up with excitement?

I was coming up to a side road that I'd never been on before. I'd only ever driven past it, so I didn't quite recognise the street name, which was partly hidden under overgrown ivy. Rugger Crescent. Rugger? It rhymed with Roger, and that was all the push I needed to turn onto a road I had not travelled before.

As I jogged past the still houses, silent in the grey of dawn, I began to notice the peculiarity of the architecture. Every building had a corner that was all glass. Some had more than one – a corner downstairs and a corner upstairs – and it was the only thing all the buildings had in common, as if the glass corners were functional, like chimneys. It was curious, so I became curious.

The glass corners were dark that early in the morning. It was too early to have the lights on, and the houses' occupants were still asleep. I noticed that there were no curtains, blinds, or anything to obstruct a nosy person's intrusion. What could these corners be for? Some sort of indoor greenhouses? A clever system to bring light into otherwise enclosed inner spaces? But then I noticed that they were bathrooms. All of them. Bathrooms with full-length clear windows of glass, with no curtains or blinds, or even plants placed to obstruct an outsider's view. But why?

A glow up ahead caught my eye. One of the corners was lit. An early riser like me. I came up to the house. An older man was taking a shower. The glass corner was the shower. The man either didn't see me, or if he did, he wasn't bothered. His skin was pale and sagging from age, and his head had lost all its hair. He began to lather his arms, and only then did he look out at me. I hadn't even realised I'd stopped to watch. I looked away and continued jogging, and when I glanced back over my shoulder, he had continued his business as if I'd not just seen him, full frontal, peeing as he showered. I hurried on. His indifference was to me as much an admonishment as the guilt I already felt from watching.

After that, all the corners were lit, and in them, people bathed, showered or sat on toilet bowls. It was uncanny. If I looked, they looked back at me, but that was all they did – look at me. No nod, no eye roll, no middle finger, no acknowledgement of any sort. Not one of them bothered to cover up or turn their backs to the peeping Tom.

It was all very strange. I saw a couple plastered against the glass in one of the buildings: a Black man in front and an Indian man behind. One thrusting and the other receiving. I stopped and gaped in awe. They watched me watching them, and they continued, as if it were perfectly normal to be seen and to be watched. I knew then that I was asleep, and that I was dreaming.

I woke up perfectly aware of the fact. It was the most vivid dream I'd ever had, and as it was a lucid dream, I figured I might have had some control over it, which would explain why it was the first time in a long while that a dream had not turned into a nightmare for me.

I lay on my back, trying to make sense of the bizarreness of it all. What had it been about? Knowing that dreams likely help us make memories, process emotions and solve the problems we've struggled with in our waking hours, I wondered what this one meant. If I'd been naked and exposed and other people had been watching me, anxiety from some insecurity could have explained it. But it was the avatars in my dream that had been naked, while I was fully clothed. I saw them, and they saw that I saw them, but they were unmoved by it. Almost like they were otherworldly. Altered humans. Unfeeling, unthinking flesh-and-blood automatons – mindless beings living in a dream world. Zombies of a dimension only accessible through sleep. Maybe it had been a nightmare after all.

I reached for my dream journal that wasn't there, and in the same instant that I remembered its loss, my eyes turned to the treadmill. I threw the duvet off and walked over to the well-used fitness equipment that took up a considerable footprint in my bedroom. I knelt beside it, lowered my body to the ground, placed the side of my face on the carpet, and there it was, under the treadmill – my dream journal. I didn't know how I'd instantly figured out that it had been there all along – in the one place I hadn't thought to search.

Rather than risk injury to my back attempting to lift the heavy machine – sciatica having been a reoccurring issue for as long as I could remember – I fetched a hanger from the closet to fish out the book. I flipped through its pages, expecting to find an explanation between the leaves. How had it got there? I imagined one of the intruders holding it like I was, turning the pages, shaking it upside down, reading my nightmares and wondering what was wrong with me. I imagined them realising it was a dream journal. Maybe they'd learnt about them from their own therapist, but they didn't believe in the exercise. In fact, they loathed the new age, touchy-feely, snake-oily, Gwyneth Paltrow-esque quality of it all, so they'd decided to save me, whose home they were in the process of invading, by hiding the bullshit journal where I wouldn't find it. It was a colourfully imaginative explanation; the alternative was that they'd flipped through it, found it uninteresting, flung it to the ground and, in their haste to beat it before I returned, unknowingly kicked it under the treadmill as they left.

I took the journal with me and climbed back into bed. I suddenly felt like revisiting my own nightmares. As I settled down to begin, I remembered that I'd gone to sleep excited about something. What was it? I scanned my room, trying to figure it out, and then it came back to me.

I'd had an epiphany the night before – not a solution, but a theory about how Roger had died. I had to test it, but first, I needed to join the dots. I couldn't get out of bed quickly enough.

Still naked as the day I was born, I hurried to my consultation room and hunted for some whiteboard markers in the drawer that held my supplies. They weren't there. The cleaner, I surmised. Not knowing where I normally kept them, she must have found a different home for them. I looked around to try to figure out where she'd most likely felt was the right place for them, then hurriedly went through each drawer and each cabinet, searching for the darn things. My body thought there was a real danger of losing my sudden insight if I didn't write it down in time.

I finally found the pens and picked out a blue marker. I wrote 'Roger' on the whiteboard and circled it. Around his name, I wrote 'D'Don', 'Accuser', 'Killer 1' and 'Killer 2' and circled them as well.

I stood back and looked at the board. How were they all related? Choosing a red marker, I used it to draw lines from the pastor and the accuser to Roger, writing 'Church investigation' against each line. Next, I got a green marker and added a fifth name to the board: 'Widow'. I stopped to think, then I added 'Me'.

Moving carefully, I plotted out my thoughts. I drew a red line from widow to myself and wrote against it: 'Said Roger called me the day he saw the pastor.'

I added a line from Roger to me: 'Made an appointment after he saw the pastor on TV.'

I added two lines from Roger to each of Killer 1 and

Killer 2, and I labelled both, 'Killed Roger on the morning of the appointment.'

The picture was crude, but it was coherent. Roger hadn't just been afraid – he'd been preparing to talk. It was all in the timing. He saw the pastor on the TV, contacted me almost immediately, and was dead on the tracks within hours. That wasn't coincidence. It was containment. Someone had wanted him silenced, cleanly and permanently.

I stood back and looked at the whiteboard. A rush of adrenaline flooded my chest, priming me for action. I knew that if I stopped to think about it, I would realise it was probably a bad idea, but still, I went to the dining table where I'd left my laptop the night before, and I fired the new computer up.

I clicked through the open tabs until I landed on the church's website and searched for the contact page. I was looking for an email address. There was one listed, but beneath it there was something even better. 'Call Pastor D'Don on . . .'

Stop, Bobby. Think.

If D'Don was involved, then calling him was indeed a bad idea. He had an army of mesmerised, brainwashed followers, as evidenced by their social media posts. A cult, really. Would they do his bidding if he convinced them that it was the will of God? Would they push a man in the face of an approaching train? I had no doubt about it. All through history, religious people have always done crazy things because a man told them to do it in the name of God. He also had a thriving church. To me that meant money – lots of it. With enough cash, anything is for sale. I'm sure you can order a hitman off the dark web. Or hitwoman, for that matter. Pastor Dolapo Daniel D'Don was a dangerous man.

But the last thing he'd expect is to be contacted by someone who knew just enough to be dangerous. I wasn't after a confession; I just wanted to know the man behind the BS.

I went to fetch my mobile and returned to read the number. Taking a series of deep breaths to steady my racing heart, I keyed it in and hit dial. After several rings, I got through to a voicemail message, which was just as well because, in my excitement, I hadn't yet thought of what to say if the pastor answered the call himself. I listened to the recorded message: 'I must be busy, or else we would be talking right now. Leave a message when you hear the beep, or don't. It's up to you.'

I ended the call and checked the number I'd dialled against the one on the website. It had seemed strange that his phone number was on the website, but surely that couldn't be his voicemail greeting. I called again, and after the call rang out, I listened to the same recording.

This time, still suspecting that the website had the wrong mobile number, I left a message: 'Hi. My name is Bobby. Bobby Fatokun. I'm a coach. A business and personal coach. I was working with . . .'

I almost blew it. I almost said Roger's name. I didn't know what fake name he'd used when he was undercover at the church, and there was no way I could find out. I hadn't thought of that.

Half panicking, half relieved that I'd caught myself, I continued: 'What I meant to say is that I believe you dismissed a client of mine from his job as a security manager at your church. This happened about a year ago. He recently passed away, and I was wondering if I could talk to you about him. Please give me a call. I hope to hear back from you soon. Have a good day.'

55

Naomi was waiting for me in front of the hobby store I'd found through a quick web search. She extended her arms, and we kissed and hugged outside the shop. The day before had not been a fluke. I was in a relationship with a woman who blew my mind in every way. My heart turned mushy – warm, joyful, giddy, youthful, energetic and just plain mushy.

'Are you going to tell me what this is about?' Naomi asked, holding my elbows and leaning back to look into my eyes.

'Trust me,' I said. We held hands as we walked inside.

After leaving a voicemail on what I hoped was truly the pastor's phone, I'd spent a considerable amount of time researching CCTV frame rates and figuring out how I could replicate the effect using my phone. Then I'd searched for a hobby shop that had what I wanted. I'd called Naomi because I needed help testing out my theory. If I was right, she would get a story out of it – so long as she treated me as an anonymous source. If I was wrong, I would have got to talk to her before our date without making a pointless call. It was juvenile, it was childish, but I couldn't get her off my mind, and frankly, I didn't want to.

After I'd bought what I'd come for, we took a taxi back to my place, where she looked around and made a joke: 'Did you do something different?'

I liked that she had a sense of humour. I also liked that she'd humoured me enough to agree to meet when I'd called and told her I might have discovered something about the CCTV footage. I'd expected her to remind me of my hyperfixation, but she hadn't. Perhaps she also wanted to see me before our date. The thought made me feel all warm and giddy inside again.

Setting the paper bag from the hobby store on my dining table, I removed the spool of nylon monofilament fishing line I'd bought and laid it on the smooth surface. Her eyes followed my every movement.

'One second,' I said, and I dashed to my office. I returned with scissors.

'Bobby?'

I remembered how much I liked the way she said my name.

'Yes?'

'Are you okay?'

I knew what was coming next.

'I'm not losing it,' I said, and gave what I hoped was a reassuring smile.

'You said this is about the CCTV.'

'Yes.'

'Are you back to thinking he was killed?'

I heard the concern in her voice. I so wanted to tell her I was sure and explain how they'd done it, but I thought it was better she saw it herself, so I simply said, 'Just trust me.'

She picked up the coil of fishing line and looked at it as if studying a piece of forensic evidence. And that was what it was – evidence. *If* I could prove what had happened.

Suddenly her eyes lit up. 'Oh, I see it,' she said. 'You think that's how they did it?'

'There's only one way to find out,' I replied.

I'd got the idea from the art installations hanging from the ceiling of the waiting area of the Burrell Street Sexual Health Centre as if suspended in mid-air. Mobiles. That was the word the shopkeeper used when I described them. Of course, it remained to be seen if it would work.

First, I cut about two metres of the nylon line, gave her one end to hold and wrapped the other end around my fist. The super-thin line was extremely slippery and difficult to hold on to, and I began to doubt my theory.

Next, I pulled out a dining chair and stood it between us. The line sagged where it rested against the legs of the chair, each of us holding one end low at our inner side. We looked at each other to know when to turn. I nodded, and we both turned outwards as if to look back behind us, tightening the nylon filament. The chair moved forward on the wooden floor. Excitement flooded my body. I was right.

'But do you think it's enough to make a man fall?' Naomi asked. She tilted the chair to consider its weight. She had a point.

I took her end of the line and tried to tie it to the leg of the dining table. It felt like an impossible task. While I fumbled with it, she unrolled a much longer length and cut it off. Nudging me to step aside, she passed the line around one of the table legs, holding the two ends in her hand.

'But we need two people turning at the same time,' I said.

She ignored me. Holding my arm to position me between herself and the table, she rolled up the two ends in her hand, bringing the line up the table leg as she did so. The transparent line sagged against the back of my legs, just beneath my knees. She began to turn away, and I felt the tension behind my legs. She turned further, and I buckled at the knees and had to take a step forward, raising my hands for balance as I did so. Just like Russell had described Roger doing in the video. Had I been standing on the edge of a train platform, and had it not been expected, I could have ended up on the tracks. Naomi gave me the ends of the line and swapped places with me. When she was well positioned, I began to turn away. I paused when I felt her weight on the line.

'Are you ready?' I asked.

She nodded. I turned all the way, and like me, she bent at the knees and stepped forward to keep from falling.

'The line won't be visible on the CCTV,' I said. 'I'm guessing there were more than two people involved. Two men to trip him, and more people behind them so no one would see what they did.'

'Well, I do agree it's a possibility,' Naomi replied. She took the line from me and examined it as she went to sit in the Egg Chair. I perched on the edge of the sofa to be as close to her as possible. 'But it's just a possibility,' she went on, still inspecting the nylon. 'We can't know for sure unless we watch the footage.'

I noticed she had said 'we'.

'We'll never get to see it,' I said.

'Well, we might not need to watch it,' she said. Her eyes rolled up from studying the line in her hand. 'The police didn't know what to look for when they did.'

I hadn't thought of what to do with the discovery, but going to the police with it was not an option. It had occurred to me that D'Don might have an informant in the Met, given the speed with which Roger was killed and the timing of the attacks on me. Or maybe the operation itself had required resources far beyond one man and one church. Or maybe I was just being paranoid. Or maybe I wasn't.

'For such a complicated operation as the one I'm proposing,' I said, 'a lot of resources would have been needed. I can only think of a few organisations with the means to carry out something like that. Or the reach.'

Naomi paused as the implication sank in.

'You think the police did it?'

I shrugged.

'But – isn't this all a lot of trouble just to kill one person?'

'Not if they wanted it to look like a suicide to discredit him,' I said. 'And for it to be public. They had to move fast. They knew he was meeting with me, and they couldn't let that happen.'

'Why was he meeting with you?'

I hadn't revealed anything about Roger to her other than that he was my client. I chose to keep it that way.

'He said he wanted talk.'

She studied me for a moment, then nodded.

'So, who wanted him dead?'

'I have no idea.'

I had my suspicions, but I really didn't know for sure. If I were a betting man, I would place my money on the pastor he'd been investigating. My theory was that Roger had discovered something while on his undercover mission. Something he had used as leverage. It had always bothered me that there was no explanation for why the woman had withdrawn her statement.

'So,' Naomi said, 'what now?'

'This is a long shot, but as a journalist, can you request to see the CCTV footage?'

Before she could answer, my phone rang. I gasped when I looked at the screen. I recognised the mobile number I'd called and left a message on.

'I need to take this,' I said. I went to my consultation room with the ringing phone in my hand.

'Hello?'

I braced myself to hear his voice.

'Hi. This is Tashique Warner of WAITRN Church. I'm an associate of Pastor D'Don. You called him about an appointment?'

The young woman. I sat on the edge of my desk. The whiteboard was right in front of me.

'Hi,' I said.

'Did you still want to meet with the pastor?' she asked.

Of course I did. 'Yes, please.'

'That's fine.' Tashique's voice was brisk. 'He asked me to arrange a meeting with you tomorrow.'

'Tomorrow?'

'Yes. He's able to free up his calendar to see you tomorrow afternoon, or you'll have to wait for a month to get another appointment. What time works best for you?'

'Can I get back to you?' I asked. She said yes.

I placed the phone down on my desk and continued to stare at my thoughts from earlier in the morning still scribbled on the whiteboard. I got up, fetched the magnetic duster from the base and wiped the board clean.

56

'Why did you leave the police force?' Naomi asked.

It was late that evening, and after the cosiness of Demon, Wise & Partners, we'd strolled over to Fortnum & Mason at the Royal Exchange and caught the final performance of an all-female jazz quartet. After another round of cocktails, she'd suggested ordering Nigerian takeout to her place in Fulham. We got jollof rice, fried plantains and fried beef stew for me, as well as egusi with goat meat and pounded yam for her. I warned her that the egusi might be a little bit too hot for her, but she told me that it wasn't her first rodeo. We ended up sharing both meals and a bottle of South African Cabernet Sauvignon that tasted of sunshine and happiness.

She had wall-to-wall shelves of records she'd inherited from her father, a famous DJ in the eighties. While I had my back to her as I inspected the collection, I heard the distinctive crackling of a needle touching vinyl, followed by the unmistakable and evocative intro of Fela Kuti's 'Trouble Sleep Yanga Wake Am'. I turned around. She took my wine goblet, placed it on a stool and then took my hands.

After dancing, we ended up in her bedroom, on her soft sheets. The pillows smelled of her perfume. She rested her head on my chest. The lights were off. The record had long since ended. We just lay there, bathed in the light of the full moon pouring in through the large bay window, and had the getting-to-know-each-other talk.

She said, 'He spent his life trying to make me not like her, and she spent her life trying to make me exactly like her. I became more like him.'

I said, 'Pink and baby blue. I discovered that when I brought my shirts home from the dry cleaners, they had arranged them according to colour. Half of them were blue, and the other half were pink.'

She said, 'Kokrobite. It's a small fishing town in Ghana. It's got a largc Rasta community. It'll bc an off-grid mid-century-type house overlooking the Atlantic.'

I said, 'An artist. When I was younger, I was actually good at it. Oil pastel. But I haven't painted in years. Wow. Since we left Nigeria, really.'

She said, 'When we do sports in school, what they're really doing is conditioning us not to work together. Because our cooperation brings success for us but not for them, they teach us to compete instead.'

I said, 'I've always felt that we abandoned him. He was buried there, and we fled here.'

Then she asked, 'Are you going to tell me why you left the Nigerian police?'

How could I explain that being a Nigerian police officer

was an extreme sport? It was a long story – one that I hadn't thought about, let alone talked to anyone about, in a long time. There was just too much trauma there. Where would I even start? Getting abducted on my very first day on the job? And not for ransom. Finding out I wasn't going to be paid what I was promised? So much happened in the few years I spent on the force that the memories resurfaced in sharp focus, as if I were witnessing a reenactment of someone else's life.

The Nigerian police force were hiring Nigerian cybercrime experts from universities over here. I'd just finished a master's degree in IT during a recession, and my thesis was on cybercrime, so I applied – much to my mother's chagrin.

Sadly, the scheme that got me employed did not survive the minister who introduced it, and it had been scrapped even before I landed in Nigeria. Despite this, I stayed, and with time, I realised that I quite enjoyed police work. Until I didn't.

The pay was bad. Really bad. If it had been all I'd had to live on, I wouldn't have survived. I'd realised then why some of my fellow officers extorted civilians. There was no guarantee of being paid at the end of the month, either. I can count on one hand the number of times my salary arrived in my bank account on time. There were moments when I questioned myself. What was I doing chasing criminals in Lagos while my mates were earning contractor day rates in London?

I didn't really need the money. My father had left more than enough for us. After his arrest, most of his assets in

Nigeria had been stolen. I thought I might be able to use my position as a police officer to try to get them back. It was a long shot, but I was young and it was worth the adventure. Or so I thought.

At one point, I was working on a project to digitise old paper records. That was when I stumbled on something that seemed impossible at first. The more I dug, the more I understood what I was looking at, and I became terrified. If I was right, I had detected a criminal conspiracy that stretched from the streets of Lagos to Aso Rock – the very seat of power. What I'd found was a violent, bloody trail that spared no one it touched. I began gathering the evidence.

Not long after, someone must have got wind of what I was up to. 'Orders from above' led to my boss's abrupt redeployment. He was a brilliant officer and my mentor. They replaced him with a tall, former national women's heavyweight lifting champion. They called her the Iron Lady. She arrived at the station asking questions about the 'sensitive files' I had been accessing.

I hadn't known my boss had been replaced. I turned up at work one morning to find press crews waiting outside. Inside, the Iron Lady was walking down the hallway with a throng of officers behind her. She looked at me and said, 'You must be the computer whiz-kid from overseas. Follow me. I will show you real police work.'

By the time we got outside, bare-chested, chained and handcuffed suspects were kneeling in front of an array of shotguns, cartridges, machetes and phones, all neatly arranged on the ground. She stood behind a podium that hadn't been there when I'd arrived and spoke into the microphones, declaring that, unlike her predecessor, the criminals terrorising the city would no longer enjoy an easy ride. She pointed to one of the suspects, a boy with scars on his exposed torso. 'Look at this one,' she said. I don't think he can be more than thirteen or fourteen. He's probably still a virgin, and he's already in a gang.'

The boy mumbled, 'I'm not a virgin,' and the press crew laughed. I laughed too. The Iron Lady's eyes darted to me. I'm sure the cameras captured her glare.

After the show, she dressed me down in front of everybody. From then on, she was on my case. She reassigned me away from the digitisation project and put me on raids. At first, I thought it was because I'd laughed, but then she began asking specific questions about the documents I had retrieved. That was when I knew it was about what I'd discovered. I felt marked.

She assigned me to a rapid response unit on the same day that a tip came in about a planned robbery. Something felt wrong, so I spoke to my former boss. An order from above sent me to Abuja immediately. The Iron Lady was furious. The raid that evening claimed the lives of every officer involved. She had me arrested as a suspect, claiming I'd tipped off the gang.

My former boss stood up for me. There was no evidence against me, but suspicion has a way of lingering. My colleagues knew only that there had been a tip-off, that I had been meant to be part of the team, and that the men had faced an ambush. I had to resign. Nigeria was no longer safe for me.

Remembering that period of my life was both harrowing and terrifying. It was the second time in my life that I'd felt helpless and hunted; the first was when my mother, my sister and I had climbed over our neighbour's fence to escape the soldiers who were coming to get us after my father's arrest.

I told Naomi everything. Once I finished, we lay quietly together. Scenes from the period scrolled through my mind as I stared up at the ceiling. After a while, she propped herself up on one elbow.

'I'm so sorry,' she said.

'What for?' I asked, my eyes close to tears from remembering my father.

'For saying what I said – for saying you'd been convicted. I only said it to make you stay. If I'd known this . . .'

'It's fine,' I said. But it wasn't. It had never been fine. I had never sought help.

57

'Remember I told you a time would come when you would have to protect her?' D'Don said.

The pastor was sitting in his chair. Kenny was across from him, noticing the familiar faces in the picture frames that lined that wall of the study behind D'Don. There was a new photograph of the three of them. Tashique had taken it selfie-style during the reception at Buckingham Palace. It was the first time he'd seen it.

'The time has come for you to do that,' the pastor continued. 'I need you to listen carefully and do exactly as I say. Do you understand?'

'Yes,' Kenny said, his eyes drifting back to the photograph.

He remembered too well. Every time he recalled the conversation, a flicker of panic returned at how close he came to losing it all that day.

D'Don stood up and walked to the window, unhurried, as if the outcome of the conversation was already decided.

'You are a gifted man,' he said, his back to Kenny. 'You

have the special power of perception.' He turned around. 'Do you know what that means?'

Kenny shook his head.

'You sense things. You feel it in here.' He patted his chest. 'You know what other people don't know. You see what other people don't see. It's your gift, and like all other gifts, it will take time to perfect it. In time, you will start to see visions as clear as day, and you won't need me to guide you or explain things to you. You are far more gifted in that area than I am or could ever possibly dream to be – just wait and see. For now, I still have to be your spiritual guide.

'Kenny, what I am about to tell you is something I should have told you from the start, but I had faith that you would come to know it yourself through your gift. This is why I did not tell you before. But now, at this very moment, principalities and powers have gathered in fear of your growing power and your imminent glory. They are fearful of you because they know I have become your mentor and protector as you learn to walk into your power. They are afraid of what you will become, so they have gathered to conspire against us, and I am afraid we are running out of time. That is why I am going to tell you what you have been chosen to do, and you just have to trust me, and do as I say. Do you understand? Will you trust me and do as I tell you to do?'

Tashique was at the cooker when Kenny opened the kitchen door. She was dressed in a colourful boubou he hadn't seen before and the smell of jollof rice filled the room. She turned around and he saw she was holding a wooden spoon in her hand.

'Hey, you,' she said. She licked her palm to taste the bit of food she had put on it to cool.

'You're making jollof rice,' Kenny said. His stomach was already responding to the sweet aroma, and his mouth was wet with anticipation.

'I wanted to surprise you, darling,' she said. 'You told me it was your favourite, so I looked up the recipe. Do you want to taste it?'

She scooped up a bit of the rice cooking in tomato sauce and blew on it. She held the spoon up to him, and he ate the grains steamed in spicy tomato sauce.

'Any good?' she asked.

'Mmm. It tastes just like party jollof rice,' he said.

'You liar. The recipe says I still need to burn the bottom when it's done. That's how you make party jollof.'

'I don't lie,' he said.

Tashique refitted the piece of foil over the pot and then placed the lid back on it. She set the spoon down, looked at him, and the smile faded from her face.

'D'Don talked to you,' she said.

Kenny nodded.

'He told you why you're here?'

He nodded again.

'And?'

'And what?'

'Are you going to do it or not?'

'Yes. I will.'

'So, why did you say, "I don't lie"?'

'I was talking about the jollof rice.'

Tashique's voice rose in frustration. 'But you lied. Kenny, I need you to look into my eyes now and tell me you've got my back.'

'You know I'll do anything for you.'

'I need you to say it.'

'Say what?'

'"I've got your back." Say it.'

'Okay. I've got your back.'

They stared at each other.

'Okay,' she said. 'Okay. That's all I needed to hear.' She turned back to the cooker and lifted the lid from the pot again.

'What really happened?' Kenny asked.

'Jesus fucking Christ.' She slammed the lid back down and turned around. 'What? What do you want me to tell you? What don't you already know? Tell me. What?'

'I'm sorry, I just . . .'

'What? You're supposed to know everything, aren't you? You just want to hear me tell you how he raped me, correct? How he forced himself on me. How he told me nobody would believe me if I said anything. How he threatened me. Yes? You probably also want to know if he came inside me, don't you? If it hurt? If I enjoyed it? What, Kenny, what? What do you want to know that you don't already know? What?'

She was furious even as her eyes welled up.

'I'm sorry,' he repeated.

'For what?'

'I'm just . . . I'm sorry I asked.'

She turned back to the cooker. 'I think you should leave me alone now,' she said.

He stayed and stared at her.

'Tashique?'

'Fucking go away.'

She picked up the wooden spoon and turned and flung it at him.

He did not flinch. The spoon flew past him and struck the door, leaving a smudge of tomato sauce before it hit the ground with a thunk. He waited a few seconds as they watched each other, then turned and left without another word.

58

'Is it okay here?' my driver asked, one hand briefly adjusting her hijab as she checked the mirrors.

She was only my second female Uber driver. We had talked about London's speed camera infestation on the crawl south through council estates and half-finished developments, and I had also learnt that she was writing a cookbook on Somali cuisine. I'd promised her I would buy it when it came out, and I meant it, but in the way people mean to keep the fleeting promises they make in fleeting moments.

I looked out of the window and opened up my messaging app to check that I'd given her the correct address. She had brought me to an industrial estate and stopped just after the gate leading into a compound surrounded by a tall concrete wall. CCTV cameras looked out onto the road. I got out, bade my new friend goodbye, pressed the call button on a dusty aluminium panel and brought my ear to the speaker.

I heard a buzz, then a noisy electric motor, and then the gate began to retract. I waited until it was fully open and I could see what was inside before stepping into the cement-floored compound. A large white industrial-style building sat at the back. It was almost as wide as the width of the plot and about a dozen cars were parked along the front, among them a Bentley coupé I'd seen on the church's website.

I had researched the youth centre before booking my ride. It was only the latest in a string of similar projects the church was carrying out, and it reeked of money laundering. Maybe it was conclusive evidence of that which Roger had been after, and potentially had found.

There were cameras everywhere, and I felt I was being watched as I walked across the compound. The door opened just before I got to it, and there was the man himself – Pastor Dolapo Daniel D'Don. He was waiting with the practised smile he had perfected for the cameras; I recognised the superfluousness of it from his pictures, and now that I was experiencing it close up, it came across as patronising.

He was shorter than I'd expected and wearing a white round-neck linen shirt tucked into white trousers. He held out his hand to me. A gold chain dangled from his wrist.

'Mr Fatokun,' he said. He went for a grip and pulled me into a shoulder bump. 'Ẹbí mi.'

I noted the attempt at camaraderie by saluting me in Yoruba. Declaring me family. If he wasn't guilty of something, why was he opening by trying to draw me in?

'I'm sorry I made you come all the way here,' he said, still holding my hand as I stepped through the door. 'I had to come and oversee something. This facility we are building is going to cater to up to a hundred athletes at a time. They will train here, get their sports physio here, everything. We also have facilities for them to stay over if needed. We already have a few residents. Do you want a tour? My associate said you have another important engagement later today. We can walk and talk?'

I had mentioned an appointment, but I had not used the word important. It was clever what he did there, referring to my appointment as 'another important engagement'. Suggesting that he considered our meeting to be important, but to whom? Me or him?

As we walked, he kept talking about the facility and the gifted but impoverished young athletes who would excel there. He walked half a step ahead of me, never looking back, as if assuming I would follow. It sounded like a well-rehearsed spiel that voice recorder-wielding journalists would have been grateful for, but to me, it felt like filibustering.

'This is the gym,' he said, stopping in front of a door at the end of a wide corridor. He pushed it open, and I heard the sound of people working out. He waited for me to step inside.

Beyond the door, the gym was a brightly lit, double-height space, larger and much better equipped than the gym I sometimes went to. All the equipment was new, and the space smelled of rubber and machine oil. Lighting units, aluminium piping and cooling vents hung from the freshly painted ceiling.

I had to scan the space twice to confirm what I was seeing. It was full of kids. Teenagers. Fourteen- to eighteen-year-olds, I estimated, and not one adult in sight. Just kids working out and kids helping other kids with their workouts. And they were ripped. All of them. As in, super-ripped. There was something disconcerting about seeing so many barely pubescent kids looking so ripped. I wondered if steroids had a hand in it. The floor spaces between the workout benches and equipment were littered with their gadgets. Tablets, GoPros, wireless speakers, phones and tripods – everywhere I looked, people were filming themselves, posing for pictures or looking in mirrors and flexing their muscles. It was as if they couldn't get enough of looking at their own bodies or recording them.

'These are the star athletes of tomorrow,' Pastor D'Don said. 'They have all been chosen for their talents. Do you know what your talent is, Mr Fatokun?'

'What?' I started.

'You must be gifted at something. God has invested a piece of talent in all of us. Some people go on to realise the full potential of that which has been planted in them, while others go through life unaware of the extraordinary gifts that they carry about unused. Still others squander their gifts. What is your gift?'

Calling bullshit, I wanted to say, but I was in his house, and there's that thing about being in someone's house.

'I once prayed over a dead chicken, and it came back to life,' I said, deadpan, and fighting the fight of my life not to let as much as a chuckle slip.

The story was true. When I was a child, I bonded with a chicken gifted to my parents as a Christmas gift by a neighbouring Muslim family, the Ibrahims. When I overcame my fear of its flapping wings by feeding it corn with the assistance of my father, who held my palm open, the bird and I became friends. One morning, after I'd fulfilled my morning obligation of finishing all of my breakfast while being supervised by Aunty Iyabo, the maid, I escaped to the backyard to find my friend, Mr Jimmy, but he was dead. I found the poor thing unresponsive in the raffia cage he had arrived in. I kept calling his name and gently prodding him with a finger, and I eventually broke into a wail that informed Aunty Iyabo of my whereabouts. She was quick to come and see what trouble I was about to get her into. On seeing the sleeping bird, she told me to close my eyes, pray and lay my hand on Mr Jimmy. I did as she directed, and to my shock, it worked! I had God's magic in my hands. That was until my father heard the story from his chuckling wife, and he, the very first atheist in my life (even though he went to church for appearances' sake while preaching science at home), sat me down and explained how chickens sleep and how prayer-mongering men and women steal in the name of God.

It was the first time I'd remembered the story in decades. The pastor didn't bother asking me to explain my avian miracle. He smiled a dismissive smile that would have been offensive had I not thrown the first jab, then he thrust his hand into his pocket. Looking at the phone that he'd retrieved, he asked me to excuse him for a moment, and he left me standing there alone in the high-octane gym.

A few of the kids had given me a once-over. A girl had even nodded. No smile, just a nod. Not even a committed one. A half nod. Or maybe it was a tic she had. I couldn't get over just how fantastically ripped they all were. Their muscle growth had to be chemically enhanced.

After a minute or so, as I was shuffling awkwardly, unsure what to do, the door opened behind me again and the pastor stepped back in, his brow creased and his phone gripped tight in his right hand.

'What time is your next appointment?' he asked.

I looked at my watch. I'd given myself one and a half hours to get to him, one hour to see him (because I could be made to wait my turn) and another hour and a half to get back to mine in time for my three o'clock client session. I was still in the ballpark of being safe.

He continued talking before I could answer. He'd never cared for my response. I got ready for the shake-off. Why had he made me come all the way? Perhaps to sum me up.

'There's a crisis in my home,' he said. 'I'm sorry, but I have to go now. Will you make another appointment?'

And there it was. The lady with a phone voice as beautiful as her pictures had warned me that if I didn't take this slot, I would have to wait a month for another chance to see the great and important man of God. What a scam.

The pastor watched me ponder my options. Fob me off once, shame on me; fob me off twice, that's my bad. There was no point in making another appointment. He had got what he'd wanted. He had set eyes on me. He now knew what the person coming for him looked like. But then he startled me.

'You can come with me if you like,' he said. 'We can talk in the car. I really have to go and deal with this crisis.'

I hadn't been expecting that. Quickly getting over the surprise, I noticed that he had used the word 'crisis' twice. He could have said he had an emergency at home, but he'd chosen the word 'crisis'. An emergency is a gas leak or a washing machine spilling its water, but crises conjure images of people breaking down and damaging stuff.

Pastor D'Don's Wikipedia page hadn't mentioned a partner or children, and one blogger had also made the bold claim that he was among the top ten sexiest single pastors in the world, so he was apparently unattached. I wondered who had called about the crisis at home.

Even at that moment, I felt the stirring touch of suspicion brush against me. It could be bait, but he'd had me at 'crisis'. I needed to know what was going on at his home. And I wanted to see it, wherever it was. Also, I had come to him to talk about Roger, and we hadn't done that.

We'd been making our way back outside as I considered his suggestion, and it was as if the sun had melted away the clouds behind which it had been hidden. The Bentley coupé gleamed with opulence. I couldn't be sure which I was more excited about: finding out what the evasive pastor had to do with Roger's murder, witnessing the sudden crisis at his home, or getting to ride in an uber-expensive, uber-luxurious sportscar for the first time in my life.

'Sure,' I said, trying to sound as nonchalant as possible. 'I'll come with you.'

59

I sat in the sumptuousness of the pastor's supercar, and it didn't bother me at all that he could see me turning my head round and round to take it all in.

'Nice car,' I said.

'It's the new Continental GT,' he educated me. 'Would you like one?'

I grinned at him. I didn't know what to make of his straight face.

'Above my pay grade,' I said.

'That was not what I asked you.'

I knew right then that mind games were his strategy. I sidestepped his challenge with, 'How long did he work for you?'

I still didn't know Roger's undercover name. With any luck, the pastor would let it slip, and he wouldn't even realise he'd done it.

He was concentrating on his driving as we left the compound, so I gave him time. But as we navigated the streets of the industrial estate, he still kept his eyes on the road. He was pretending I'd never asked the question.

'I asked how long he worked for you,' I said.

I watched for his reaction. Nothing. He just kept looking straight ahead. I felt a slight unease. I'd quickly got over the novelty of riding in a Bentley Continental GT and was now fully focused on him. If I had to ask a third time and he still remained silent, I might have to jump out of the moving vehicle. He knew my name and who I was. That had been a calculated risk on my part, but now I was beginning to question the accuracy of my calculations. Just to be sure, I tested him.

'I was asking—'

'What is the Body of Christ?' he asked, his voice calm and steady, ignoring the fact that he'd just cut me off.

My scalp tingled with alertness. It was not as if we'd started talking at the same time. No. He'd waited until I started to say something, then he'd spoken. The silence, the timing – it was deliberate. He was onto me. Was I being kidnapped?

My heart leapt into action, pumping oxygenated blood to where it was most needed. My fight-or-flight response had kicked in.

'What?' I asked.

He kept his eyes on the road as he spoke.

'Is it the members of the church? Who is a member of a church? A person who comes to it? And what is a church? A building? A place of worship? "Where two or three are gathered in my name, there I am." So, then, what is the Body of Christ? What does it mean to be saved? Saved from what?'

If I thought that a client was actively avoiding my

questions, I would call it out. I would say something like, 'I notice that you did not answer the last three questions I've asked you. I wonder if you meant to, or perhaps you are not aware you are doing it.' But the pastor was not a client, and there was no doubt in my mind that he was aware of what he was doing. And he knew I was aware of it too. What had I been thinking when I'd agreed to go with him to his house? I also questioned the risk assessment I'd carried out when I'd booked an Uber to take me to him in the first place. Could I be the crisis he had at home? This trip felt like a meaty piece of bait that I'd sunk my teeth into, fully aware that it was bait and yet unable to resist the hook.

I cut in with, 'You're avoiding my question.'

'On the contrary,' he said, not missing a beat, his eyes still steady on the road. 'Sometimes we ask the wrong questions. All the answers you seek are waiting for you when we get to the house.'

I felt myself being reeled back in. I'd been watching out for slow traffic so I could open the door and just walk away. Now I wasn't so certain that was what I wanted. Sure enough, the chance came only once, and I didn't take it. The rest of the ride was on motorways and winding country roads. Now my heart was working double time, partly from fear and partly from excitement at what I could discover at his house.

It turned out to be a mansion in Hertfordshire. A beautiful, huge mansion that was no doubt paid for by his gullible followers, who also probably paid for the car and who, from my experience, would boast to their Christian friends from other churches about their pastor's big car and big house – the conclusive evidence of his being called into ministry by God himself.

I was in the wrong profession. My day rate would never compare to a congregation of tens of thousands of people willingly handing over ten per cent of their income every month to a person who claimed to be their hope of salvation in heaven and largesse here on earth. And should either fail to happen, there would be no comeuppance for the pastor: in the one instance, his followers would be dead, and that would be that; and in the other, it would be their own lack of faith that had cheated them of their cure, made them fail their job interview, or separated them from the source of their blessings. A good scam. A perfect con. I wondered how much the mortgage for a house that big was. Perhaps I'd ask him. He would probably see the snare behind the question. He would have heard the accusation in it too.

Just as he had opened the door at the youth centre before I'd got close enough to open it myself, a young man opened the front door of the house before we got to it. He stood aside for the pastor and me to enter. I noticed that he did not look at me. As he turned around after shutting the door, I extended my hand to him.

'Hi, I'm Bobby,' I said. 'Bobby Fatokun.' My face was full of smiles.

The lad looked at my hand, and then he looked at the pastor. I understood that this wasn't in the script. I couldn't wait to learn what was going on here and what it had to do with me and Roger. I was nearing one hundred per cent convinced now that the so-called crisis had something to do with my turning up. Why else would Pastor D'Don have invited me to his home?

I was also aware of my elevated heart rate and of the effects of adrenaline on my system. My body had experienced my alarm in the car as if I were definitely walking into a kill mob. On an intellectual level, I'd not even thought about what I feared would happen. I began to calm down now that I was in the house.

The young man finally shook hands with me but failed to tell me his name. I held on when he thought the handshake was over, and I noticed the panic in his face. I continued to beam at him.

'And you are?' I asked.

Once again, he looked at the pastor, who then answered for him.

'His name is Kenny. He lives here with his girlfriend. Shall we go into my study, please?'

I was having fun making Kenny feel uncomfortable with whatever he'd been conscripted into. I held on to his hand, and I kept freaking him out with the smile on my face. I was sure I was freaking him out from the way he'd look down, then look back up to see me still grinning, and then look down again.

Okay, Bobby. That's enough now.

I let go of the teenager and went with the pastor to his study. I should have expected the assault of framed photos. He and an array of famous people, all staring down at me in multitudes from the walls. There was also a selfie of him, the young woman and the boy at some function.

I sat in one of the chairs at the mahogany desk while he walked around to his throne. A large window to my right overlooked a vast field with woods at the end of it. I didn't see a fence or any other form of demarcation. The land could belong to the house. Ah! Yes. The Gathering. It could have happened out there. Possibly some fraudulent ploy to get away with listing the mansion as a property of the church, which no doubt was listed as a charity, as all churches are, thus qualifying for charitable organisation rebates.

As soon as my eyes swept back to him, Pastor D'Don launched straight back into his repertoire. He seemed to have forgotten about his crisis. He leant forward in his chair, planted his elbows on the desk, laced his manicured fingers beneath his chin and opened with: 'Leviticus 19:34: "You shall treat the stranger who sojourns with you as the native among you, and you shall love him as yourself, for you were strangers in the land of Egypt; I am the Lord your God."'

No, you're not.

'Even as you and I are strangers in this land, I welcome you into my home, as this land has welcomed us both.'

He continued with his vacuous nonsense, using eloquence to sell bullshit, and I contemplated reminding him of his suddenly not-so-urgent crisis. But that all changed in a moment, when he blindsided me with: 'I have been wondering how long it would be before you turned up seeking answers.'

60

Let the games begin.

'Answers to what?' I asked the man of God.

'To the questions you have,' the charlatan replied.

'What questions do I have?' Are we really doing this?

'I am not a mind reader, Mr Fatokun,' he said. 'But I know a man who is seeking answers when I see one.'

'You do know who I am, right?'

'Oh, no. Not at all. Not in the least. I know your name, yes, and I know what work you do, but the man you are, that I do not know. However, I am confident that I will know you by the end of today.'

The end of today? What had happened to his crisis?

'Have you been following me?' I asked.

The surprise on his face looked genuine.

'Following you? No. Why would I do that? Why would you even ask such a thing? Do you think someone has been following you?'

'Actually, I do.'

'And what would that have to do with me?'

'You tell me.'

His preacher man's effervescence fizzled away, and lines of apprehension creased his brow.

'Mr Fatokun. What was it you wished to discuss with me?'

Did I have him on the ropes? I already knew I would have to bluff everything. I figured that being a pastor, he already had the advantage of practice, but I knew a thing or two about the human psyche that you can only learn from science and not the Bible. It was my turn to mess with his head.

'I know everything,' I said. I let the silence percolate.

He watched me. I maintained my poker face. My search for the truth was made complicated by unknown unknowns, but there was no way he could know that.

He was the first to fold. He sniggered and said, 'What do you know?'

'Everything,' I said. 'Your former security manager told me everything.'

Fingers crossed Roger was the only security manager dismissed from the job.

The pastor paused. 'And what exactly did he tell you?'

I smiled. 'If I told you, I would be breaking client confidentiality, and you could report me and get me deregistered,' I said. A bluff. I was banking on him not knowing how the coaching profession was regulated.

'In other words, you do not know anything,' he said.

'I do. And even though I cannot speak about it, I can still act on what I know. I am here, am I not?'

'Yes, you are. And I am still waiting for you to tell me why you are here.'

'Did you know he died?' I pivoted.

'Yes, the police called me.'

'Why did the police call you?'

Did he know that Roger had been working undercover at his church?

'We had a case against him.'

'But the case was closed,' I said. Hopefully, throwing in something about what I really did know would make him think I knew a lot more than I did.

He shook his head. 'Like I said, you don't know anything. Do you want to know why I know that?'

'Humour me.'

To insist that I knew when he said I didn't would have put the onus on me to prove my knowledge.

'Because he was an errand boy, and even he didn't know everything.'

He said it with a snort of arrogance. Errand boy. What did he mean by that? Maybe he had known that Roger was working undercover after all. But how? He had only fired Roger after the accusation had been made.

The pastor sat silent. He had played his card, waiting for me to show mine. If only he knew how good my waiting game was.

We waited. He folded. Frustration cracked through his calm.

'And you too,' he said, his voice rising, the British inflection wavering under the strain, 'you are less than an errand boy, and you are here trying the same thing he did. I will tell you why he died. I placed a curse on him.' He beat his chest.

'Yes. I placed a curse on him for what he tried to do to me, and God answered me. He ran mad and jumped in front of a train. Look at this.' He stuck his tongue out and pointed to a discoloration in the middle of it. A birthmark.

'This is àṣẹ,' he said. 'You are a Yoruba man; if you don't know what it means, go and find out. I was born with this. Anything I curse here on earth is cursed in heaven.' He pointed at the ground and then at the ceiling. 'Everything I bless here is blessed in heaven.' He skipped the pointing this time. 'I took my clothes off and stood naked in this very room, and I cursed him. The same way I will curse you at midnight today for attempting to blackmail me.'

Blackmail. I knew it. Roger had found something on him and played it as his get-out-of-jail-free card. If the pastor kept talking, he'd give away even more.

I feared that he might see the excitement on my face, correctly read it as me finding out something new and know to make a course correction. I need not have fretted. He had got to his feet and was firmly in the grip of an emotional hijack. He became increasingly animated as he spoke, gesticulating from where he stood behind his desk.

'You want to know what he did before he left this congregation? He raped that boy's girlfriend.'

He pointed at the door, but I understood he meant the young man who had welcomed us to the mansion. Kenny, who wouldn't say his own name.

'He sexually assaulted her, and when the boy confronted him, he said he must forgive him just like Jesus forgives all sinners.'

'Well, mustn't he?'

I promise, I do not know where that came from. I was not in any way condoning what he had done – far be it from me – but I wasn't buying any of the show. The pastor had a narrative he wanted me to hear, and from the way the young man, Kenny, had looked at him when I'd deviated from their script, it was obvious the kid had been recruited into this charade. I wasn't going to get any answers here, just more questions.

The pastor stared at me open-mouthed as if I'd taken all the sins in the Ten Commandments, rolled them all up together into one and committed that single sin of sins.

After a moment, he recovered and marched to the door. I took it to mean that my invitation had been revoked. I got up to leave, not waiting to be told, and I saw him stick his head out and shout at the top of his voice, 'Kenny!'

The young man arrived as if he'd been behind the curtains waiting for his cue. The pastor returned to his chair, and the young man stood close to mine. I sat back down. I wondered when the girl would make an appearance too.

Pastor D'Don asked the young man, 'How is she?'

I looked at the boy. He shook his head. Was he mute?

'You remember Philip?' the pastor continued.

So that was Roger's undercover name. Philip. I committed it to memory.

The young man nodded.

Back and forth, I turned to the examiner and the star witness as they ping-ponged their rehearsed performance.

'This man wants to know what he did to her.'

The young man answered, looking at D'Don. 'He assaulted her.'

'Did you witness it?' I asked, looking up at him. He continued to gaze at the pastor.

'Tell him,' the pastor said. He sat back down.

I watched the boy. He stared straight ahead.

'She told me he was harassing her for sex. On the day it happened, I was away at the gym. When I got back, she told me what had happened. I confronted him the next day, and he did not deny it.'

I waited for him to continue, but that was it. There were so many holes, I didn't know where to start. If only they knew I used to be a police officer.

'That must have been hard for you,' I said.

No reaction.

'Why didn't you believe her when she told you?' I asked, slipping words into his mouth.

That startled him. His eyes shot to me, then just as swiftly, they moved to his director for further instructions.

'I believed her,' he said, sounding unsure. I'd thrown him. I guessed he was ad-libbing now.

'I'm a bit confused,' I said. 'If you believed her, why did you have to ask him?'

The boy was confused. He looked at the pastor, who decided my interrogation was over. He spoke instead.

'Like I said, you do not know anything.'

'I know she withdrew her allegation,' I said.

'Yes, she did. Because she forgave him. As a Christian, it was her duty to do so.'

'And you, did you forgive him too?'

'It was between them.'

'How was he blackmailing you?'

He looked at me as if he had just noticed something about me.

'You really don't know anything, do you?' he said.

I felt the tables turning against me.

I kept quiet. I did not know what I did not know, and I was aware of that. I wasn't going to speak and inadvertently expose something that would let him know he was right.

'Mr Fatokun,' he said, 'not everything is what it seems to be.'

Roger had said the same thing. Maybe not in the same words, but the same thing. Not everything is what it seems to be. What were they both referring to? What bigger or different picture was I still missing? All these thoughts buzzed in my mind while I sat there in the luxurious study. There was more to this than the lie the young man had corroborated. I looked at him. He looked down. He was way too young to be the beautiful young woman's boyfriend.

The pastor's 'errand boy' remark was nagging me.

'Do you know what Philip did for a living?' I asked.

'You may leave now,' the pastor said.

61

My invitation had finally been revoked. I stood up, and the pastor asked me, 'Where are you going?'

It was then that I saw the young man slinking away, probably relieved that his part in the put-on show had ended. I checked the time. I was now eating into my buffer. I sat back down.

'He was your client,' the pastor said. 'You should know what work he did.'

'He worked for you,' I said. 'You should know what he did.'

'My church welcomes over five hundred thousand worshippers and hundreds of workers worldwide every week. You expect me to know everything about all of them?'

His website boasted a million members. Unbeknownst to him, he had answered the real question. It was an interrogation technique of mine. If he did not know why I was asking, he might have asked me why. Instead, he'd distanced himself from the answer. He knew what Roger was. What I still didn't know was how much he knew – whether Roger was a policeman moonlighting at his church, or whether Roger had been working undercover there.

'I lost a client,' I said, 'and he told me some rather troubling things before he died. I was hoping you could shed some light on what he did here before I go to the police.'

I studied him.

'Like I said, you do not know anything. Do you know why Judas betrayed Jesus?'

'For thirty pieces of silver,' I said.

'I see you know your scripture. If Judas betrayed Jesus for money, why then did Jesus say to him, "Go and do what you must do"? Jesus knew he was to be betrayed, and he knew which of his disciples would do it. You see it as mere betrayal; I see it as destiny. Jesus had to die on the cross for you and me. Judas had to do his part for mine and your salvation. Philip was Satan's errand boy. He was destined to work here and do what he did. His sin serves a bigger purpose. Do you think it is by chance that you are here today?'

No, I didn't. I suspected him of murder; that was why I was there. I was there to check out my hunch.

'You know the story of Jonah and the whale?'

I nodded. I noted the return to preacher mode, the effortless switch back to his calm, even voice. Almost hypnotic. A technique. Charisma is one thing – a honed ability to captivate and mesmerise – but the uncanny gift of instant self-regulation was something else entirely. Was he trained for this? Did he take acting classes? Attend a hypnotherapy course? Or did evangelism for profit attract a certain personality type, just as billionaires and most world leaders tend to be megalomaniacs?

'What is your whale, Mr Fatokun? What is your mission? You have to know how to differentiate the two. What brought you here is not the reason you are here. You are meant to be here today. I was meant to see you today.'

Yes. I made an appointment.

'I asked you what your gift is. You are an executive coach. Your website has countless testimonials from those you have helped, but is that your true calling? Are you truly where you should be? Our brothers and sisters don't have the privilege of coaches and therapists. That's an advantage white people have over them. When I listened to the message you left on my phone, I sensed the purpose of the universe moving in me. I knew I had to see you. The instant I laid eyes on you, I knew I was right. You do not know, but since yesterday I have been inspired to pray for you. I asked God what They wanted me to do, and They showed me a vision – a man wandering the earth, unaware of his preeminent purpose in life.'

I guess I was the wanderer in his vision.

'Didn't you just threaten to place a curse on me?' I asked.

He ignored me.

'In my vision, I saw you searching for me online. You thought it was the man you were searching for, but no, it is not. It is not me that you have come here for, but They who sent me. It is They who will lay their hand on you through me today, and you will be saved. Tell me, what did you find out about me? Who do people say I am?'

What was this with the 'They'?

'I saw my own vision too: my Sunday school teacher

reading from the Bible. And Jesus said to the disciples, "Who do people say I am?"'

Come on. This man was sitting there trying to persuade me that God had called him and that it was God's will for me to follow a trail of clues to some country house so a stranger could put his hand on my head, save me, and conscript me into working for him for free. And wasn't this man the same guy who, a moment ago, had been threatening to strip naked to place a curse on me? I wished I'd asked him what nudity had to do with it.

I was watching a first-hand demonstration of how people like him manufactured belief. His vision of me researching him online was no different from a TV psychic fishing in a room full of grief: 'I see an old woman. She's in pain. Her daughter is here today.' A numbers game.

'Your surname – Fatokun – you know what it means, don't you? Your ancestors worshipped Ifá. It was handed down through generations until it reached you. Even without practising it, you have inherited it spiritually. The innocent blood of all the human sacrifices made at the altar of Ifá is part of that inheritance. Tell me – have you found that things seem to work out better for you than for other people? As if by magic?'

I felt insulted. He really thought he could manipulate me like he did his devotees. What had given him the impression that I was as malleable, as gullible as them? If his assessment of me had led him to believe that I would kneel before him and offer the crown of my head to his fraudster hands, then he was not so clever after all. There was no point educating him on Ifá, not least because he'd already pitched his tent in the tabernacle of Christianity.

Everything suddenly fell into place.

Roger was guilty. I had always believed this. He'd found something on the preacher, and he used it to buy his way out. His widow had read it wrong. Seeing the pastor on TV hadn't upset Roger; it was seeing his victim standing beside the pastor that had undone him. Guilt can be a powerful force – at least for those capable of feeling it.

Roger took his own life. The man sitting opposite me was nothing more than a con artist. Like all the rest of them.

With every word he spoke, my anger turned inwards. This man wasn't a mastermind. He was a charlatan. His greatest crime was fleecing his congregation every Sunday or whenever the spirit conveniently moved him. He might even believe his own nonsense.

He was not capable of engineering a perfect murder in open view on a train platform. That theory was mine. All of it. Sitting there, drained of momentum and adrenaline, I could see it clearly. Desperate to absolve myself of guilt over a client's suicide, I'd built an elaborate conspiracy out of scraps.

He really believed he cursed Roger into suicide. He truly believed he could talk me into kneeling before him. Lunatic. A conman drunk on his performance.

And there it was. Roger had killed himself. The fishing line fantasy had never happened. I had created a mountain out of thin air and carried it straight into a stranger's house. This man didn't kill anyone. He sold miracles, not murder.

Damn you, Bobby. Damn you to hell.

I checked the time. I wasn't going to miss my session for this.

Then, as if all the previous madness he had uttered had not been enough, D'Don followed up with: 'Mr Fatokun, you are in imminent danger. There are people you don't know who are plotting to kill you. But Jesus will protect you. He has brought you here to be saved. Kneel down. Please, let me pray for you.'

'I never searched for you online,' I said, straight-faced, and I remained in my chair even though he'd pushed his chair back, already rising, ready to lay his misguided hand on my head.

'Why are you trying to deceive the man of God?' he cried.

I couldn't help myself. I had had enough of his bullshit, and it was time to call it.

'Ẹbí mi.' I said with a snigger, 'come on. It's me you're talking to. What scam are you running here, eh? How much have you made? Let me buy a franchise.'

Eyes blazing, he shot up from his chair, slammed his fists onto his desk, and shouted at the top of his voice, 'I am the world's next superpower!'

62

It was clear I'd definitely overstayed my welcome. I was most definitely not getting a ride back to town in his Bentley.

Just as dramatically as the Hyde in him had burst out, the pastor suddenly shrank back into the calm, metrosexual preacher I'd seen earlier. He slid into his chair and smiled at me, a smile that did nothing to diminish the effect of his earlier eruption. I had seen his anger, and it had scared me. Violent fury had filled every inch of his face in that brief moment, and it was hard to unsee. This man was psychotic. I thought of his followers, of the viral posts I had seen. One returned with alarming clarity: 'I am not afraid to follow you to the end.'

'The knowledge you are seeking has never been sought,' he said. 'I cannot protect you from what you may find. I will pray for you, but you have to pray for yourself as well. I am but a mere messenger. My message to you is to be careful. You do not know what you are looking for. Not everything is what it seems.'

Again, 'not everything is what it seems'. That probably

had to do with the blackmail. Despite myself, I was shaken. What had Roger found? Whatever it was, if he'd stumbled onto something he used to coerce his victim, he probably hadn't reported it to the Met. Roger had got away with his crime, and the pastor had too – or so it felt. Roger had paid with his life, but what had he let the pastor get away with? Financial fraud. Money. That much cash moving every week could cover almost anything.

As much as I wanted to leave and never think of him again, my gut told me to persist.

'Where do you have to be?' D'Don asked, interrupting my thoughts. His voice sounded resigned. Defeated.

'Home,' I said.

'I'll take you,' he offered.

I wasn't expecting that. We stared at each other. Nah. I didn't want to be stuck in a car with this man again. I did not want him to know where I lived.

'Or I'll get you a taxi,' he said.

'Never mind,' I said, already hailing my own ride.

'You have my number,' he said, almost pleading. 'Whenever you are ready to learn God's purpose for your life, I'll be waiting for your call.'

'I'm not going to call you,' I said.

'You will.'

The young man, Kenny, was waiting at the front door. I wondered if he'd been there all along. Like a robot, he opened the door and stood aside. No spirit in his movements. No soul in his demeanour.

'I'll be waiting for your call,' the pastor said again.

I turned to the young man. He still wouldn't meet my

gaze. I stared intently until he finally did, his eyes tentatively connecting with mine. I felt sorry for him. Whatever his part in all of this, he was trapped in the performance. Perhaps the young lady was his girlfriend and he had confronted her attacker, just as he'd described. I could only hope he saw the apology in my face.

As my ride pulled away from the mansion, the pastor's words remained with me: 'I am the world's next superpower.' What did he mean by it? I turned it over in my mind as we drove. The more I thought, the more unsettled I became. A man who thought himself Jesus-like, hosting the Gathering, trying to talk me into kneeling in front of him, running a youth centre full of disturbingly ripped teenagers. I kept remembering the viral posts from his backyard event – a clarion call of some kind. Something was wrong with the picture. I thought I knew what it was, but I couldn't prove it. But what if I wasn't wrong about this?

I reached a decision. Fetching my phone, I stared at it, wondering what to do. I typed one-four-one to hide my number, then entered 999 for the police. Before I made the call, I caught the driver's face looking at me in the mirror. I couldn't make the call in his presence. Another thought hit me. I held down the back button to delete the numbers, brought up the browser, and typed: Can you block your caller ID when calling 999?

I should have known the answer. Realising how close I'd come to an unforced error, panic surged, hot and sudden. I imagined the police calling me back after my 'anonymous tip', even though I'd blocked my number.

'I need to stop at a phone shop,' I said to the driver.

He had two phones mounted on the dashboard, each displaying a different GPS app. He flicked through one.

'We can go through Tottenham Court Road,' he said. 'There are many shops there.'

63

I went with the driver's suggestion, checking the time as he navigated the route. I was cutting it close for my client session, but for what I needed to do, I had to get a cheap pay-as-you-go phone that I could afford to throw away after just one use. I mentally rehearsed exactly what I would say.

When we reached Tottenham Court Road, we stopped in front of a shop that had every type of mobile phone in its window. I told the driver I would be in and out as fast as possible, and he said he would circle back to avoid getting a ticket.

I hurried into the shop and realised I didn't have cash on me. I was being paranoid, I knew, but if I made the call and the police decided they needed to find the caller, I didn't want to be traced because I'd done something stupid like pay for a burner phone with my bank card.

I asked one of the men behind the long display counter if they had a really cheap phone.

'How cheap?' the Pakistani man asked.

'I'm only in town for a couple of days,' I said. 'I won't need it after that.'

'You don't mind a used phone?'

'That would be perfect.'

'Do you want a SIM card as well?'

'Yes, please. And some credit.'

He showed me an old phone that looked more like a toy. 'How much is that?' I asked.

He looked at me as if to weigh my pocket, then he said, 'Thirty pounds.'

'Plus the SIM and the credit?'

'How much credit do you want?'

'What's the lowest?'

He fetched a SIM-card packet from behind his counter. I didn't recognise the brand name. 'This one comes with five pounds on it,' he said.

Perfect.

'How much is it?'

'Five pounds.'

'So, that's thirty-five pounds in total?'

'Yes. Do you want a charger?'

'Is it charged?'

He nodded.

'Where's the closest cash machine?'

After I paid for my burner phone, he inserted the SIM and switched it on to prove that it worked. The battery was ten per cent charged.

Out on the pavement, I paced up and down and looked for my driver as I dialled 999 with sweaty fingers. The call was answered almost instantly.

'Emergency. Which service?'

I cupped my hand over the mouthpiece. 'The police,' I said.

'Hold on.'

I heard the click as another person picked up the call.

'Police. Where are you?'

'I have information.'

My heart kept pounding as I read out my rehearsed lines. As soon as I was done, I ended the call. My hands were shaking. Switching off the phone, I looked around as I pried open the back, glancing down briefly to remove the SIM before I returned to scanning the area for anyone who might be watching me. I slipped the SIM into my mouth and chewed it between my molars. At the same time, I slipped the mobile into my waistline and let it fall down my trousers. As I shook my leg, the phone slid out the bottom, and I subtly pushed it against a bin. I pretended to cough into my hand. I'd spat the chewed-up piece of plastic into my palm. I dropped my hand to my side and let the mashed-up SIM card fall to the ground, and then I walked away to the next shop to await my driver.

I looked up and found myself staring into the black, reflective eye of a CCTV camera mounted high on a lamp post.

64

Rod sat up. Something on his screen had caught his attention. He leant forward and frowned at the green text scrolling against a black background. He typed commands into his screen and monitored the results. His face lit up as he typed in more commands.

'Shit,' he swore out loud. He turned to face the other spies as they looked towards him.

'What is it?' Libby asked, her fingers hovering over her keyboard.

Rod pushed himself back in his chair and stood up. 'You're not going to believe this,' he said, his face bright with excitement.

Dempsey moved his earphones to his neck. 'What is it?' he asked.

'We have to call him,' Rod replied.

'What did you find?'

'Come listen to this,' Rod said.

A young family of four had occupied the bench facing the pond in St James's Park. Francis walked past them with a folded copy of the *Guardian* in his hand and continued until he eventually sat down on the bench where he had his meetings with John. The traitor's bench was empty. A herring gull landed on the bin next to it, head cocked, watching him. He stared at it for a moment, then looked around and scanned the sky. He placed his folded newspaper down on the bench and opened it, revealing his lunch wrapped in a paper napkin. He peeled back the napkin and brought the sandwich to his mouth, just as his phone vibrated against his chest. He paused. He waited for another ring, then took a bite, placed the paper napkin back over the rest of his lunch and refolded the newspaper to cover it.

He tracked the flight of a ring-necked parakeet as he reached into his jacket, then cupped his hand over the phone screen to shade it from the sun. It was a new message from the dating app on his phone. He opened it. Someone had responded to his pictureless profile. Suzy Bellingham wanted to know if they could meet for coffee.

He tucked the phone back into his jacket and looked for the parakeet. Turning back to his unfinished lunch, he wrapped the newspaper more securely around it, got up and walked to the bin.

Dusting his hands on the sides of his jacket, he searched for the bird again. He spotted a blackbird standing in the grass, side-on to him, but watching him, nevertheless. A moment passed, then Francis turned and began to walk out of the park.

*

When Francis entered the basement beneath the gun shop, the three agents were on their feet, lined up and facing the sofa.

Francis held up his hand. 'Before you say anything,' he said, 'I owe you all an apology.' He heaved a deep sigh. 'I am sorry that I spoke to you in the manner that I did. I realise that you are all working hard, and I appreciate all your efforts. I will do better next time.'

He searched each of their eyes. None of them responded. He noticed grins on their faces.

'All right, then,' he said, 'what's all the excitement about?'

He settled into his sofa.

Dempsey and Libby looked at Rod.

'I picked up some chatter,' Rod said.

'Chatter? What chatter?'

'Well, since we don't know what we're looking for, I thought I might as well monitor what other people are saying about the pastor and the woman.'

'Other people?' Francis raised his brows.

'The police. I wanted to know if they were also interested in him.'

'I told you to stay away from the police,' Francis said.

'I didn't hack the police. I wrote a listener. If anything came in about the church or either of them, I'd be notified. It's an interceptor.'

'I know what a listener is. What did you pick up?'

'An anonymous caller. He said he had information on the church.'

Francis leant forward. 'What did he say?'

'I think it's better that you hear it.'

Rod sat down and pulled his swivel chair up to his workstation. He hit a button on his keyboard. A recording played from the speakers at the sides of his screen: 'I have information. My church is planning a mass suicide. WAITRN Church. That is Whisky, Alpha, India, Tango, Romeo, November. The pastor's name is D'Don. Delta, apostrophe, Delta, Oscar, November. D'Don.'

The recording ended.

Francis sat still, his eyes resting steadily on the speaker that had gone mute. The other agents were silent too, exchanging glances and waiting. Then Francis shot up onto his feet.

'This confirms another piece of intel I've received,' he said. 'This is what all this has been about. Well done. What are the police doing?'

'Nothing. It's been flagged as a hoax call.'

'Send me a copy and shut everything down.'

65

In windowless backrooms, basements, and a boarded-up flat between Leicester Square and Marble Arch – all within a one-mile radius of Clarence House – young agents deleted hard drives, disconnected devices, wiped down surfaces, and took their trash with them.

Francis walked onto the bridge over the lake at St James's Park. A couple were taking pictures of the scenery while their toddler watched the world from its pram. Francis made silly faces at the baby, making it chuckle and point its chubby finger at him.

As Alex climbed onto the bridge, he watched Francis entertain the child. Meeting in the middle, the two men turned to the water and crossed their hands over the railing.

'All set?' Francis asked.

'Affirmative,' Alex replied.

'I want eyes,' Francis said, watching the water.

'Sure.'

'When it's done, we go dark.'

'Understood. Do you have a date?'

'Tonight.'

'Tonight?' Alex asked.

Francis looked at him. 'Will that be a problem?'

'No.'

'Good.' Francis pushed himself back from the railing, making as if to leave.

'There is one thing, though,' Alex said.

Francis turned around to face him.

'I am to inform you-know-who before you-know-what,' Alex said.

'Is that so?'

'Yes.'

'And were you to let me know this?'

Alex shook his head. Francis searched the young man's face.

'Okay,' Francis said. He turned and began to walk away, and the baby in the pram pointed again at what it saw.

66

I felt exposed in the back of the Uber. I had called in a mass suicide plot I couldn't prove, and all because a man had told me he was the world's next superpower. In that moment, when he shouted and the mask slipped, I'd seen how real the danger in him was. Until then, I'd pegged him down as a weirdo – someone increasingly frustrated that his gravity hadn't pulled me in the way it did his million followers. I would have left his mansion regretting nothing more than the waste of my time and that would have been that. But that eruption spooked me. My gut picked up on something that had been there all along. Was I right? Maybe not. I hoped not. But someone had to look into him. Someone had to take him seriously.

But . . .

What if the police investigated and found nothing? No stockpile of incriminating material, no boxes of pamphlets outlining or justifying some apocalyptic plot. Nothing. Making a hoax call was one thing; making a malicious hoax call something else entirely. What if, once D'Don was found squeaky clean, he pressed charges and forced the Met's hand, compelling them to reveal the source of the allegations – allegations that could easily be framed as racially motivated?

The police are extremely sensitive to anything race-related. I should know. I've worked with enough officers whose supposed sins, diagnosed as unconscious bias, struck me, a Black man, as tremendous overreach on the part of the complainant. Once, an officer brought watermelon slices dipped in chocolate to a Black colleague's leaving party. I still struggle to see the offence there, and so did my client, who concluded – after our six sessions – that she 'did nothing wrong, but if someone says they're upset, their discomfort is real and therefore valid'. My shock came later, when I learnt the complaint had been made by a white officer.

I had no doubt that the police would reveal the source of the allegations. 'An anonymous tip' would not be enough. I'd used a burner phone and had discarded it immediately, but now it dawned on me how easy it would be to trace the number back through supplier networks to a batch of SIM cards sold to a specific phone repair shop on Tottenham Court Road.

Shit.

If the police came knocking, what would I say? That a man had said something that sounded crazy? That he had gatherings in his house? That his followers reposted batshit declarations? That my gut told me he was dangerous? They'd ask why I hadn't made the call as myself. Why I'd gone to such lengths to hide my identity.

I wondered what would happen to my contract with the

Met. To my membership of the International Coaching Federation. To my coaching practice. I wondered what would happen to whatever Naomi and I might have had. If I'd run this past her first, she'd have pointed out the obvious: I had no evidence. None at all. And maybe, just maybe, I would have listened to her.

I called Margaret, my supervisor coach. My voice trembled as the call connected.

'Hi, Maggie,' I said. 'I have done something stupid. Do you still have that therapist's number?'

67

Francis was in his study, sitting in his striped pyjamas and reading Michelle Obama's *Becoming* by the warm glow of a banker's lamp. His phone beeped with a new message. He glanced at the lit-up screen where it lay next to his laptop, then he placed the book face down on his desk and picked up the phone to read the message properly: 'Table booked for three. Hold or cancel the reservation?'

He placed the phone back down, locked his fingers behind his head, leant back into his chair, and looked up at the ceiling. Try as he might, he could not explain to himself in any satisfactory way why the young agent had offered up this piece of information. Why had he taken sides with Francis? Why had he risked his relationship with John? What had motivated him to volunteer information that could end his career or put him under Francis' control? What was his game? What did he stand to gain? No matter how Francis looked at it, there was no obvious upside for Alex, so why had he done it?

After months of work – of enduring the pastor and catering to his whims – to learn at the very end that John's hand secretly hovered over a stop button had caused Francis twice the stress of all the previous months combined. Could it be due diligence on the spy catcher's side, or was it a trap? If Francis didn't go ahead after instructing Alex, John would know what the young agent had done; if he did go ahead, John would know when and possibly how. Why did he need that information? Not knowing would have been the strategy Francis would have chosen if he were in John's shoes. Why had the spy catcher risked compromising himself?

These unanswerable questions had wreaked havoc on Francis' mind. Perhaps he was simply being paranoid. John had read the pastor's letter. He knew what was at stake. Maybe he was watching out for Francis. It's what friends should do, after all. However, in their world, friendship was a commodity too often readily exchanged for gain.

There was one other explanation: John wanted Francis to know he knew. He didn't trust Francis, and he wanted him to know that he didn't. He wanted to be certain that Francis did everything to make sure that nothing went wrong. If so, then it was really up to Francis to give it the final go.

He picked up the phone and noticed that his hand was shaking. He put it back down, held out his hand and spread his fingers. He watched, breathed, and waited until he regained control.

Then he picked up the phone and replied, 'Hold.'

He set the phone back down on the desk, picked up his bourbon glass and found it empty. He picked up the bottle and found it empty, too.

68

Kenny woke up with a racing heart. It was still dark, so it wasn't morning yet. Something had woken him, but he could not place what it was. He stayed perfectly still on his back while he tried to sense what it was. Had he heard something? Why was his heart beating so fast?

Not finding anything to panic over, his mind turned to the events of the day. Who was the man D'Don had made him lie to? Had the man believed him? Why was Tashique still so angry with him? Would she ever talk to him again?

Why had D'Don asked him to lie in the first place? He'd said Kenny would understand one day because he had special powers that allowed him to see and know things that other people don't see or know. But Kenny knew he didn't have any special powers. He hadn't seen D'Don lift off the ground the day he'd been chosen. He'd just said he had because D'Don had asked if he did. He did not see things, he did not know things, and he would not one day understand why he'd had to tell the lies he'd told about Tashique to that man. He didn't know anything.

He didn't even know if he and Tashique were ever going to be together.

That man – who was he, anyway? What was his involvement with what had happened to Tashique? Was he a policeman? A lawyer? D'Don hadn't said anything about it, only that a man was coming and that Kenny had to lie about Tashique.

He remembered the way the man had looked at him as he'd left the mansion. It had reminded him of the way his former foster parent had looked at him before leaving for good, and how the next day his wife had tried to burn the house down. Had Kenny not smelled smoke and woken up, they would all have died. Looking back, it was as if her husband, Kenny's foster father, had been trying to warn him when he'd looked at him that way.

Kenny got up. He couldn't shake the feeling that something wasn't right. With no clue as to what it was, his heart began to beat even harder. Something really was wrong. He opened his eyes wide. He thought he smelled something. He sniffed at the air. It smelled like gas. He tiptoed to the door and made his way downstairs, and as he descended the stairs, the smell grew stronger, until he had to cover his nose. He hurried to the kitchen, but the door wouldn't open. He tried again. How could it be locked? His lungs began to hurt from holding his breath, and even then, not breathing in, he could still smell the gas. His eyes burnt. He had to let it out of the house. He made it to the main door, but the key wouldn't turn in the lock.

He looked around desperately. Maybe the windows

would open. He realised that he was standing in the exact same spot he'd been standing in when the man had looked at him the way his foster father had to try to warn him. Kenny's body tingled all over. Just like then, they were all in danger, and just like then, he was the only one who could do something about it.

69

Libby straddled him, pinning his hands to the headboard as she brought herself to climax. When she opened her eyes, Rod was looking at her. She rolled off him. She'd kept her black bra and her thigh-length black stockings on as they had sex in her room in the house that she shared with six other housemates, and now she sat on the edge of the bed, picked up her bag of tobacco from the bedside stool and began to construct a roll-up.

Rod linked his fingers beneath his head and watched her.

'What do you think he's going to do with the intel?' he asked.

Libby turned to him and held up a finger. 'No. No shop talk in my crib.'

'Aren't you concerned? Even a bit?'

She licked the adhesive on the edge of the paper. 'Nope.'

'But what if it was just a hoax call?'

'So what?'

'Doesn't that bother you?'

Libby shrugged. She searched the stool for her lighter. Rod sat up in bed.

'You've got level five access, don't you?' he asked.

'Yes, why?'

'I just want to check something.'

'It's over. We're done.'

'It'll only take a minute.'

He got up and walked to fetch his clothes from the chair that also held hers. Moving their stuff away to get to his backpack, he fetched his laptop, sat on the bed with one leg folded beneath him and began to log in.

'What are you doing?' she asked him.

'I just want to check something.'

'What?'

'The anonymous caller.' He typed on the keyboard.

'What about him?'

'I'm working out where he made the call from.'

'What do you need my access for?'

'Got it.' Rod looked up at her as he answered her question. 'So, I have the location from which the call was made. Now I need every mobile that was active in the area when it was made. Please.'

'Oh, fuck,' Libby groaned. 'I knew I shouldn't have shagged you.'

She got up and walked to her desk.

'Send me the location,' she said.

She sat down and logged in to her laptop. Moments later, she said, 'Okay. Sending you all the mobile phone pictures and video recordings made in that location in a ten-minute bracket.'

'Can you make it one minute?'

'You make it one minute.' She hit the return key. 'Sent.'

'Thanks. Got it.'

Rod went to work on his laptop while she sat and watched him from the chair, a cigarette smouldering between her fingers.

'When did you last get tested?' she asked.

'What?'

'We just shagged without a condom. When did you last get tested?'

He looked up. 'I don't know. Maybe a year ago, I guess.'

'Why did you get tested then?'

'I . . . Hold on. Let me finish this.'

'You better not give me any STDs.'

'I've filtered down to the exact time the call was made. There are quite a few pictures.' He continued typing at the keyboard. 'Got him. Oh, fuck.' He looked up at Libby. His mouth was wide open.

'What?' She stomped out her cigarette and went to sit next to him so she could see his screen.

'No way,' she said. 'It's the coach guy.'

'Should we tell him?'

'Tell who? Francis?'

'Yes.'

'Why? It's over, remember?'

'It's actionable intel.'

'How do you figure that out?'

'He's one of the subjects. We have to tell him.'

'No. It's already too late. And you were not supposed to be working on it.'

'But—'

'No "but", Rod. Remember, he asked you if you thought you should stay on the coach, and you said no. You. If this is a fuck-up, it's your fuck-up. Do you understand? Look at me. This could be bad for you. Do you understand? This never happened, okay?'

70

Kenny missed a step and fell onto his knee as he rushed upstairs. His lungs were bursting and his eyes were burning. He gripped the bannister and gasped as he hauled himself to his feet. He darted to Tashique's room. She wasn't in her bed. He dashed to her bathroom. It was empty. He ran to D'Don's room. There was light under the door. He gripped the handle, and it turned in his hand. He threw the door open and froze in the doorway as a whip came down on the pastor. Thwack.

D'Don was on his hands and knees on the bed. His eyes were on the door. He was sweating, and he was naked. Tashique was on one knee behind him. Her breasts were glistening with sweat and her other foot was planted wide on the bed. She had one hand on D'Don's waist, and in the other, she held a black whip. She stared at Kenny as he stood at the door. Strands of her hair were glued to her face. She looked pissed.

'Kenny!' D'Don exclaimed.

The pastor fell to one side and grabbed at the sheets to

cover himself, and Kenny saw the glistening black strap-on around Tashique's waist. She laid the whip down on the mattress, stood up, planted her feet wide, placed her fists on her hips and glared at Kenny.

Pulling the sheet around his body, D'Don fumbled himself off the bed. 'Kenny, I can explain,' he said, holding out a hand as if to stop the younger man. But Kenny was not moving. He stood in the doorway, eyes and mouth wide open in shock.

Tashique kissed her teeth and began to undo the straps around her waist as she also got off the bed.

'Kenny,' D'Don said. 'Listen to me. I can explain.'

But in that moment, Kenny knew more than he had before. He realised right then that the girl who screamed hadn't seen D'Don lift off the ground either.

'We have to go now,' Kenny shouted.

'Kenny, relax,' D'Don said.

'Something terrible is about to happen,' Kenny said. 'We have to leave now.'

'Nothing terrible has to happen,' D'Don responded.

Tashique shook her head and walked to the settee beside the bed. Kenny caught sight of her rolling her eyes. She sat heavily, crossed her legs, picked up her phone from the cushion, and turned her attention to its screen.

D'Don took a moment to compose himself, slightly bowing his head to breathe in some courage, and then, standing straight and with his chest out, he said, 'Kenny, listen to me!'

'No!' Kenny cried. 'You don't understand. I see things.

I know things. A terrible thing is about to happen. I saw it. It was the man who brought the fish. I saw his horns. The house is full of gas. We have to go now!'

71

Francis watched the grainy aerial footage from Alex's drone. He flinched at the sudden flash. The screen momentarily went white. He watched as the image zoomed out, showing the burning building from a distance, and then the camera swept away over dense foliage. It was over. He reached forward and closed the laptop, but as soon as he did, he lifted the screen back up again. His eyes went to the top left-hand corner just as the time on the digital clock changed from 11:11 to 11:12. He huffed at the screen. It became a one-cheeked smile. The smile became a chuckle. Laughing through his nostrils, he stood up, picked up his glass of bourbon, switched off the lights, and shut the door as he left the study. The darkness howled silently after him.

Abraham stood by the wall, and with his index finger, he parted the curtain just a crack to peep out into the deserted street. A fox strutted across the pavement below the orange light of a streetlamp. It stopped to investigate something tucked beneath a concrete bench.

Abraham looked in the other direction along the road that ran in front of the block of council flats. He let the curtain fall back into place, plunging the living room into darkness again. With his back to the wall, he slid down into a squat, then rested his bum on the floor, folded his legs into a lotus position and held them in place with his hands.

D'Don and Tashique were sitting on the floor against the adjacent wall. D'Don was wearing a pair of trousers and a white dress shirt, both too large for him. Tashique was wearing a pair of blue men's jeans and a black Nike T-shirt, both of which were baggy on her.

The three of them watched Kenny. He was snoring on his side on the floor. His lips were slightly parted as he slept.

At first, D'Don thought that the boy had gone mad because of what he'd seen – catching him and Tashique like that. But then Kenny mentioned the horns.

In that moment, D'Don saw past his panic. It was not the boy who stood at the doorway; it was a man – ignoring what he'd seen and focusing on the danger.

The horns. Of course. He should have seen them too.

'We have to get out!' Kenny had commanded, turning and running.

The smell of gas choked the air as they flew down the stairs. At the landing they headed for the front door, but Tashique stopped and grabbed Kenny. D'Don bumped into them.

She pointed at a window, her palm over her nose

and mouth, her eyes wide with urgency. She had seen something.

Kenny ran in the opposite direction – towards the passage leading to the guest cloakroom, the utility room and the garage. They rushed into the utility. Tashique listened, peered through the window, and scanned the sky before opening the door. Fresh air rushed in.

Kenny pushed past her, gulped air, and moved aside for D'Don. Tashique kept listening, glancing up at the house and then at the sky. She pointed up and back, toward the house, then forward at the woods at the end of the driveway.

They ran.

Kenny had led, forcing them to keep up. Tashique ran behind him, strap-on still in situ. D'Don followed, naked as the day he was born, watching his family ahead of him and realising how badly he had underestimated Francis.

They had barely reached the canopy of the great elm trees. The house exploded. The blast hurled them into the undergrowth.

They stayed where they fell, pressed to musky earth, afraid to move. Orange flames licked out from the shattered windows of their home.

Then, Tashique's phone beeped.

And after a while, they called Abraham, Kenny's former counsellor – the man who had groomed and recruited him for WAITRN.

72

Floating on his back, Francis admired the splendour of the ceiling above the pool: the floral motifs, heraldic symbols, and other intricate classical mouldings adorned in gold leaf; the large crystal chandeliers that cast a brilliant light across the water; and the emotive frescoes that had watched over generations of royals taking their first swimming lessons.

He recalled the first time he had enjoyed the privilege of using the pool. The water had been warmer then, before the King, who had been the Prince of Wales at the time, had ordered the heating be turned down. If the green monarch had his way, all of the Crown Estate would be net zero.

Feeling relaxed, his day's calendar sparse and free of urgent tasks, Francis turned his mind to mentally drafting the King's response to the tragedy. D'Don would have liked that. He smiled. It would be unprecedented for the palace to comment on the death of a relatively unknown, flamboyant Pentecostal preacher, but this was not a problem to hide from; it was a problem to run at.

*

From Buckingham Palace, Francis walked through Green Park, past Lancaster House and towards his office at Clarence House. It was a cold autumn day, but he was still warm from his swim, when his mind had been focused on nothing but the water, the timing of each turn and the countdown to the fiftieth lap. Now, as he walked to his office, with the angst of the past year behind him, no longer suspicious of unfamiliar faces, no longer stopping to tend to his shoelaces anytime his gut told him to look behind him, he enjoyed the macabre beauty of trees bereft of leaves, their branches frozen into static clumps against a grey and sombre sky.

With his gloves safely in his pocket, he squeezed his fist around the straps of his duffel bag in defiance of the cold, and with the fingers of his free hand, played conductor to an orchestra playing 'Hunter's Chorus' in his carefree mind. He had just stepped through the door when, out of habit, he glanced back, and his instinct recognised the first stirrings of a media scrum: a woman dressed for television and another in a pair of jeans and a camera operator's vest, both scouting for a vantage position. Their target was his building. Clarence House.

The sick feeling in Francis' stomach built as he climbed the stairs to his floor and hurried to his office. Everything had gone according to plan and he had shut down the operation without a flicker of concern, but now his gut told him that something had gone terribly wrong.

He pushed his door open and froze. The old Chubb Manifoil MK4 safe in the corner was wide open. The discomfort in his belly became a gut-wrenching pain that radiated through his entire body. With his eye fixed on the safe, he shut the door behind him and dropped his bag. His head rang with alarm, driving pain through his jaws and into his ears. Pulses of terror gripped his heart. Each step towards the safe was like a step closer to a coiled viper. When he stood before the old metal box and looked inside, the emptiness rushed at him like a screaming banshee. He gasped and clutched at his chest. His phone vibrated. With shaking hands, he fetched it from his inside pocket. It was a new message. He had two. The first was from his son. He skipped it. The second was from 'No Caller ID.' He opened it. 'Watch the news,' it said.

He had lost control of his breathing while he stumbled towards his desk and sat down. As he waited for his computer to boot up, he felt the open safe watching him. Unable to resist, he turned to look at its stunning emptiness and moaned. He brought up the live news on the BBC. His heart raced as he listened and scanned the scrolling text at the bottom of the screen, but his brain had lost its ability to read. The mobile phone buzzed again. He turned to it. He had a new voice message. First, he read the message from his son: 'Thank you, Dad.'

Then he listened to the voice message his boy had left him: 'Dad, I was out in the forest last night. There was no reception. When I got back to the village, there was a power failure, as usual. They just started the generator this morning, so I just got to charge my phone. All this to say, that's the reason I'm only just returning your call. Does this mean I can come back home now?'

As Francis listened to the message with his eyes fixed on

the TV screen, his grip on the mobile tightened, and his face morphed from desperate fear into a twitching scowl of profound and ferocious anger. He watched a man with a microphone speaking against the backdrop of Clarence House.

He dialled his son's phone and stood from his chair. He went to the window, and with a finger, he lifted the curtain to peep outside. Police officers had formed a line marking the boundary that the media was not allowed to cross.

His son answered the call: 'Dad? I just left you a message. Dad, thank you. Listen, I know you don't believe me, but I really didn't touch the woman.'

Francis' hand shook. His nostrils flared with forceful breaths. Through gritted teeth, he responded to his son. 'She filmed you, you bloody idiot!'

'In three . . .'

The producer continued the rest of the count with her fingers.

The reporter straightened her back and lifted her brows for the camera. When she spoke, mist engulfed the microphone.

'If you are just joining us this morning, we are reporting live from outside Clarence House in the City of Westminster, where we are following a breaking news story. A short while ago, a video, which I must point out is yet to be verified, was posted online. The short clip purportedly shows a sexual act between an allegedly underage woman of Afro-Caribbean origin and the married son of a prominent aide to the royal household. A lawyer who claims to represent the woman and who also claims to be her pastor has released a statement saying that the video is genuine. He also hinted at the existence of further evidence implicating the accused party, whose name is yet to be revealed.'

73

Naomi returned from the kitchen with a mug of coffee in one hand, a bowl of cereal in another, and a slice of toast between her teeth.

She and Bobby were meeting for coffee at the members' bar in the Tate Modern, and then they would stroll by the river to Borough Market to while away the time before heading to Bond Street, where they had reservations for lunch at Chishuru. Sometimes she wondered if they would have ever got together if he had liked her back on that dating app. She had discussed it with him, and he had confessed that he had also thought about it. However, in his own words, the question was whether they would have ended up together if she hadn't stalked him. She smiled. She liked his sense of humour. It wasn't so much the things he said, but the way he said them – deadpan and with great timing. His humour had a sharpness to it when it wasn't self-deprecating, in which case it was unforgivingly mean. She had pointed this out to him, and he'd replied, 'Okay, shrink.' Then there was the tenderness about him. It was the way he listened to people. She saw it when they were out with friends or even in the back of a chatty Uber driver's car. She'd mentioned this too, and he had simply put it down to his job. But she knew it wasn't just his job; it was who he really was. She was lucky to have him, and he was lucky to have her. They were lucky to have each other.

She settled down on the sofa, set the bowl of cereal on the coffee table, took a bite of the toast and raised the coffee to her mouth while listening to the morning news on her television.

Then she spat out the mouthful of coffee, grabbed the remote control, and increased the TV volume.

'Holy shit!' she exclaimed.

They say that admitting you have a problem is the first step. I knew that I had paranoid delusions, and I knew that my episodes of psychosis were becoming more frequent and more intense. It was the next step that I struggled with.

After making the anonymous tip to the police, it felt as if every siren I heard, every police vehicle I saw and every stranger that looked my way was the authorities coming for me. I was about to ask Google if it knew how often hoax calls were investigated, but I feared that should I be arrested, they would go through my browsing history and conclude that I had known it was a hoax call when I'd made it. I was a mess, and I knew that I wasn't going to stop being a mess until a lot of time had passed without an early-morning knock on the door or police cars waiting for me outside my block of flats. I tormented myself with thoughts of how I could have stopped to challenge my thoughts before I'd made the call. I was convinced that that one crime would get me arrested, be the end of my practice as a coach, cause me to lose my flat and my friends, and ultimately get me deported. If they could do it to Shamima Begum, who was born in England, what would stop them from putting me on a flight to Lagos, where old enemies would have climbed higher up in politics and in the police force?

It was death by increments. I had to do something. I called the therapist my supervisor coach had recommended, and we arranged to meet at Store Street Espresso, just off Holborn, close to where she would be when she could squeeze me in for a fifteen-minute initial chat.

I arrived early and bought a large black coffee so I wouldn't feel guilty sitting and waiting. The café was quieter than the busy chains on Holborn – high ceilings, polished wood panelling, and dark timber tables that reflected the soft light streaming in through the windows. Leather-backed chairs lined the walls; a few stools hugged the long counter.

I could see why she'd chosen it. We could have a conversation here.

I chose a seat near the back, where I could see both the door and the window. Even years after the Nigerian police force, I still needed a clear line of sight. From my vantage point, I watched the ebb and flow of the café, the occasional passer-by outside reflected in the glass. That was when I noticed him.

He had just settled onto a stool at the counter against the window with a muffin on a porcelain saucer and a coffee in a takeaway cup. I saw something others wouldn't. He was carrying a gun.

Appendix carry. Not the obvious bulge – though it was there if you knew what to look for – but the subtle pinch of fabric, the way his fingers adjusted his shirt as he lowered himself into the chair. Instinct. I had done it myself, long ago.

He examined the muffin, lifted a crumb from the saucer, and popped it into his mouth. One bite left. I studied him in the reflection of the polished wood behind the counter. Short-sleeved shirt, black trousers, black loafers with uneven rubber heels. Gold signet on his little finger. No jacket.

Wrong weather. Wrong outfit for Holborn.

Then it clicked. He'd come from somewhere warmer. My senses tingled.

Maybe because I was finally meeting a therapist about my paranoia, I recognised the beginning of an episode. On a good day, I would have put him down as a foreign agent. I would have searched for the closest embassies. And of his unseasonal dressing, I would have concluded that he hadn't changed because he wouldn't be staying. He was briefed and ready, and he knew where his target would be, but he just had to stop for one last blueberry, spelt and almond muffin at the coffee house.

My phone rang. I kept my eyes on the assassin as I slid the mobile out of my pocket. It was Naomi. I smiled at the screen and briefly scanned the café. No one else seemed to notice him. They would all go on with their lives, never knowing they once shared a coffee house with an armed person. Probably government, I told myself.

'Good morning, you,' I said, answering the call.

'He's on telly,' she said.

Her voice threw me. It sounded like panic, excitement or even anger. There was energy in it.

'Who?' I asked.

'The pastor. D'Don. Watch the news. Now. He posted a video.'

'What video? What channel?'

'Any channel.'

'Naomi. What's wrong? You sound—'

'Watch the news!'

'I'm in a coffee shop waiting for a client.'

I squeezed my eyes at my own lie. Why was I ashamed to be seeing a therapist about my mental health?

'Watch the news now!' she screamed, and I had to take the phone away from my ear to recover.

'Okay. Hold on. I'll check on my phone.'

I typed 'UK live news' into the browser and clicked on the first link. *Sky News*. I turned down the volume before playing the livestream. I set the phone down and searched for my earbuds so I could talk to Naomi as I watched, and as I did, I saw D'Don's face on the screen.

'Are you watching it?' Naomi asked.

I recognised the front of the youth centre. D'Don and Kenny, the young man I'd met at D'Don's mansion, were standing next to each other, both dressed in black suits and black shirts. The pastor wore a clerical collar. I sighed and shook my head at the small screen in my palm. What was the idiot up to now?

I found my earbuds in my jacket's inner pocket.

Something about Kenny seemed different. He looked confident. He stood tall, with his feet slightly apart, and his arms were like ready weapons by his sides. It was the superhero stance favoured by male politicians in the United Kingdom. They thought it made them look strong, but it suited young Kenny. Maybe it was the suit. D'Don bowed his head as he read from a prepared note, only occasionally looking up and into the camera. Kenny appeared relaxed, his head slightly tilted upwards, casually observing the press crew in front of him. Had I not met him before, I would have thought he was in charge and that D'Don, who often forgot to look up from the paper he was reading from, was the puppet whose strings the younger man controlled.

I pressed an earbud into my ear and adjusted the volume.

'Following our previous press release, we have encountered additional nefarious and suspicious activities that aim to inflict physical harm, including death, on my client, myself – their lawyer – and other members of Christ's body. Our lives are in danger, so it is now incumbent upon us to make further revelations. As you are already aware, my client, whose partner stands with me today, was the victim of sex trafficking and rape committed by the son of a high-ranking aide to the royal household. Last night, at approximately eleven minutes past eleven, an explosive device was detonated at my official residence as the general overseer of WAITRN Church, where myself, the victim, and the victim's partner have been residing. This brazen attack on a property owned by the Body of Christ was a desperate attempt at a cover-up after several failed attempts at frustrating our efforts to bring the crime to light.

'The bombing is just the latest in a long history of attempts to intimidate and silence us through various means, such as following us, bugging the church, placing a spy among our workers, offering bribes to both myself and the victim, and making direct verbal threats, including the threat of deportation.

'They have failed, and now, as a direct consequence of their evil actions, we have no choice but to release all other evidence in our possession for the safety of our lives and the sake of justice. We will release the full, unedited video, the names of all parties involved and evidence of extended bribes, which we were forced to accept or face the consequences.

'We will release all of this information, along with more, on the WAITRN Church website, all social media platforms and all media channels at a precise time that I will reveal to you. But first, remember that Ecclesiastes 3:8 in the Bible states, "There is a time to love and a time to hate, a time for war and a time for peace." Matthew 11:12 says, "For the kingdom of heaven is violent, and the violent take it by force."

'Let everyone who has ears hear me. This morning, at precisely eleven o'clock, everything will become clear. And for Christ's army, remember Jeremiah 51:20: "You are my war club, my weapon for battle – with you I shatter nations, with you I destroy kingdoms."'

Kenny raised his fist and held it up, and the cameras began to flash away.

My mouth was wide open as I stared at my phone. It took a few more seconds for it all to sink in, and then fear permeated my entire being. I was right. I had been right all along!

'Are they coming for us?' Naomi asked.

I'd forgotten she was still on the phone. She sounded exactly like she had when I'd freaked her out in my apartment.

'Bobby, are you there? Are they coming for us?'

I looked up from the screen. A worker was clearing away the assassin's saucer and wiping down the empty bench. Every inch of my body tingled. They were coming.

Acknowledgements

Special thanks to Oyinka Rotimi, Mike Timbers, Zukiswa Wanner, Wole Adenle, Emma Shercliff, Onome Osikolo, Gabriel Gbadamosi, Andy Russell, Dr Alessandra Bassey, Wuraola Abulatan, Simon Shercliff, Thoko Budaza, Maaza Mengiste, Yemie Sonuga, Sarah Ozo-Irabor, Florence Amerley Adu, Ayo Onatade, Dr Kate Hammer, Yvonne Ibazebo, Sophie Goodfellow, Tolani Ibiduni, Tola Ilaka, Lola Bubbosh, Aysha Rafael, Colin Scott, Lise Belporn, Sandrine Oyeyi, Amanda Lees, Othuke Ominiabohs, Peter Langdale, Ibhade Aimakhu, Georgina Leighton, Katherine Armstrong, Charlotte Osment, Gabriella Nemeth, Natasha Onwuemezi, Oliver Cotton, Izzy Hall, Lisa Moylett, Zoë Apostolides, all essential workers everywhere on the planet, and the lady who sits in the corner at Lumberjack – thank you for always watching my laptop when I need to take a break.

Bobby Fatokun will return in
his thrilling next adventure . . .

SEPTEMBER 2027

SIMON &
SCHUSTER